Two M-203 grenade launchers barked, and as their projectiles arced across the thirty meters of ground toward the objective, Tex Benson pumped the trigger of his SAW, sending three short bursts of 5.56-millimeter rounds straight into the enemy fighting position. As soon as the two grenades struck their target and exploded, the entire section leaped to their feet and made a quick rush toward the objective. No fire was being returned, and Cruiser continued the attack completely up the slope without resistance. They reached the top and could see the ripped-up body of a Zaheya soldier sprawled in his own blood on the dirt inside his post.

Suddenly more enemy soldiers appeared from a bunker exit fifteen meters away. They jumped back as soon as the SEALs opened up on them. Cruiser knew that he and his section had pressed their luck about as far as they could. It would be only moments before the whole enemy force responded to the assault.

"Haul ass!"

Titles in the SEALS series by Jack Terral

SEALS
SEALS: GUERRILLA WARFARE
SEALS: BATTLECRAFT
SEALS: ROLLING THUNDER
SEALS: BATTLELINE

SEALS
BATTLELINE

JACK TERRAL

JOVE BOOKS, NEW YORK

THE BERKLEY PUBLISHING GROUP
Published by the Penguin Group
Penguin Group (USA) Inc.
375 Hudson Street, New York, New York 10014, USA
Penguin Group (Canada), 90 Eglinton Avenue East, Suite 700, Toronto, Ontario M4P 2Y3, Canada
(a division of Pearson Penguin Canada Inc.)
Penguin Books Ltd., 80 Strand, London WC2R 0RL, England
Penguin Group Ireland, 25 St. Stephen's Green, Dublin 2, Ireland (a division of Penguin Books Ltd.)
Penguin Group (Australia), 250 Camberwell Road, Camberwell, Victoria 3124, Australia
(a division of Pearson Australia Group Pty. Ltd.)
Penguin Books India Pvt. Ltd., 11 Community Centre, Panchsheel Park, New Delhi—110 017, India
Penguin Group (NZ), 67 Apollo Drive, Rosedale, North Shore 0745, Auckland, New Zealand
(a division of Pearson New Zealand Ltd.)
Penguin Books (South Africa) (Pty.) Ltd., 24 Sturdee Avenue, Rosebank, Johannesburg 2196,
South Africa

Penguin Books Ltd., Registered Offices: 80 Strand, London WC2R 0RL, England

SEALS: BATTLELINE

A Jove Book / published by arrangement with the author

PRINTING HISTORY
Jove mass-market edition / August 2007

ISBN: 978-0-515-14335-5

JOVE®
Jove Books are published by The Berkley Publishing Group,
a division of Penguin Group (USA) Inc.,
375 Hudson Street, New York, New York 10014.
JOVE is a registered trademark of Penguin Group (USA) Inc.
The "J" design is a trademark belonging to Penguin Group (USA) Inc.

PRINTED IN THE UNITED STATES OF AMERICA

10 9 8 7 6 5 4 3 2 1

This book is dedicated to

The 456th Parachute Field Artillery Battalion
82nd Airborne Division
World War II

U.S. 75-millimeter pack howitzers dropped by parachute
vs.
Dug-in German 88-millimeter cannons

Special Acknowledgment to
Patrick E. Andrews
82nd Airborne Division and 12th Special Forces Group
(Airborne)

NOTE: Enlisted personnel in this book are identified by their ranks (petty officer third class, chief petty officer, master chief petty officer, etc.) rather than their ratings (boatswain's mate, yeoman, etc.) for clarification of status and position within the chain of command. However, when a man's rating is significant in the story, he is identified by that designation.

TABLE OF ORGANIZATION
BRANNIGAN'S BRIGANDS

HEADQUARTERS

Lieutenant William "Wild Bill" Brannigan
(Commanding Officer)

PO2C Francisco "Frank" Gomez
(RTO)

PO3C James "Doc" Bradley
(Hospital Corpsman)

SNIPER TEAM

PO2C Bruno Puglisi

PO2C Josef "Joe" Miskoski

PATROL TEAM

PO1C Michael "Connie" Concord
(Team Leader)

PO2C Mikael "Mike" Assad

PO2C David "Dave" Leibowitz

PO2C Garth Redhawk

PO2C Edward "Matty" Matsuno

FIRST ASSAULT SECTION

Lieutenant Junior Grade James "Jim" Cruiser
(Section Commander)

PO3C Earl "Tex" Benson
(SAW Gunner)

ALPHA FIRE TEAM

PO1C Guttorm "Gutsy" Olson
(Team Leader)

PO2C Peter "Pete" Dawson
(Rifleman)

PO3C Enrico "Rick" Morales
(Grenadier)

BRAVO FIRE TEAM

PO1C Montgomery "Monty" Sturgis
(Team Leader)

PO2C Andrei "Andy" Malachenko
(Rifleman)

PO3C Wallace "Wally" Halonen
(Grenadier)

SECOND ASSAULT SECTION

Ensign Orlando Taylor
(Section Commander)

PO3C Douglas "Doug" MacTavish
(SAW Gunner)

CHARLIE FIRE TEAM

PO1C Paul Schreiner
(Team Leader)

PO2C Reynauld "Pech" Pecheur
(Rifleman)

PO3C Uziel "Uzi" Melech
(Grenadier)

DELTA FIRE TEAM

PO1C Antonio "Tony" Valenzuela
(Team Leader)

PO2C Arnold "Arnie" Bernardi
(Rifleman)

PO3C George Fotopoulus
(Grenadier)

THIRD ASSAULT SECTION

Senior Chief Petty Officer Buford Dawkins
(Section Commander)

PO3C James Duncan
(SAW Gunner)

ECHO FIRE TEAM

PO1C Lemar Smith
(Team Leader)

PO3C Guy Devereaux
(Rifleman)

PO3C Paulo Garcia
(Grenadier)

FOXTROT FIRE TEAM

PO1C Thomas "Tom" Greene
(Team Leader)

PO3C Chadwick "Chad" Murchison
(Rifleman)

PO3C J. T. Snooker
(Grenadier)

FIRE SUPPORT SECTION

Chief Petty Officer Matthew "Matt" Gunnarson
(Section Commander)

FIRST MACHINE GUN CREW

PO2C Charles "Chuck" Betnarik
(Gunner)

PO3C Arlo Bartholomew
(Rifleman/Ammo Bearer)

SECOND MACHINE GUN CREW

PO2C Dennis "Tiny" Burke
(Gunner)

PO3C Humphrey "Hump" Dobbs
(Rifleman/Ammo Bearer)

THIRD MACHINE GUN CREW

PO2C Gregory "Greg" Beaver
(Gunner)

PO3C Terrence "Terry" O'Rourke
(Rifleman/Ammo Bearer)

Prussian General Karl von Clausewitz, *Principles of War*, as paraphrased by PO2C Bruno Puglisi of Brannigan's Brigands:

You're always open to attack unless you're attacking, so what you gotta do in the meantime is cop a defensive attitude and use all the cover and concealment you can until you're ready to come out and kick some serious butt.

PROLOGUE

THE newly organized unit was the spearhead of the Iranian Army's special warfare operations that had been put together for a desperate gamble in that part of the world. It had been officially designated as Zur Jamie Entegham (Strike Force Vengeance) and was referred to by its Farsi acronym of Zaheya. It numbered four officers who commanded sixty noncommissioned officers and enlisted men, and although it was nowhere near brigade size, the overall commander was a brigadier. His name was Shahruz Khohollah, one of the organizers of Iran's recently established Special Forces. This able leader had been chosen to lead the Zaheya not because of its size, but because of the far-reaching consequences of the mission assigned it.

This objective was both military and political, with the ambitious goal of bringing all the Shiite Muslim insurgencies in the entire Middle East under the command and control of the Iranian government. This ambitious project was designed to ultimately create a modern Persian Empire that would rule that part of the world while benefiting from its massive oil reserves.

The opening salvos of this newly hatched imperialistic plot was happening along the Iran-Afghanistan border, but at this point in time, neither the civilians in the Iranian government nor the General Staff of the national army wanted to create an attention-grabbing incident. Certain political and diplomatic events that they hoped were only temporary limited their grandiose scheme for conquering surrounding nations. Thus an all-out war of fully equipped division-size units would do more to impede those ambitions than advance them.

Thus Brigadier Khohollah suggested that a smaller group of elite troops could make very effective probing attacks into Afghanistan to eventually gain control over a large, isolated area in the mountains. These tactics would not attract undue attention, and the territory gained would provide a central base of operations from which a larger invasion could be launched in the future.

The Zaheya consisted of a group of twenty well-trained Arabs in a unit designated as al-Askerin-Zaubi (Storm Troopers). They were led by a deserter from the British Army named Arsalaan Sikes, who was respectfully addressed as Sikes Pasha by his men. Additionally, a handpicked unit of twenty Iranian Special Forces troopers led by hard-core Captain Naser Khadid of the Iranian SF served as an essential part of the assault element. A fire support group was under the direct command of Brigadier Khohollah. He had chosen his newly appointed adjutant, Captain Jamshid Komard, as the actual field commander of the heavy weapons organization. They were set up for rapid deployment to specific areas when needed.

Khohollah could also expect infusions of Arab insurgents from time to time. These would be graduates of the Iranian Special Forces Training Center, set up to prepare the mujahideen for unconventional warfare. After the tough eight-week course, the volunteers were destined to be funneled into Sikes Pasha's unit. This Brit turncoat enjoyed the very real possibility that he might end up with a hundred or so fully equipped and well-trained assault riflemen under his direct command.

The fortified position occupied by the Zaheya along the Afghan border had been constructed a year and a half before by Iranian Army personnel under the supervision of Russian military engineers. They and their construction equipment and machines had been flown in undetected by a small fleet of Mi-10 flying crane helicopters at a time when the site was largely ignored. A high mountain area with an empty, flat terrain at its apex offered a perfect landing spot. The personnel, equipment, and stores needed for construction went from there to the site of the fortification on a road hacked out of the side of the mountain.

The Russian supervisors took advantage of a series of caves in the area, connecting them with deep trenches and well-fortified fighting positions that faced eastward, toward Afghanistan. Wells were also sunk to bring up pure cold artesian water. No doubt the veterans of the Soviet-Afghan War among the job bosses were delighted to be constructing a project that had a realistic potential of dealing death and destruction to the Afghan fighters who had made their lives so miserable back in the 1980s.

The Iranian officers coordinating the effort emphasized the need for protection against aerial attack, since the chance of Western air forces being engaged against the site was almost a certainty. The Russians complied by reinforcing the fortifications with tiers of heavy logs and packed earth. The caves required no additional construction or alterations.

0700 HOURS

BRIGADIER Shahruz Khohollah stood in front of his assembled force in the field that once served construction helicopters. To his left he looked on Sikes Pasha and his twenty-man force of al-Askerin-Zaubi. The Storm Troopers looked magnificent and nearly exotic with their keffiyehs as they stood at a strict position of attention. They gave the impression of soldiering in the old British colonial days when white officers, often from working-class backgrounds, turned

to the dangers of isolated areas in Queen Victoria's empire
as their only chance for military glory and high rank. The
old tradition was now being carried out in a twisted manner by Archibald Sikes, an English lad from working-class
Manchester.

The middle formation of the brigadier's force was made
up of Captain Naser Khadid and the twenty Iranian Special
Forces troopers. They had adopted the name Shiraane Salta-
nati (Imperial Lions). The Shiraane—as they were referred
to within the Zaheya—were clad in camouflage battle dress,
sporting the black berets of Special Forces. These were modern empire builders, drawn into an impending do-or-die war
by a fiercely ambitious government.

And over to the brigadier's right was the fire support
group led by Captain Jamshid Komard. They were dressed
in the same uniforms as the Special Forces, except their
headgear consisted of small black turbans styled in the manner of those widely worn in northern Iran. This detachment
was divided into three two-man crews for the Spanish LAG-
40 grenade launchers, and seven two-man crews for the German MG-3 machine guns. These were pragmatic, determined
men who had taken no special name for themselves. It was
enough knowing that the riflemen would depend on them for
covering fire to accomplish assigned missions, whether attacking or defending.

Now Brigadier Khohollah called the Zaheya to stand at
ease. "Soldiers!" he addressed them. "You have been brought
here as a vanguard. This is a great honor for a small fighting
group such as we. There are great plans that will result in our
nation and religion avenging the past injustices and encroach-
ments of the West. These are humiliations that have been
forced on us for more than ninety years. When you have finally prevailed in this holy struggle, the people of the Middle
East will revere you; the people of Europe and America will
fear you; and Allah will reward you."

He had chosen his words carefully to placate Sikes
Pasha's men. They would be needed, like all their brethren,
to advance Iran's ambitions. Later, when that area of the
globe was completely dominated by Iranians, the Arabs' native countries would be ruled by military governors sent

from Tehran. This was the colonial modus operandi of the ancient Persian Empire.

Now Khohollah began pacing as he continued. "There have been setbacks, as we all know. But such unfortunate instances were expected, and we do not reel from these small defeats. The big attack will begin from here and by you. Are you ready?"

Cries of *"Bale, Satrip"* and *"Aiwa, Zaim"* came from the Zaheya troops as they made affirmative replies in Farsi and Arabic. The enthusiasm in their voices was in perfect tune in spite of being shouted in two separate languages.

"Detachment commanders!" Khohollah bellowed. "Take charge of your commands and move them into their fighting positions."

Sikes Pasha, Captain Khadid, and Captain Komard called their separate units to attention, then faced them to the west to begin marching to what was to become their front lines.

SHELOR FIELD, AFGHANISTAN
5 JUNE
1430 HOURS

TWENTY-THREE men arrived on the latest flight from Kuwait to be added to the roster of Brannigan's Brigands. However, one was not exactly a reinforcement. PO2C Arnie Bernardi was a Brigand reporting back from Kuwait, where he had been on TDy, on a training mission. Bernardi's initial joy at being reunited with his old outfit was dashed when he learned of Milly Mills' death. His mood spiraled rapidly down as he experienced a combination of sadness and guilt at not being with the detachment during the battles out on the desert. He truly felt he had let his buddies down, and nothing they said to the contrary eased his feelings of remorse.

Bernardi's fellow passengers had been dispatched into the OA for this one specific operation, of which they knew nothing. They would have been surprised to learn that their new commander was as uninformed as they. This new mission had evolved out of an earlier one, titled Operation

Rolling Thunder, and was renamed Operation Battleline by the powers-that-be who ran Special Operations in the Middle East. The Skipper, Lieutenant Bill Brannigan, found it irritating to be moved laterally from one tactical situation to another without feeling the first had been satisfactorily wrapped up as an undeniable victory. Bruno Puglisi, the detachment's ever-verbose weapons specialist, felt the same, and was not bashful about expressing his disenchantment: "The whole thing is too fucking half-ass to suit me," he stated candidly and loudly. "It's like changing opponents at halftime in a football game. There ain't no final score!"

The C-130 that brought the personnel to Shelor was one of a quartet that had been arriving since the day before. The earlier trio was crammed with ammunition, equipment, rations, and other warmaking matériel. The logistics of Shelor Field were under the control of a diminutive senior airman named Randy Tooley. Randy had been going crazy coordinating unloading, storing, quartering transit personnel, and all the other headaches that go with the preparatory activities for a campaign in the mountains.

Randy's basic attitudes would not be considered militarily correct. He found it inconvenient to wear a uniform, salute, or use the title "sir" or "ma'am" when speaking to commissioned officers. In fact, his normal apparel consisted of T-shirts and cut-off BDU trousers, and he openly disliked observing any military protocol whatsoever. However, he was the base commander's fair-haired boy. Colonel Watkins always looked the other way when it came to the little guy's transgressions, and for good reason. The kid was fast and efficient, keeping the operations of the facility going smoothly and on time through his totally dedicated efforts. The CO's life was made easier and less stressful because of Randy's innate talents. And due to this new set of circumstances that had evolved into a problematic turmoil, the colonel became even more tolerant of Randy's unconventional behavior. Packing him off to the stockade for insubordination would not only accomplish nothing in reforming the young guy, but also would create a loss to the Air Force during his incarceration. Things ground to a standstill badly enough when Randy became upset by a dressing down from some chickenshit NCO or officer, and he would go off by himself to sulk for a day or two. There was an unofficial standing order that he was never to be carried AWOL on base personnel reports.

Randy had a misappropriated desert patrol vehicle that a grateful Lieutenant Bill Brannigan had given him for past services rendered. The young airman, knowing well when guile and subterfuge were necessary, immediately had it painted Air Force blue and stenciled some phony registration numbers across the hood. He happily zipped around in the purloined conveyance as he tended to his duties.

The new SEAL arrivals, after disembarking from the C-130, were ushered quickly to the hangar Brannigan's Brigands used as a headquarters, living quarters, and warehouse. The newcomers found bunks and mattresses waiting for them but no blankets or sheets. That meant they would be slumbering in sleeping bags and/or poncho liners. SCPO Buford Dawkins had chow passes for them through the efforts of Randy Tooley, which meant the newcomers could get hot food in the base mess hall rather than have to consume MREs in the hangar. All the facilities at Shelor Field were open to them: BX, base theater, NCO and enlisted men's clubs, and the swimming pool. The only downside to their stay was being confined to the base. For reasons of the tightest security, no one was permitted to wander off the Air Force property unless on official duty.

One of the new arrivals was a young African-American officer named Ensign Orlando Taylor. After walking down the ramp from the C-130, he went inside the hangar to find the detachment officers. Brannigan and Lieutenant JG Jim Cruiser were in the corner cubicle used as a headquarters of sorts, going over the roster as they began to organize the assault sections for the coming operation. Ensign Taylor dropped his gear by the door and knocked. The Skipper looked up and noted the somber young black man. "You must be our newly assigned Ensign Taylor. Come in."

Taylor stepped inside the office and rendered a faultless salute. "Sir! Ensign Taylor reporting to the commanding officer as ordered."

"Welcome, Taylor," Brannigan said, offering his hand.

"This is Lieutenant JG Jim Cruiser. Take a seat and join the party."

"Thank you, sir," Taylor said. He took a chair as invited, sitting stiffly and formally.

Cruiser gave him a friendly smile. "How was the trip over?"

"Everything moved on schedule," Taylor said. "I am anxious get into the program. When will I be able to meet my men?"

"Right now, Ensign," Brannigan said, "you don't have any men. Jim and I have been mulling over how to reorganize the detachment for the new operation. We went from a total strength of eighteen men to forty-one. Besides the increase in personnel, we also have some added weaponry. All that has to be married together into an effective fighting team. I know that sounds melodramatic, but it's fact." He pushed the rosters and other papers aside. "Well, now, tell us a little about yourself."

"Sir," Taylor said. "I received my commission through NROTC at college. I attended a mostly African-American institution of learning in Georgia. I have only recently completed BUD/S, and this is my first assignment. I have, however, completed the HALO course at Yuma, and am properly prepared for any duties assigned me."

Cruiser smiled. "Well, I guess you must be chomping at the bit, Ensign."

"Yes, sir!" Taylor said. "I look forward to this auspicious beginning of my naval career. Although I hold a reserve commission, I plan to make a career of the U.S. Navy."

"Fine," Brannigan said, reaching back for his papers. "I've got a couple of ideas to discuss. Jump in any time you feel froggy."

"Aye, sir," Taylor said. "Thank you, sir."

"Okay," Brannigan said. "The first thing I want to do is organize a patrol team."

"I take it you'll start with the Odd Couple," Cruiser said. "And don't forget Redhawk. He's a natural."

"Right. And I think I'll put Connie Concord in charge of it. He's a first class and about ready for chief. It's time to start grooming him, don't you think?"

"Yes, sir," Cruiser said. "And I noted that there's a Petty Officer Matsuno on the roster. I know him. He'd make a good addition."

Brannigan wrote down some notes. "Done! And I'll leave Gomez and Bradley in headquarters with me." He sank back into thought for a moment. "Another thing has just this instant occurred to me. This coming operation will be perfect for a sniper team."

"Puglisi and Miskoski," Cruiser said. "That goes without a second thought."

"It shall be done, sayeth the gods of war," Brannigan said, writing down the names of the two SEALs. "Okay. I can see we'll be able to have three assault sections with two fire teams each."

"Don't forget a SAW gunner for each one," Cruiser urged him.

"Right, Jim. You take the First Section," he said, writing down the assignment. He glanced over at Taylor. "The Second Section is yours, Ensign."

"Yes, sir," the young man said.

"And, of course, the Third will be honchoed by the intrepid Senior Chief Petty Officer Buford Dawkins, the pride of Alabama."

"You have some guys left over," Cruiser pointed out.

"It's all part of my cunning master plan," the Skipper said with a wink. "That will be our support section of machine guns. Seven-point-six-twos, as a matter of fact. I'll let Chief Gunnarson run that particular show." He gave Taylor another look. "Any suggestions?"

"Negative, sir."

"This operation is going to be your baptism of fire, is it not, Ensign?" Brannigan asked.

"Yes, sir."

"In that case, I have some advice for you," Brannigan said. "You'll be the leader of an assault section, understand? You are the commander, but you listen to the advice of the senior petty officers. Developing that habit will be invaluable to you not only in the beginning of your career, but even after you're a salty old dog yourself."

"Yes, sir."

When Brannigan slid the diagram of the organization over to Cruiser, the impassive Ensign Orlando Taylor gazed steadily at the two veteran officers. The one thing he wanted to conceal from them was his fear; not the fear of death or injury, but the fear of failure. He had been raised in an African-American family well tuned into the twenty-first century. It was headed by a capable, ambitious father. The outcome of this paternal supervision was a fierce rivalry among the four Taylor brothers, who had been taught that anything short of success was not an option.

Cruiser handed the quickly sketched manning chart to Brannigan. "I'd say it's good to go."

"Fine," the Skipper said. "So let's put it into reality, shall we, gentlemen?"

"Lead on, sir," Cruiser said.

The three officers got up to go outside. Taylor followed the two seniors, his apprehension growing.

OVAL OFFICE
WHITE HOUSE
WASHINGTON, D.C.
5 JUNE

A rapping at the door caught the President's attention. He looked up from the press briefing he was preparing and called out, "Come in."

Arlene Entienne, the White House chief of staff, entered the office. She was a beautiful woman of African-Cajun ancestry, with green eyes and dark brown hair. She looked stunning that morning, even though it was obvious she was tired. "Good morning, Mr. President."

"Hello, Arlene," he replied to the greeting. "I heard you came in at four A.M. today."

"Yes, sir," she replied. "I received a call from Edgar Watson of the CIA a little after three. Operation Persian Empire has kicked into high gear."

The President got up and walked over to the side of the room where a coffeepot was plugged in. He poured a cup of the brew, then brought it over to Arlene. "Here. You need this."

"I sure do!"

"Did we hear from Aladdin again?" the President asked, sitting back down. He referred to a mysterious individual who had been sending anonymous but accurate intelligence from the Iran-Afghanistan border.

"Edgar said it was a quick transmission," Arlene answered. "Evidently Aladdin is in a particularly dangerous area. At any rate, he informed us that a compact group of Iranians and Arabs are occupying a fortified area in the far west of the Gharawdara Highlands. When the time is right, they'll make their move. Their objective, of course, is to gain control of that mountainous area in western Afghanistan."

"A 'compact' group, hey?" the President remarked. "They evidently don't want to make a big fuss. That's good. We don't want to either."

"Mr. President," Arlene said, "you gave me authorization to put your special executive order into effect. I did so at a little past five this morning."

"All right," he said. "It's amazing when one considers the fact that this sensitive international crisis is going to be settled by dozens rather than thousands of troops."

"Without a doubt it's a most unique situation."

"And now our own so-called compact group will answer the challenge," the President said. "A small, deadly operation within a larger one, with global implications."

"Operation Battleline folded into Operation Persian Empire," Arlene said.

The President sighed. "The worst part of this job is having to put the lives of our finest young people at risk." He stood and walked to the window, gazing out pensively. "I cannot describe how much it distresses me."

Arlene got to her feet and went over to him, standing close to the chief executive. "Would it make you feel better if I reminded you they were all volunteers?"

"Not really."

CHAPTER 1

THE procedure is called "isolation," and the name can be taken literally.

This is a routine of segregating a detachment as it begins preparation for a highly classified mission. Its members are either moved to a secure area, or their present quarters are sealed off. Segregated from the outside by security personnel, the people concerned are first briefed with what is actually a very complicated WARNO. This involves a detailed presentation, usually given by an operations and/or intelligence officer that spells out the what, where, and when of an upcoming operation.

This is called the *briefing*.

The people receiving the information then write up an OPLAN based on everything they've learned during the briefing. When the commander of the mission is satisfied with it, the OPLAN is presented orally to the briefing team.

That phase is called the *briefback*.

This can lead to more discussion until everything is hashed over and given a final approval. At that point it becomes an OPORD, and the situation shifts into high gear for implementation and application.

The SEAL operations officer, Commander Thomas Carey, and his cohort, Lieutenant Commander Ernest Berringer, an intelligence officer, worked off the USS *Combs*, a DDG that served as a surreptitious SFOB floating around in the Persian Gulf. The commander was a grumpy U.S. Army Special Forces brigadier general named Leroux. He likened his assignment to being encased in a steel box that rolled and pitched 24/7 without ceasing. From all appearances, the vessel was just part of a CVBG carrying on normal duties rather than acting as a direction center for SPECOPS within that operational area.

Both Carey and Berringer had arrived at Shelor Field only hours before. Their appearances were always unexpected and heralded the beginning of exciting times, but this latest presence raised moods of the deepest suspicion and apprehension among Brannigan's Brigands. The pair of visiting officers had someone with them, and this person gave strong evidence that something very special was about to go down. Carl Joplin, PhD, an Undersecretary of State, was already well known by the SEALs, and his usual bailiwick was in the State Department Building in Washington, D.C.

Immediately after their arrival, Carey and Berringer placed the recently reinforced SEAL detachment Brannigan's Brigands in isolation. The SEALs were taken into their special hangar, cut off from the rest of the air base, meaning they no longer ate in the mess hall, no longer visited the theater or service club, and had to curtail their favorite pastime of making out with female Air Force personnel behind the beer garden. Security was provided by Shelor's APs to make sure the Brigands were kept out of circulation.

They and all their belongings were now in total confinement.

SEAL HANGAR
0700 HOURS

SCPO Buford Dawkins checked the names on his clipboard with the faces seated in the four rows of folding chairs.
Brannigan's Brigands had gone from its customary strength
of some twenty-one individuals to a total of forty-one. Since
Dawkins didn't know all twenty of the new men prior to their
arrival, he used this method to familiarize himself with the
newcomers. After taking the silent roll call, he was satisfied
nobody was lost or wandering around. He turned to his commanding officer, Lieutenant Wild Bill Brannigan. "Ever'
swinging dick is present and accounted for, sir."

"Right, Senior Chief," Brannigan responded from his
chair. He nodded to Carey and Berringer, who stood at the
front of the group with Dr. Joplin. "We're ready to rock and
roll, sir."

"Alright!" Carey said. "Consider this an official welcome
to Operation Battleline. We discussed this before, but now
the day is here. First thing we'll do is review the overall situation. Your preliminary enemy in Operation Rolling Thunder has been defeated. The Arab and Iranian bad guys are
out of that operational area. The Pashtun rebel group who
occupied the Gharawdara Highlands gave it up, and now live
under the gentle care of Dr. Bouchier's UNREO team in a
pacified area farther east."

CPO Matt Gunnarson frowned. "It seems to me them
Pashtuns is getting off pretty light."

"This particular group of people are being tolerated because of their very strong anti-Taliban attitudes," Carey
replied. "And their leader went to the Afghanistan government and declared what is called *nanwatai*. This is a code in
which a loser begs for mercy and humbles himself. Custom
demands he be granted mercy. We Americans, therefore,
cannot insist on more severe punishment. Thus the Pashtun
chief and his people are being well treated."

Bruno Puglisi, sitting comfortably with his arms folded
across his muscular chest, grinned. "In that case, it don't
sound like there's much more to do around here, sir."

"Unfortunately, that's not the case, Petty Officer Puglisi,"

Carey said. "But I'm getting ahead of myself. You are all aware of Operation Persian Empire. That is an all-encompassing situation that has been boiled down to a small but very complicated matter with delicate political and diplomatic criteria. I'll let Dr. Joplin explain that further."

The African-American, looking dignified even in the BDUs he wore for the occasion, stepped forward. This intellectually gifted expert in the complicated environment of international diplomacy gave his audience a warm smile. "It's really nice to see you fellows again. It's been a long time since South America. I promise we'll have some beer together before I leave. And, by the way, I'm buying."

A spontaneous cheer broke out from the group, with whoops and shouts of gratitude. Joplin's smile spread into a grin. "I knew somehow you would be pleased."

Senior Chief Dawkins announced, "Dr. Joplin has already put in an order for a good number of cases from the BX. But you guys ain't drinking a drop 'til the operation is over and done with."

"Now with that settled, let me review the Iranian situation for you," Joplin said. "You're already acquainted with what's going on, but things have slipped into a sort of different perspective." He paused to organize his thoughts. "As you all are well aware, the government of Iran has become rather belligerent lately. They began their latest mischief with their nuclear program and support of the renegade Hezbollah terrorists in Lebanon. Now they have now begun using their intelligence operatives to bring Shiite insurgencies throughout the Middle East under their control. The objective is to take over the whole of that part of the world with its people and oil, and establish the first steps of a modern Persian Empire. If they succeed, this will spill over to all parts of the globe. The economic effect on the Western world would be catastrophic."

Lieutenant Jim Cruiser, sitting on the front row with Brannigan and Ensign Orlando Taylor, showed a serious expression. "What you're describing seems to be a situation that could lead to a world war."

"We're already in a world war, Jim," Joplin replied. "And your main duty in this upcoming operation is to keep a lid on this volatile situation. A small force of Iranians and Arabs is now in the Gharawdara Highlands in the border country. They are called the Zaheya, which is a Farsi acronym for Strike Force Vengeance. This includes Arabs you've fought before when they were an armored car company. And, as I'm sure you remember, they are led by a deserter from the British Army. I must warn you that he has whipped them into an elite unit of infantry. So you may anticipate that they will be much harder to deal with in the future."

Mike Assad interjected, "We'll deal with 'em, alright, Dr. Joplin. Don't worry about that."

"There is no doubt in my mind you can handle it, Mike," Joplin said, keeping his apprehension to himself. "They are joined by some hard-core Iranian Army Special Forces who have completed a most demanding program of training and preparation. These men are totally dedicated to their national aims. So your work is cut out for you."

"How many of them are there?" Joe Miskoski asked.

"A few more than you," Joplin said.

Brannigan frowned. "I thought you were talking about a world war. But we're not dealing with forces of thousands or even hundreds of troops here. This is literally a clash of dozens. I don't understand."

"I'll try to explain this complicated and confusing issue to you," Joplin said patiently. "Neither we nor the Iranians want a big to-do to settle this thing. The bigger it is, the more dangerous it becomes for everybody concerned. And believe me, it would fuel the fire of this world war we're now involved in. The Iranians want a foothold in Afghanistan to renew the Pashtun revolt. They plan to accomplish this illegal goal unobtrusively."

"Well, hell!" Connie Concord said. "Why not just bomb 'em to ashes?"

"We could certainly do that," Joplin said. "But that would cause a backlash in the Middle East. Therefore we must follow Iran's example and also be as low-key as possible."

CPO Matt Gunnarson raised his hand. "What is so important about Afghanistan to the Iranians?"

"They can accomplish two things in that country," Joplin replied. "First they have an immediate expansion of their territory; and second, by ruling Afghanistan it would be only a matter of time before they took over Pakistan. If that happened, the international implications are bound to be catastrophic. It would be exactly like the situation that brought about the start of World War One. Before that conflict erupted, the leaders of the affected European nations—the kings, emperors, czars, and what have you—were more afraid of what would be thought of them if they *didn't* go to war, rather than if they did."

"Excuse me, Dr. Joplin," Puglisi said, "but what the fuck are you talking about?"

"I'm talking about egotistical assholes within the Islam world not wanting to be considered candy-asses," Joplin said, choosing words the SEAL could relate to as a fighting man. "Their only consideration would be whose side to be on in the inevitable war to come."

"Alright!" Puglisi said. "I can dig it."

"So if the thing is settled in a small, unobtrusive manner, then the government in Tehran can back off without losing face if they are defeated here in Operation Battleline," Joplin said. "The problem goes away."

"That's fine if the Iranians lose," Gutsy Olson remarked. "But what if *we* lose?"

Joplin took a deep breath. "My dear friends, you *cannot* lose! The country couldn't afford it. You see, we don't have the luxury the Iranians have. If you're kicked off that mountain, then Israel will move in big time to squelch Iran's master plan. As you know, they will employ considerable force that would entail the use of one of their own WMDs. Such a destructive attack would change the present global situation for the worse. Muslims in all parts of the world would rise up, including those in Indonesia, Bangladesh, India, Turkey, Nigeria, and even China. All in all, we're talking about one point two billion people who would respond in a most violent way."

"Then nuke *all* the motherfuckers," Monty Sturgis, one of the new guys, suggested with a smile.

"That wouldn't be very good for this planet we're living on," Joplin replied. "It would be a thousand times worse than what Israel would do."

"Excuse me, Dr. Joplin," Chad Murchison said. "Couldn't our government proscribe Israel from taking such a cataclysmic step?"

"They would not listen," Joplin said.

"How do we know that?" Brannigan asked.

"Because the Israelis said so," Joplin replied. "Having a Persian Empire ruled by people who have sworn to wipe Israel off the map is not the same as dealing with Hamas in Palestine or Hezbollah in Lebanon. The leaders in Jerusalem are not willing to take that chance." He shrugged. "Therefore—and please forgive the cliché—losing is not an option. With your victory in a contained campaign, all those big problems will go away."

Somewhere within the group of SEALs could be heard a single utterance of frustration. "Shit!"

"Yeah," Joplin agreed. "Any questions?" When nobody spoke, he gave them another smile. "No matter the circumstances, I really enjoy being with you again." He stepped back as Carey retook the floor.

The operations officer took a moment to study the faces of the Brigands. Everyone was glum, showing that Joplin's dissertation had convinced them of the seriousness of the upcoming operation. Carey cleared his throat. "Ahem. So, although it is not necessary but customary, I will continue this briefing with the mission statement. You are to engage and defeat the Iranian forces now occupying an area of the Gharawdara Highlands on the Iran-Afghanistan border. The reasons behind all this have been rather well presented by Dr. Joplin, so we'll move on to the execution."

The SEALs all had their notebooks out, with ballpoint pens poised to begin taking notes.

Carey continued, "On seven June at oh-six-hundred hours you will depart from Shelor Field via an Air Force Pave Low chopper to fly up into the Gharawdara Highlands. Your destination is a stronghold formerly used by that Pashtun rebel group mentioned earlier. There are excellent defensive positions already constructed that you can occupy as well as a number of caves available for bunkers and storage areas. These are artillery- and bombproof."

"Sir," Dave Leibowitz said, raising his hand. "Before you go any further, I'd like to know if we have any assets available."

"There is one," Carey said, "and you already know about him. It's the guy code-named Aladdin."

"Wait a minute!" Brannigan blurted. "Isn't he the one who is such a mystery to our own intelligence community?"

"Yes," Carey answered. "I would like to emphasize that he has been officially—I say again—*officially* approved. Since I spoke to you last he has managed to get off a couple more transmissions. That's how we know the physical setup of your base camp. One more thing: There will be neither discussion nor argument about his reliability."

"Aye, sir," Brannigan grumpily acknowledged.

"To continue," Carey said. "The choppers will land on an LZ behind the base camp. It is a small, flat area that can accommodate aerial deliveries and extractions, including medevacs. After offloading, you will proceed down to the former Pashtun area and establish your base camp. When it is properly prepared, you will launch your operations. Any questions about that?"

"Yes, sir," Jim Cruiser said. "Will we have air support?"

"Not unless Iranian aircraft come on the scene," Carey replied. "Anybody else? Good. Now I'll let Commander Berringer give you the intelligence portion of the briefing."

Berringer had no notes with him. He walked up to the front of the group and assumed a relaxed position of parade rest. "The intel we have on the bad guys is a couple of days old, so figure there's probably going to be some changes and alterations, understood? Their approximate total strength is sixty, with an overall commander and three subunit commanders. Two of those subunits are infantry assault troops, while the third is a support element of some kind. That probably means a combination of machine guns and mortars."

"Can you be more specific, sir?" CPO Matt Gunnarson asked.

"No," Berringer replied in a flat tone, then continued with his dissertation. "They are situated in a preprepared fighting position that was constructed under the supervision of Russian military engineers. We know nothing of the layout or defensive capabilities of the area."

"In other words," Brannigan said, "we'll have to dig up our own intelligence."

"Yes," Berringer answered. "Our knowledge is limited because the asset Aladdin is unable to transmit long, detailed messages to us. And we do not know the actual location of his radio. He might be moving it around for security purposes. Any questions?"

"Yes, sir," the former preppy Chad Murchison said. "What is the physical milieu of the area between the warring factions?"

Berringer hesitated before speaking. "I think you want to know what the terrain is like between the SEAL positions and those of the enemy, do you not?"

"Yes, indeed, sir," Chad replied. "I am, of course, referring to the area similar to what they called 'no-man's-land' during the trench warfare of World War One."

"Well, Petty Officer Murchison," Berringer said, "no-man's-land is a valley floor about two hundred meters across. There is cover and concealment available, but the area is under full visibility by either side. You'll have to go up some fifteen meters of steep slopes to reach the fighting positions."

"Ah!" Chad said. "So one must *descend* into the valley, cross it, and then *ascend* the slopes on the opposite side to reach the enemy for any close—hand-to-hand— engagements."

"That is correct," Berringer said. "Any more questions?"

"About a thousand," Mike Assad said, "but I guess we're not going to get any answers."

Berringer spoke up sharply. "If you're a nervous Nellie, Petty Officer Assad, we can pull you out of Operation Battleline."

Now Brannigan's temper flared. "With all respect, sir, but I have to remind you that Assad spent many long weeks undercover within the al-Mimkhalif terrorist group and came out with enough valuable intelligence to put them out of business."

"I don't care if he's been fucking Usama Bin Laden in

the ass," Berringer snapped back. "I will not tolerate insubordinate remarks!"

"Aye, sir," Brannigan said. He looked over at Assad. "Shut up!"

"Aye, sir!"

Berringer went back to join Dr. Joplin as Carey retook the floor. "Alright, that's it. You'll be fed additional information by us and the Air Force as it becomes available. In the meantime, take what you've got and turn it into an OPLAN. That is all."

Brannigan called the detachment to attention as the two officers and the diplomat left the hangar. He turned to the SEALs in the chairs. "Alright! I want to see Lieutenant Cruiser and Ensign Taylor in the cubicle. Senior Chief Dawkins, take over the detachment and set 'em to work."

Operation Battleline was now official and functioning.

ZAHEYA POSITIONS
IRAN-AFGHANISTAN BORDER
1400 HOURS

ARSALAAN Sikes, born Archibald Sikes in Manchester, England, was a commissioned major in the Iranian Army. He had insisted on the appointment to solidify his position within the Zaheya to avoid any loss of his prestige as commander of the al-Askerin-Zaubi. Sikes Pasha, as he was called within the strike force, did not trust officers of any army, and that included the ones in the Zaheya.

Now he stood alone on the front lines of his unit's defensive position, using his binoculars to peer across the valley at the area about to be occupied by the enemy. He knew the place well, having lived there for many long weeks. Every defensive position, bunker entrance, and the paths up and down the mountains were familiar to him. This had been the stronghold of the rebel Pashtun leader Yama Orakzai, who had surrendered to the Afghanistan authorities after the American SEALs ripped his organization apart. Part of the dismantling process had included shutting down his opium poppy smuggling operations. That illegal activity provided financial support not only to the Pashtuns but also benefited the very armed force in which Sikes now served.

The sound of footsteps interrupted Sikes' study of the area, and he turned to see the Iranian Army officer Captain Jamshid Komard approaching. Komard was the commander of the fire support unit made up of Spanish LAG-40 grenade launchers and German MG-3 machine guns. The Iranian saluted the Brit. "Good morning, Sikes Pasha."

"Sob bekheyr," Sikes replied in Farsi.

Komard smiled. "So you are learning more Farsi with each passing day, *rast,* Sikes Pasha?"

"Right," Sikes replied in the accent of northern England. "I figger it's the bluddy least I could do since I'm a major in the army, yeah?"

Komard pulled his binoculars from the carrying case. "I am ready for you to point out the positions across the valley."

"Right," Sikes said. "We'll work from left to right." He grinned. "That might be a bit sticky for you, since your lot do your reading and writing from right to left."

"I shall manage, Sikes Pasha," Komard said.

"Right then," Sikes said. "Now look slightly up to where the ridgeline runs from the mountaintop. That's the farthest out the bastards can go to the north, and them Pashtuns laid it in good to protect that flank. I'd look for both heavy weapons and infantry to be there."

"I see it plainly," Komard said. "I expect they might try to camouflage it better once they move into the area."

"More'n likely," Sikes agreed. "You can see it well enough now, since the brush around it is dead and dried out."

Komard took his compass and shot an azimuth on the location. After entering the information in his notebook he said, "I'm ready for the next one."

The two men spent the next half hour meticulously noting all the fighting positions the Pashtuns had established in the past.

ARCHIBALD Sikes had once been an excellent non-commissioned officer in the British Army's crack Royal Regiment of Dragoons. This armored infantry unit had a long and colorful history in the colonial days of Queen Victoria's domains. The sun did not set on the British Empire, nor did it set on the battlefields on which the Dragoons had fought and died in the greatest traditions of Great Britain.

Sergeant Sikes had been an ambitious soldier and decided he would like to earn a commission to continue his career as an officer. He was approved by both his platoon leader and company commander to go before the board for attending officer training. He passed the examinations and interviews with flying colors, but when he requested his commission be made in his home regiment, he was turned down. The major in charge of the examining board told Sikes he was not socially acceptable for the officers' mess of the Royal Dragoons.

Sikes had no idea of the rigid class system of the regiment's elite. In reality, they were all from wealthy families with the right connections and a standard of living far above that of the typical British unit. To keep up appearances, the officers had to use more than their army pay. They had high dues and subscriptions in their mess, all uniforms were tailor-made, they kept privately owned polo ponies in the regimental stables, and they enjoyed a lifestyle of the truly rich and famous. Television and movie stars visited their mess along with powerful politicians and industrialists. It was hardly the place for a young Brit whose father worked in a building materials supply warehouse as a stockman.

This snobbery turned Sikes off. When informed of the when and why of the refusal of the regiment to accept him as one of its officers, he was infuriated. It didn't matter that he could have been commissioned in any other regiment—with the exception of the Brigade of Guards—Sikes wanted the Royal Regiment of Dragoons. He had especially picked it out to serve in when he joined up. The same evening of the turndown, he went to town, got drunk, and ended up being arrested for brawling. He was reduced from sergeant to corporal. More misconduct resulted in his being busted down to the rank of private.

When his unit went to Iraq, his conduct did not improve. His regimental sergeant major informed him that when they returned to Britain, he would be kicked out of the Army with a bad-conduct discharge. An Iraqi civilian employee at the camp had taken special notice of Sikes and became friendly with him. This was Khalil Farouk, an undercover agent for a terrorist group that was aligned with Iran. He knew that Sikes was really an excellent soldier, just the sort of man the terrorists needed to whip their mujahideen into shape. The bottom line was that, under Farouk's influence, Sikes deserted, converted to Islam, and joined the Iranian-sponsored Jihad Abadi, which was actually an army-in-the building in a scheme for Iran to control the Middle East.

Sikes, because of his background, was given command of an armored car company at the Chehaar Garrison in the salt swamps on the Iran-Afghanistan border. They used a secret road through the bogs to enter Afghanistan and conduct combat operations. Sikes had discovered an UNREO unit working with the Pashtun natives in the area and ordered them out. When he returned the next day to see if they had left, he was ambushed by an American unit of DPVs. It turned out the Yanks had no AP rounds and could not damage his armored cars. But because of the possibility of CAS aircraft coming onto the scene, Sikes ordered his men back across the border.

The next confrontation with the Americans in Afghanistan occurred ten days later. This time they had AP capabilities, and used the nimble DPVs to advantage in quick strikes and envelopments. Sikes lost thirteen of his twenty vehicles and retreated across the international border. When he complained to the Iranians about the lack of reserves along with no artillery or air support, they disbanded his armored cars. He and his men were transferred as infantrymen to Pashtun allies in the Gharawdara Highlands.

Things went to hell again when the Americans wiped out the Pashtuns' opium poppy smuggling operation. The Pashtun leader surrendered, and Sikes took his command back into Iran, where they ended up in the present operation to strike into Afghanistan and grab a big hunk of territory to lure the Pashtuns back to their cause.

Sikes had now worked his way up to the rank of major in the Iranian Army, and he stood ready with his Iranian comrades and his own Arab followers to do battle with whoever would be moving into the old Pashtun stronghold across the valley. This time Sikes and his men were well equipped with the latest night vision capabilities of goggles and binoculars, LASH radio sets, and heavy fire support. Reinforcements and resupply were also available to sustain this latest operation.

Sikes Pasha smiled to himself, his confidence buoyed by the strong support from both the Iranian government and Army. The tide had at last turned.

CHAPTER 2

THE folding chairs had been arranged into a semicircle, with two to the direct front for Commander Tom Carey and Lieutenant Commander Ernest Berringer. Dr. Carl Joplin would not be present at the briefback for security reasons. The Undersecretary of State was a trusted individual with a top-secret and cryptography security clearance, but his exclusion was because of that traditional requirement of not having a "need to know."

When the two staff officers walked into the area, Carey let it be known it was unnecessary to call the detachment to attention when he loudly proclaimed, "Carry on!" He and Berringer went to the chairs obviously set out for them and settled down. They had left their briefcases behind and did not produce as much as a notebook in which to jot down the highlights of the briefback.

Brannigan took the obvious hint to hurry things along.

He spoke from the center front chairs, where he sat with Lieutenant JG Jim Cruiser and Ensign Orlando Taylor. "Before we start the briefback, Ensign Taylor has an announcement to make. It's a bit of information that every member of this detachment will take to heart. Lieutenant Cruiser and I only learned the facts last night."

Taylor stood and turned to face the SEALs. "I told the Skipper and Lieutenant Cruiser last night about a cousin of mine who had served with the SEALs. He was KIA on an operation, but our family was never given the full details of the incident. We did not know his whereabouts when he sacrificed his life for his country, nor were we aware of the exact circumstances. Naturally my cousin had told the whole family about the possibility of such a thing happening because of secret missions. When I mentioned his name, the Skipper told me he was a Brigand, and was killed in action on your deployment to South America." Taylor paused to get hold of his emotions. "I was very close to him and I am honored beyond belief that circumstances have permitted me to take his place in this detachment. His name was Lamar Taylor, and he's left me some pretty big shoes to fill."

Connie Concord nodded to the ensign. "I was his fire team leader, sir. Lamar was a hell of a fine man. A real SEAL."

"Alright!" Brannigan barked. "Let's get this briefback rolling along. Lieutenant Cruiser!"

"Aye, sir!" Cruiser stood to address Carey and Berringer. "My portion of the briefback will cover the movement from Shelor to the OA. I won't be using any maps or aerial photos, since we all know the exact location of the place. So! I'll start with an announcement of my own. Two choppers are going to be used, and I'll discuss them one at a time. We'll be utilizing an Air Force Pave Low MH-fifty-three J chopper for personnel, equipment, weapons, and ammo. It's more than adequate to handle all our needs for the mission. We have set up a new departure time of zero-six-hundred hours. That will be for the first chopper. The Pave Low will follow at zero-seven-hundred hours."

"Where does this additional first chopper come in?" Carey asked.

"We want to drop in a recon team to scope out the area prior to landing and deplaning. All available aerial photos indicate the site is secure, but we want to make sure. I've made arrangements through the Army transportation company to have the use of an Afghanistan Army Huey helicopter for this parachute infiltration."

This piqued Lieutenant Commander Berringer's interest. "Why did you go to the Afghans? We could easily arrange for something larger."

"The sight of an Afghan aircraft will not excite the enemy too much," Cruiser explained. "They make frequent flights in the OA as part of their normal activities. The local AF-SOC folks can spare us three T-Ten chutes. Petty Officers Leibowitz, Assad, and Redhawk will jump in at approximately zero-six-thirty hours and make a recon."

"That's a good idea up to a point," Carey opined. "But don't you think when the Iranians catch sight of three parachutes descending into the area they'll figure something special is happening?"

"The jump will be made at five hundred feet," Cruiser explained. "I'm hoping the chutes will not be spotted from the enemy positions, since a mountain range is between them and the LZ. Or the DZ in this case."

"I don't know," Carey said. "Exiting the aircraft at five hundred feet can be extremely risky."

Brannigan interrupted. "During our operation against the al-Mimkhalif fortress in the Yemen-Oman desert, that is exactly what we did. A jump altitude of five hundred feet will afford the jumpers a minimum time between the aircraft and the ground."

"Alright, Lieutenant," Carey said. "If you're not concerned, then I'm not concerned."

Puglisi spoke up with a silly grin on his face. "Hell! If you want minimum time between the aircraft and the ground, don't use parachutes."

"Shut up, Puglisi!" Brannigan snapped.

"Aye, sir!"

Cruiser continued, "When we receive the all clear from the recon team, the Air Force chopper will go in. We'll disembark bag and baggage and move into our fighting positions to get the show on the road."

"I'm glad you came up with the recon idea," Carey said. "That hadn't occurred to me. It sounds like you guys should be able to make a smooth infiltration."

"Right," Berringer agreed. "Our intel says the place is empty, but it's wise to check it out before committing a deployment."

Cruiser sat down, and Brannigan stood to give the organizational portion of the briefback. "We have three officers, two chief petty officers, and thirty-six petty officers for a total of forty-one guys. I've set up a headquarters for command, commo, medical, and special tasks. My Headquarters will be Gomez as RTO and Bradley as corpsman. Puglisi and Miskoski make up the Sniper Team, with each toting his own A-fifty sniper rifle. We will assign them spotters when possible. A special Patrol Team for recon and combat patrolling will be utilized, with Petty Officer Concord as the leader. His personnel will be Assad, Matsuno, Redhawk, and Leibowitz."

Carey was curious. "Were there special qualifications for assignment to the Patrol Team?"

"Yes, sir," Brannigan answered. "Assad, Leibowitz, and Redhawk have already demonstrated their skills in this area during past operations. Lieutenant Cruiser personally recommended Matsuno."

"I agree, sir," Senior Chief Dawkins said. "I've been on operations with him before, and he is from a Japanese-American background, where he did some serious study of ninja techniques. He's damn good at sneakin' and peekin'."

"Seem excellent choices then," Carey said.

"The rest of the detachment is going to be broken down into three assault sections. These will be commanded by the two officers and a senior chief. Each of them will have a SAW gunner tagging along with him. The rest of the section consists of two fire teams of a team leader, rifleman, and grenadier."

"What about the guys that are left over?" Berringer inquired.

"That's the Fire Support Section, sir," Brannigan replied. "Chief Gunnarson will honcho three M-sixty machine guns. Each will have a gunner and a rifleman who will also be the ammo bearer."

The next speaker was PO2C Frank Gomez, who gave the commo portion of the briefback. "All the gear will remain the same as on Operation Rolling Thunder, sir. I will use my Shadowfire for long-range commo, while everyone will tote AN/PRC-one-twenty-six radios with LASH headsets. Call signs are Brigand Boss for Headquarters, Hit Man for the Sniper Team, and Sneaky Pete for the Patrol Team. Brigand One will be for the First Assault Section, with the others being Brigand Two and Three, respectively. The fire support will be Brigand Four. All the fire teams will use their designations. Alpha, Bravo, Charlie, and so on."

Hospital Corpsman Doc Bradley came forward for the medical side of the operation. "We're in good shape with personal medical kits that have the usual battle dressing, Ace bandages, et cetera. This also includes codeine, morphine, and the array of sedatives, stimulants, and pills for normal sickness that occurs in the field. I'm planning on setting up a treatment station in one of the bunkers. And I'll have my field surgical kit for the big hurts. I've checked everyone's shot records, and they're up to date. The LZ will be used for medevac. So, medically speaking, we're ready to go."

"Sounds good," Carey remarked. "Next!"

PO2C Bruno Puglisi represented the weapons and ammo side of the operation. "All the guys is gonna be packing issue Beretta nine-millimeter auto pistols in drop holsters. "The headquarters weenies—"

Mike Assad interrupted, saying, "Who're you calling headquarters weenies?"

"The headquarters section," Puglisi replied. "Who else? And remember I'm in headquarters too. Being called a weenie just goes with the territory."

"Stick to the briefback!" Senior Chief Dawkins snarled.

"Right, Chief," Puglisi said. "So, as I was saying before that rude interruption, the *elite personnel* of headquarters, along with the section commanders, fire team leaders, riflemen, and machine gun crews will tote M-sixteens. The grenadiers is gonna have the same along with M-two-oh-three grenade launchers. And, as the Skipper said in his organization spiel, we'll have three M-sixty machine gun crews. The SAW gunners will be packing their M-two-forty-nines, as can be expected. We can have all the ammo we want, so I laid in for plenty. Also, the load will include a couple of flare guns and a crate of smoke grenades for signaling on the LZ, since we'll be depending on aerial resupply."

"You've nailed it, Petty Officer Puglisi," Carey said. "Also keep in mind that because of the static situation, you'll have no trouble obtaining additional weaponry and ammunition."

That pleased Brannigan. "Great, sir! I'm thinking there's a possibility we'll be needing some mortars to soften up enemy positions for any big pushes."

"I'll see that some are available for immediate use," Carey promised. "Okay. Who's next?"

SCPO Buford Dawkins stepped forward. "Our organizational and personal supply situation is excellent, sir. I ran an inventory on every swinging dick and they were standing tall. We have everything we need, including additional night vision apparatus. Enough night vision binoculars have arrived that each section commander and team leader will be issued one. That also includes the Skipper, Patrol Team, and Sniper Team."

"Now, there's a pleasant surprise," Berringer said. "I wasn't aware of that."

"What about creature comforts at your base camp?" Carey asked. "I'm talking about ergonomics."

"Well, sir," Dawkins said, "the guys will be well off with plenty of room. We're starting out with MREs, but if circumstances permit, Randy Tooley said he could arrange for some cookpots, pans, and hot chow from the mess hall from time to time."

"Randy Tooley?" Carey said. "Isn't he that weird little guy who drives around in the DPV?" He looked at Brannigan. "That reminds me. You were supposed to submit a report about that DPV that was lost in action. The Army S-four at Station Bravo has been bugging the hell out of me about it."

"Right, sir," Brannigan said. "I've got the first draft done. I just need to tweak it a bit."

"Get it to me PDQ!"

"Aye, sir!"

Carey glanced at Berringer. "Do you have anything to add, Ernie?"

"Negative, sir," Berringer replied. "It sounds complete to me."

"I agree," Carey said, standing. He gestured to Brannigan. "Turn it into an OPORD. You'll depart Shelor Field tomorrow morning."

ZAHEYA POSITIONS
1330 HOURS

MAJOR Arsalaan Sikes—known as Sikes Pasha by his men—finished off the last of the Iranian field ration. The food was canned in this case, and he had grown weary of the various soups the menus offered. The canned bread wasn't too bad, but the cheese spread that came with it was more than an Englishman's palate could stand. He longed for the varieties offered in the dehydrated chow available in Western armies.

He sat outside in front of his bunker, gazing down at the maze of trenches that made up the defenses of the base. He could see his second-in-command, Warrant Officer Shafaqat Hashiri, walking slowly down the line, inspecting the men on duty. Sikes grinned when he saw the veteran soldier give a dressing down to one of the Storm Troopers. The Brit had sharpened the men up from the time he commanded the armored car company at the Chehaar Garrison near the salt swamps farther south. Now, thanks to a fearful drubbing by Americans, they were an infantry unit. But they still demonstrated a marked fighting spirit, and responded well to discipline.

"Sikes Pasha!"

He looked up the path at the sound of his name, and saw Captain Naser Khadid of the Iranian Special Forces approaching. Sikes lifted a hand in a gesture of greeting. "Out for a stroll?"

Khadid shook his head as he walked up and took a seat

on the ground. "Brigadier Khohollah wanted me to drop by to see how your Arabs are doing."

Sikes gestured downward. "They're 'standing to,' as is said in the British Army."

"The Brigadier is extremely pleased to note how well you have trained them," Khadid said. "He is particularly pleased that their morale has remained high in spite of the previous setbacks. I thought you might be interested in the fact he speaks highly of you to others."

"That's always nice to know, ain't it?" Sikes remarked, pulling a packet of cigarettes out of his pocket. He offered one to Khadid and took one himself. "Them lads o' mine are damn good, no doubt. Good thing for them they're here, ain't it? If they was back in Iraq, they'd prob'ly all been sent to blow themselves up as suicide bombers by now."

"Indeed," Khadid said, lighting a match to serve both of them. "That is the one thing my government wanted to stop. That was the driving force behind the concept of Iranian control over all Shiite insurgencies."

"Here now, Naser," Sikes said. "I ain't completely stupid, y'know, hey? You Iranians want to own the whole bluddy Middle East. Even I figgered that out though nobody sat me down and actually said it."

Khadid looked at him carefully. "How do you feel about that, Sikes Pasha?"

"I got no problems with it," Sikes said. "I'm a major in the bluddy Iranian Army, ain't I? So when this all happens, I'll be sitting pretty." He took a drag off the cigarette and slowly exhaled. "But I'm a bit confused about this here operation, know what I mean then?"

"What is bothering you?"

"Aw, there ain't nothing bothering me, but I can't quite figger out what we'll be accomplishing here, hey?" Sikes said. "What if we win? What if we lose?"

"Although there are not many troops here, this is an important operation," Khadid said. "For both sides. Our objective, of course, is to get a good foothold in Afghanistan, then have large units of the Iranian Army follow up to occupy our conquered area. A victory on our part will bring Yama Orakzai and his band back to us. When that happens, more Pashtuns will rally to our cause. Afghanistan will be completely dominated by Iran within six months."

"Then what in the bluddy hell are we waiting for, hey?" Sikes asked. "There ain't a single, solitary Yank across that valley sitting in Orakzai's old stronghold. All we got to do is make our way over there and it's ours."

Khadid shook his head. "The Americans would simply contain us there, then push us back here. What we must do is defeat them here as they attack us, understand? In the meantime, do not forget that more and more Shiite Arabs are joining our ranks. If we can keep the infidels occupied long enough, we shall have a strong force."

"Alright," Sikes relented. "I'll take yer word for it. Tell the Brigadier that me Arab Storm Troopers are ready to fight."

Khadid stood up. "He will be glad to know he can depend on you, Sikes Pasha."

"Tell me, something, Naser," Sikes said. "Do you miss your Pashtun wife?" They had both entered temporary Muslim marriages with teenage Pashtun girls during the time they were stationed with Orakzai's people. When the leader pulled out to submit to the authority of the Afghanistan government, the marriages were ended. "I sure miss Banafsha."

"And I long for Mahzala's charms," Khadid said. "But we will be without women for a long time." He got to his feet. "I must go, Sikes Pasha. Good day."

"*Ruz bekheyr*," Sikes said. "And tell the Brigadier that I'm working hard at learning me Farsi."

"You learned a lot of Arabic quite rapidly," Khadid said. "I am sure you will have an excellent working knowledge of Farsi within a few more weeks." He nodded a good-bye, then went back down the path.

Sikes settled back and lit another cigarette off the first. In truth, he didn't have that much faith in his Islamic brothers-in-arms, but he had no choice but to stay with them. He would face years in a military prison if he returned to Blighty. He had cut himself off from his native land the moment he deserted and joined the enemy. But if the Iranians succeeded in their plans and really controlled the Middle East, he had much to gain.

His twenty-man Arab Storm Trooper detachment would eventually be expanded to division or perhaps even corps size as the Persian Empire began spreading outward. Brigadier Khohollah had once told him they would branch out to the east and south after conquering Afghanistan and Pakistan, swallowing up Iraq, Saudi Arabia, and Syria. After that came the destruction of Israel before continuing to scoop up other nations until the Great Army of the Empire of Persia was in Turkey, ready to invade Europe itself.

Sikes glanced down at his soldiers on duty in the trenches. They wore Iranian camouflage uniforms and keffiyeh head-dresses, giving them an exotic yet fierce appearance. While he and Warrant Officer Hashiri wore Iranian insignia of rank, their noncommissioned officers wore British chevrons. Some-how, the sight of the familiar badges made Sikes feel more confident.

He finished the cigarette and flipped it over into a stand of rocks. God! How he would love to go down to his favorite pub in Manchester for a few pints with his old mates.

CHAPTER 3

THE Afghan pilot who flew the Huey chopper was good at his job. He had made countless insertions of U.S. Army Special Forces teams into combat situations all over Afghanistan, and instinctively reacted to every aspect of the parachute insertion.

Now, as he swung his aircraft along the proper azimuth over the DZ/LZ, he made note of the wind by studying the directions of the dust clouds being kicked up at ground level. He swung farther away from the western edge of the area to give the three jumpers in his troop compartment more space. However, he knew that at low altitude it probably didn't make much difference. They were headed for a very short trip between aircraft and terra firma. The pilot sincerely hoped it wouldn't be *too* quick.

Mike Assad, Dave Leibowitz, and Garth Redhawk sat on the deck, their legs dangling out of the aircraft. Mike was the jumpmaster, and he waited until he was certain they were in the middle of the flat area designated for the DZ and LZ. When he was satisfied, he pushed himself out. The down-blast from the rotors pressed him hard, and he turned to his side slightly as he rushed earthward. He could see Dave and Garth at slightly different altitudes above him. Suddenly his canopy opened and two beats later he hit the ground hard, unable to make a decent PLF. Pain shot through his legs up into his lower back, but when he got to his feet he was sore but obviously had suffered no serious injury. After hitting the quick-release box, his harness dropped to the ground and he retrieved his M-16 rifle. A moment later Mike and Garth walked up to him, both limping slightly.

"Shit!" Garth said. "I don't know why they bothered to give us parachutes."

"I think we ought to have a rule in the SEALs," Mike said. "From now on, low-altitude jumps from choppers will be performed by officers only."

"Good idea," Dave said. "Be sure and mention that suggestion to the Secretary of the Navy."

"That'll be the first thing I'll do the next time he calls me up for some advice," Mike said. "Alright! Dave will take the point, and Garth, you're the Tail-End Charlie. Let's go check this place out."

The three trekked westward for some fifty meters before finding a trail. It led downward toward the area they were to occupy, and the patrol moved gingerly, keeping on the alert. The photoreconnaissance that showed it unoccupied was forty-eight hours old, and a lot could have happened during the passing of two days.

It was a short fifteen-minute walk down to the area that was obviously the site where the Pashtuns had lived when they inhabited the locale. The SEALs went into the nearest cave, pausing for a moment. "These'll make great bunkers," Mike remarked. "I'll check out this first one." As soon as Garth and Dave were ready to cover him, Mike rushed in with his M-16 ready. The place was empty and also very clean and swept out. Further investigation along the mountainside revealed the same in all the grottoes.

"Them Pashtuns are neat freaks, ain't they?" Mike remarked.

"Y'know," Dave said, "I think this place could pass inspection from the senior chief."

"Are you shitting me?" Garth said. "Dawkins would gig an operating room."

"There's another path," Mike said. "Let's check it out."

The lower level had more caves and some small stone houses. Three mountain springs in the near vicinity produced streams of cold, clear water that gave more favorable indication of the livability of the place. When the SEALs turned their attention to the dwellings, they found clay baking ovens. Countless fires had turned them brick hard, while scorching the interiors to a deep charcoal black. Dave was thoughtful for a moment. "All this orderliness means only one thing. Those people were planning on coming back here someday."

"I think you're right," Mike said. "Well, let's check out the defensive features of our new neighborhood. Then we better hotfoot it back to the LZ."

A short but efficient walk-around brought the discovery of several well-maintained fighting positions. The trio of SEALs gave each location a professional study. Garth stepped into one and looked around. "This place is solid as if it were carved out of rock. The camouflage is all dried out now, but it's easy to tell it was effective when fresh. Everything blends perfect with the surroundings."

"That's why it's called camouflage, wiseass," Dave remarked.

"I don't like stone defenses," Mike complained. "When a mortar shell hits it, the stuff splits up and adds to the shrapnel."

"Well, this place ain't exactly Sherwood Forest," Dave said. "If they got no trees to cut down, then rock is their next best choice."

"Their *only* choice around here," Garth added. "I'm glad there's a shitload of empty sandbags coming in on the Pave Low. It'll be a lot of work to fill 'em up, but they'll strengthen the defenses and make 'em safer for the guys using 'em."

"Okay," Mike said. "Let's get back up to the LZ. The rest of the detachment ought to be coming in pretty soon."

"I hope to hell that Connie and Matty remembered to put our gear aboard that Air Force chopper," Dave said.

"If they didn't, we'll take their stuff away from 'em and split it up," Garth said sourly. "It'll be share and share alike."

Mike could hear the approaching Pave Low in the distance. He spoke into his LASH. "Brigand Boss, this is Sneaky Pete. The Oscar Alpha is secure. Over."

"This is Brigand Boss," came back Brannigan's voice. "We're coming in. Out."

OA LZ
0710 HOURS

THE Pave Low helicopter nosed up slightly as it eased down to the ground. The three-man recon patrol double-timed over to the aircraft as the rear ramp slid open. The first guy out was the Skipper, followed by the two officers and the senior chief. Immediately the rest of the detachment unassed the chopper, falling into formation by sections, with the officers standing off to the side.

Mike, Dave, and Garth joined the Headquarters crowd, falling in beside Connie Concord and Matty Matsuno. Connie nodded to them. "You're gear is aboard on the starboard side."

Before the three could respond, Dawkins called the detachment to attention. "Alright! We got mucho crapolla to get off the chopper and down to our new home. Alpha and Bravo fire teams form a relay line starting in the aircraft. Charlie and Delta join the line and stretch it over to the edge of the LZ where that path begins. Echo and Foxtrot continue it down to the bottom and stack it there." He looked over at Chief Gunnarson. "Matt, take your men and machine guns down to the front line and pick out three good spots to set up your weapons. Have your bullet toters take along some ammo boxes so you can go into business ASAP."

"Right, Senior Chief," Gunnarson said. He turned to his six men, shouting, "Let's go, Fire Support Section!" He led the gunners and ammo bearers toward the chopper to pick up their personal gear along with the M-60s and ammunition.

Dawkins turned his attention to Headquarters. "Gomez! Bradley! Get your radios and medical stuff below. Then hold up down there and wait for word where to set up. When that's done, get on line with your M-sixteens and keep an eye peeled across the valley. Consider yourselves on watch."

"Say, Senior Chief," Puglisi called out, "can me and Joe take our AS-fifties and whack somebody over there?"

"No, Puglisi," Dawkins responded in an irritable tone. "Not now. There's other things to do. Find a place in the relay line and lend a hand." Dawkins noted the three officers off to one side at a stand of boulders. He gestured to Connie Concord. "Take your team up there, where the Skipper is. He wants to see you Sneaky Petes. Alright! Ever' swinging dick turn to!"

By then Chief Gunnarson and his machine gun crews were already heading for the ledge. Concord took his four scouts up toward the location where Brannigan, Cruiser, and Taylor gazed over at the enemy positions through their binoculars. It took the Sneaky Petes a couple of minutes to reach the spot, and when they reported in, Brannigan put his binoculars in their case while Cruiser and Taylor continued to study the Zaheya area.

"You guys take a seat," Brannigan said to the team. He sat down with them on the ground, pulling a map out of his side trouser pocket. "Okay. Tonight you're going to make an area reconnaissance. And I want to emphasize the word *reconnaissance*! You are going to avoid combat at all costs. Your mission is to scope out the enemy's positions. I want to know the extent of their fortifications, routes of approach to and from their fighting positions, and how many men they have along their front line. This includes any other interesting tidbits of intel you're able to pick up. Keep in mind that the information you're looking for will be used to set up combat patrols."

Concord nodded. "It sounds like you're not planning on any all-out assaults for the time being, sir."

"Right," Brannigan replied. "I want to look around for weak spots to probe. You'll leave our lines at zero-one-hundred hours, and you should be able to find advantageous positions for observation relatively quickly."

"Yes, sir," Concord said, now pulling out his own map. "I'll split us up into two teams. The Odd Couple will work from north to the center, and I'll take Redhawk and Matsuno from the south to the center." He checked the lay of the land as indicated on the topographical sheet. "We'll meet here, behind this hill."

Matsuno looked over at the spot. "That doesn't look like much of a hill to me."

"Well, semihill," Concord allowed. "At any rate, it will provide us with cover to converge for the return to our side of the valley."

"Mmm," Assad said. "It looks like me and Dave have a bit longer to travel, so we'll get there a little later."

"You guys come up with a challenge and a password," Brannigan said. "Use the odd-number system."

"Aye, sir," Connie said. He turned to his team. "Listen up. Say I choose an odd number like thirteen for the password. So the challenger says a number less than that, like nine. That means the guy being challenged has to come up with a number that equals thirteen." He winked at Mike. "Don't count on your fingers. The answer is four."

"Don't use 'thirteen,' Connie," Matty Matsuno said. "It's unlucky."

"Alright," Connie said. "The number is fifteen."

Brannigan folded his map. "Okay. That's official. When you go through our lines, you'll have to check out with the officer or chief of the watch for the challenge and the password."

"Our *lines*!" Dave Leibowitz exclaimed. "It really does sound like we're in the trenches in World War One, like Chad was talking about in isolation."

"That's exactly the case," Brannigan said. "I'll cover that with the guys later. Meanwhile, Concord will work out the routes of the patrol on the map, and you guys get some rest. You'll be gone for a few hours."

"Aye, sir!"

The Skipper started to get up and stopped. "Oh! Another thing. Just before we left Shelor, we learned our enemy is up-to-date. They've got night vision capabilities. Keep that in mind while you're sneaking and peeking out there."

1800 HOURS

THE work of settling into the new area had gone on without a break. The old fighting positions of the Pashtuns were occupied, and the construction of several new ones had begun. Ensign Taylor's assault section was detailed to begin filling sandbags for the effort.

Brannigan didn't like the idea of static points of resistance when it came to defense, and his main plan was to have more sites than they needed. That way, they could shift daily or even hourly to different defensive patterns to keep the enemy off balance. He also set up a CP for the front line. This was where the watch officers and chiefs would be positioned during their duty hours. Additionally, he issued orders that all sections would have three men "standing to" at all times day or night. With two fire team leaders, six fire team members, and a SAW gunner, that meant a one-third alert. The Fire Support Section was set up the same way, by keeping one machine gun crew on duty.

This system permitted using the Navy's regular watch organization of four hours on and eight hours off during the seven periods of watches. The exceptions were the two dog watches, which went from 1600 hours until 2000 hours. These were two on and four off during the evening mealtime, as was normal aboard ships. The system also kept men from having to keep the same duty hours every day.

Normal administrative, medical, and communication functions would be in the Headquarters bunker, in the center of the position. It was a large cave and, like the others, offered a comfortable temperature in the interior because of small entrances as well as the natural insulation. Frank Gomez found a small hole some three feet in diameter up in the ceiling, and he positioned his Shadowfire Radio on a rock shelf nearby. He would place the set outside when he transmitted or received. Thick brush around the area offered concealment, and the location was also an excellent OP if necessary.

Hospital Corpsman Doc Bradley had an excellent chamber for his rustic clinic. A small stream came out of the rocks and made its way across the deck to descend into an opening that led outside. His potable testing kit showed the water to be free of bacteria and contaminants, meaning it would serve well when required in the treatment of the wounded. Bradley also arranged his medical and surgical kits, operating table, medicines, and drugs in an orderly manner. Although his patients would be required to sleep on the rocky floor, he had enough foam mattresses to take care of half a dozen casualties. They would be able to rest comfortably.

The rest of the headquarters group—like Gomez and Bradley—were exempt from standing watches. In naval parlance, the seven men of the Sniper Team and Patrol Team were called "idlers" because of their status. However, in Brannigan's Brigands phraseology, they were "weenies." Mike Assad especially resented this, since there would be times when they would be on duty for long hours at a stretch, but the name stuck even when he threatened to break Andy Malachenko's nose for referring to him thusly.

NOW, tired from the hauling, stacking, and digging, the detachment sat down to their first meal in their new garrison. It was no more than MREs, but the SEALs consumed the food gratefully as the men on stand-to patiently waited for their reliefs so they could chow down in turn. Meanwhile, the Sneaky Petes huddled together in the Headquarters bunker, making a careful map reconnaissance of the area they would patrol that night.

CHAPTER 4

CONNIE Concord signaled the patrol to halt and gather around him. They had reached the east side of a small hill at the bottom of the valley between the warring factions. The SEALs all wore NVGs, and viewed their surroundings in the green, gray, and black the devices provided. Everyone was stripped down for action with empty pockets, one ammo pouch, K-Bar knife, and canteen on their belts. Additionally, all the rifle slings had been removed and the swivels taped down. Before leaving their position, Brannigan had made the Sneaky Petes jump up and down to make sure there were no rattling noises that might give them away during the mission.

"Alright!" Connie said, whispering into his LASH. No matter how softly he spoke, the others could hear him clearly in the earphones. "This here's that raise in the ground we picked out on the map. This is gonna be both our ERP and RRP, okay? So let's get this little show of ours on the road.

Mike and Dave, you guys head north. Keep close track of the time because you gotta be back here no later than zero-four-hundred. Here's another important item: You guys got to take off your LASH sets so's you can listen good for whatever's going on around you. Them Zaheyas might have a patrol or two of their own prowling around out here."

"What if we got to say something?" Dave whispered back.

"We can wave at each other or something and point to our ears," Mike suggested.

"Just don't make any noise to attract each other's attention," Connie remarked seriously. "And let me remind you what the Skipper said about the bad guys having night vision. D'you remember the challenge and the password when we go back through our lines?"

"Yeah," Mike replied. " 'Grin' and 'grapple.' "

"Right," Connie said. The Skipper wanted all challenges and passwords to have the letter "r" in them, since it was difficult for speakers of Farsi and Arabic to pronounce it the American way without rolling the sound with their tongues twittering. "So take off, guys, and good luck."

Dave took the lead as he and Mike moved north to follow their assignment of traveling the entire length of the enemy positions in that direction. When they reached the outermost point, they would work their way back to the ERP. The rest of the detachment referred to the two as the Odd Couple because Mike was an Arab-American and Dave Jewish-American. In spite of a situation that could have caused an ethnic clash, the pair was 100 percent American and disinterested in Middle East conflicts except how the events might affect the United States. They were also the best of buddies and spent all their off-duty time together swilling beer and chasing young women.

THE terrain in the no-man's-land between the two mountaintops was fairly smooth, with a few dips and rises. Stands of boulders—some as large as automobiles—were scattered throughout the area. The ground itself was smooth, hard-packed, and rock-strewn, while the vegetation was scrub brush with thorny plants that were tall and thick enough in places to offer good concealment.

It would be impossible to move across the valley undetected in daylight. Such movement would be extremely dangerous and would have to be done in short rushes. But at night or when the mountain mists and fogs lay heavily over the terrain, a quiet, determined force of properly clad men would be able to move unseen. During those conditions, even NVGs had difficulty detecting movement, since the shapes of camouflaged individuals would blend in well with the natural features of the area. IR devices, of course, would have no trouble identifying living beings because of body heat imaging.

Navy SEALs had been trained for years in the tradition of conducting operations with "one foot in the water"—that is, close to the sea. They generally went into their OAs in boats or SCUBA gear. They stayed on dry land only long enough to perform their missions; then it was back to the friendly environs of the ocean, lake, or river for exfiltration to naval vessels. But the latest demands of combat in the Middle East had changed all that. The introduction of war against terrorism meant that they now went ashore and stayed there for weeks, practicing their deadly trade far from beaches and seashores. Brannigan's Brigands could be numbered among the many SEALs who had gone so far as to employ desert patrol vehicles on missions in which they raced in and out of combat in the midst of gunfire and roaring motors.

Now, in that valley of the Gharawdara Highlands of Afghanistan, the Sneaky Petes moved slowly across the mountainous terrain, their feet as dry as if they were trodding over the sands of the Sahara.

0245 HOURS

MATTY Matsuno was on point as Connie Concord and Garth Redhawk followed him. They had stayed more or less on the eastern side of the valley while they made their wary southern trek toward the far reaches of their patrol area. Now they had worked their way into a north-northwest direction to reach the base of the slopes that led up to the enemy positions. Matty glanced back, as he did from time to time, to see how his companions were coming along. This time he saw Connie gesturing to him. He went back and joined the team leader and Garth.

Everyone slipped on their LASH headsets. Connie pointed upward. "That's where the bad guys live. We need to take a look and see if we can spot something interesting. Be sure and make a note of personnel and the strengths of their defenses. That's the main reason we're out here."

"I'll go," Garth volunteered.

"Okay," Connie agreed. "Matty needs a break after being on point for so long. We'll both follow you and keep about ten meters to the rear. We'll spread out a little so we can cover both the right and left flanks."

"I'm ready," Garth said.

He was of Kiowa-Comanche Indian ancestry, making him a mixture of two of the fiercest fighting tribes of the Southern Plains. He carried a traditional medicine bag for good luck and spiritual guidance. It was a rawhide sack of two by six inches in which he had placed his issue SEAL trident qualification badge, a piece of wood from a tree struck by lightning in his native Oklahoma, and a pebble taken from an enemy mortar position in the Selva Verde Mountains of South America. He had gone on a one-man combat patrol into enemy territory, sneaked into a mortar bivouac, and dropped thermite grenades down the tubes of the weapons to disable them. His instincts told him his medicine was strong at that particular spot in the world, and he had taken the pebble to carry some of that power with him when he exfiltrated safely from the area. This was the same highly classified operation in which the new Ensign Taylor's cousin Lamar had been KIA.

This scion of great warriors such as Lone Wolf, Medicine Feather, Wild Horse, and Hears-the-Sunrise wore the camouflage paint on his face in the lightning streak patterns of the Southern Plains tribes. And with the traditional warmaking skills of his people, Garth Redhawk moved in fluid silence up toward the enemy fighting positions.

0300 HOURS

ON the opposite end of no-man's-land, Dave Leibowitz had discovered a natural path that was some five meters below the ridge where the Zaheya were dug in. A section of the cliff had given way under a primeval earthquake of long past aeons, leaving a narrow ledge just wide enough to walk on. The cloudy night allowed no moonlight to illuminate the shadows that hid the place where the Odd Couple trod softly in a southerly direction.

Dave moved no more than ten paces before stopping to look upward. Mike kept his attention on his best buddy, making occasional glances behind to make sure no Zaheya soldiers were following them along the protrusion. After ten minutes had passed, Dave stopped and signaled Mike forward. Both donned their LASH sets. "Look up there," Dave said. "That rock formation has some good foot- and hand-holds."

"Yeah," Mike agreed.

"I'm gonna climb up and see if there's anything interesting," Dave said.

"Be careful."

Dave showed a crooked grin. "Hey! Y'know! That's a good idea. I never thought of that. Any more suggestions?"

"Yeah," Mike said, "but you'd have a tough time keeping quiet while you shoved that M-sixteen up your keister."

"Wiseass," Dave said.

He handed his rifle to Mike, then carefully placed his foot on a rock and tested it. He did the same with another he had grasped to pull himself up. When he was satisfied they would hold his weight, he began the ascent. Dave repeated the procedure slowly until he had reached the top. He looked around, happy to note that there was nobody there. He could see a well-constructed trench that had obviously been scooped out of the mountain by machine. It would have taken a jackhammer to break up the rock that was hauled away. The floor of the thing was even and level, while the sides were reinforced with sandbags.

Mike watched him descend back to the path to his location. "Anything special up there?"

"Yeah," Dave replied, taking his M-16 back. "We got a big job ahead of us if we're gonna take this fucking mountain."

"And the powers-that-be expect us to take it without sophisticated help like airplanes and heavy artillery," Mike said. "Shit! Let's keep rolling. Don't forget we got to be back at the ERP in"—he looked at the luminous dial of his watch—"a little less than an hour and a half."

0330 HOURS

GARTH Redhawk had found a partly natural, partly man-made bastion at the apex of the slope. It was on the Zaheya defensive line where he could nestle in the available concealment and enjoy an undisturbed view of the enemy positions. One guard was on duty, and the guy wasn't sleeping or goofing off. He stood his watch like a professional soldier, his short assault rifle slung across his chest as he stood alertly and well balanced on both feet.

The sight of the facilities caused Redhawk to take a silent but sharp intake of breath. The fighting positions built along the wall were reinforced with logs. These had obviously been brought into the treeless area from somewhere else. Additional cover was provided by sandbags, and locations of support weapons had roofs made of layers of timber covered by more sandbags and packed earth.

Redhawk turned to look down the other way. It was more of the same, and now he noticed the camouflaged bunker entrances offering ingress into what would no doubt be shelters, living quarters, and/or storage for ammo and supplies. He also could make out the figures of more men standing-to. These guys were disciplined, well armed, and would be doing their fighting behind extremely strong defenses.

The SEAL slowly and stealthily began a descent of the slope to rejoin Connie Concord and Matty Matsuno.

SEAL BASE CAMP
0445 HOURS

CHAD Murchison stood his watch with his M-16 locked and loaded as he gazed through his NVG at the figures moving upward toward his position. After a few moments he could recognize Mike Assad on the point as they drew nearer. Even though the recognition of his fellow SEAL was unmistakable, Chad followed the SOP.

"Grin," he said softly, issuing the challenge.

"Grapple," Mike replied with the password. "Four guys behind me."

"Roger," Chad said. The procedure of the first man giving the sentry the number of men following him was to keep enemy infiltrators from joining the rear of returning patrols in the darkness. If Chad counted more than four, then the unexpected guests would be dealt with in an extremely prejudicial manner.

When Matty Matsuno came across the fighting position, he whispered that he was the last man. At that point, Chad gave the frontal slope a meticulous surveillance to make sure that no bad guys were lurking in the vicinity.

SEAL HEADQUARTERS
0515 HOURS

"SHIT!"

That was the sixth time Lieutenant Bill Brannigan had uttered the expletive during Connie Concord's vocal report on the results of the recon patrol. Ensign Orlando Taylor, the detachment's acting N-2, was taking notes with the anxious concentration typical of an eager young officer.

The other four members of the Sneaky Petes were sitting in a semicircle on the bunker floor around the two officers. Garth Redhawk scratched his chin. "The damn thing looked like a fucking underground castle, sir."

"Same from where I got a look, sir," Dave Leibowitz said. "That place wasn't constructed in a couple of weeks. Somebody took months to put that facility into the side of the mountain."

"And they had plenty of up-to-snuff equipment to do it," Redhawk added. "It sure as hell ain't like this place." He gestured around him. "This is just natural shit with a few additions."

"That's right," Mike Assad said. "All we got here is some caves and fighting holes."

"I *know* what we got here, Assad," Brannigan snarled. "You don't have to tell me."

"Another thing," Redhawk said. "I got a good look at some of their people. These guys are real soldiers, not a bunch of crazy-ass mujahideen. And they're armed with them little French rifles. What do they call 'em? Bullpups, I think."

Brannigan nodded. "Yeah. I'm familiar with the weapon. Officially they're FA-MAS automatic rifles. That's kind of a misnomer, because they have a selector for semiauto too. The French soldiers call them *clairons*. That's their word for bugles."

"Uh-huh," Dave said. "They kind of look like that."

"Did you see any mortars or artillery?" Brannigan asked.

"Negative, sir," Connie replied.

"Shit!" Brannigan said again. "How many people do you think that place can hold?"

"Well, sir," Connie said, "if their entire line is like the parts that Garth and Mike saw, I'd say they could easily take in a couple of thousand."

"Remember what Dr. Joplin said," the Skipper pointed out. "They have only a few more guys than we do."

"Maybe so, sir," Connie said. "He told us they didn't want to make a big deal out of this, but now I'm not so sure. If we start kicking their asses real bad, they'll call in reinforcements quick. Maybe artillery and CAS from the Iranian Air Force. We could be wiped out quick before our side could react."

Matty Matsuno glanced at the Skipper, asking, "Are we at that place they call between the rock and the hard place?"

"Yeah," Brannigan said. He stood up. "Okay, guys. Good

job. Get some rest and you better sleep fast. You might be going out there again real quick."

"Aye, sir!"

The Sneaky Petes got to their feet and followed Connie out of the bunker entrance.

CHAPTER 5

AT the end of the morning watch, Lieutenant Jim Cruiser's entire First Assault Section were informed they would not be returning to sentry duties on the first dog watch, as they normally would have. They were to go back to their bunker to fix some chow and stand by for further orders. Now, after two and a half hours of waiting, the seven men lounged on their foam mattresses, catching up on lost sleep.

The sights and sounds inside the cavern were ones of dozing men and deep breathing punctuated now and then with snores. When Cruiser stepped inside the rocky abode, he grinned at the spectacle. "Isn't this a cozy picture?" he remarked. "It reminds me of my happy boyhood days at summer camp." He chuckled. "Well, except for the M-sixteens and the SAW."

Gutsy Olson, the Alpha Fire Team leader, raised his head.

"What's going on, sir?" he asked. "The senior chief said we was off watch 'til further orders."

"Right," Cruiser said. He emitted a loud, sharp whistle at those still slumbering. "Let's go! Wake up!"

Monty Sturgis got to his knees and stretched. "And I was having such a beautiful dream."

Pete Dawson, now on his feet, grinned at him. "About a good-looking woman, I bet."

Monty shook his head. "Nope. I dreamed you paid me back that fifty bucks you owe me."

Andy Malachenko laughed. "You must have really been dreaming. He's owed me fifty for three months now."

"Well, hell, guys," Pete said. "I'd rather owe it to you than beat you out of it."

Now everyone was up and looking expectantly at their section commander. Cruiser motioned them to follow him away from the living space to the area near the entrance that was used for section get-togethers. He turned to face them. "Sit down and get comfortable, guys."

Like everyone else in Brannigan's Brigands, the First Assault Section had constructed tables and benches out of the wood from the crates that had been emptied of supplies and ammunition. They situated themselves among the rough-hewn furniture to get the word.

"The Skipper gave me a WARNO," Cruiser said. Whatever sleepy feelings were left over from their naps immediately evaporated, and they instinctively sat up straighter and leaned forward. "Combat patrol," he continued, giving an answer to the unasked question.

"Ambush or raid?" Gutsy Olson inquired.

"Raid," Cruiser responded. "The objective is to test the enemy's ability to respond to a small surprise attack on part of their line. In this case, the north flank."

"Uh-oh!" Gutsy said. "This reminds me of that one attack we made down there in South America." He glanced over at the others. "Andy, me, and Lieutenant Cruiser were on that operation against a bunch of neo-Nazi rebels. They were tough bastards, let me tell you. All professional soldiers from South America and Europe. We was going up against 'em for the first time, and the Skipper wanted to find out how much of a fight they could give us. He told us about an old Chinese saying that says that the best way to test a tiger is to let him out of his cage."

"Actually, he said you could do it that way," Andy said, "or go into the cage with him."

"I remember that particular action only too well," Cruiser said. "I was hit and medevaced out of there. It was touch and go for a while if I was gonna be able to walk again." He paused as the unpleasant memory flitted through his mind. "Anyhow, that's exactly what we're gonna do—test the tiger."

"I'm on pins and needles about the execution phase of this thing," Monty Sturgis said. "I got to tell you guys that this is the strangest operation I've ever been on in my ten years in the SEALs."

"Okay," Cruiser said. He laid his map out on the floor so they could all see it. "This is gonna be an RON. We'll leave at thirteen-hundred hours from headquarters. There's a hole in the top of the bunker just big enough for a man to pass through. Gomez is using the place for commo. He sets his Shadowfire radio out there for long-range transmissions. There's plenty of concealment around the place, so we'll leave from there, and head east far enough to drop below the horizon. Then we move north about fifteen kilometers to this point on the map. It's near the desert where we ran our DPVs in Operation Rolling Thunder." He used his laser pointer to indicate the spot. "We should arrive there at approximately seventeen-thirty hours. As you can see from the wider contour lines, it's not so steep in that area. That's always a welcome break. At that time we'll turn west to this point"—he employed the beam once again—"which we'll reach at twenty-hundred hours. From there we turn south to an area that is at a direct right angle to the enemy lines. That's where we start climbing back up into the Gharawdara Highlands. When we're within a couple of kilometers of the enemy sometime after zero-one-hundred hours, we stop. I'll send two of you guys forward for a recon on the objective, which is the Zaheya positions." He glanced up at his team leaders. "Each of you guys give me one man for that chore."

"Morales," Gutsy Olson said.

"Halonen," Monty Sturgis announced.

"You two guys will go for a look-see and bring back any helpful intel you can get," Cruiser said. "Do a good job, because at oh-five-hundred hours we attack the place. We'll stay engaged only long enough to get them to respond, then we haul ass straight across the valley and up the slope to our home positions."

"Will we be making a fire-and-maneuver withdrawal, sir?" Monty Sturgis asked.

"No," Cruiser replied. "We're going to be running as fast as we can. Minimum time is of the essence when we cross that two hundred meters of no-man's-land."

"Damn, sir!" Dawson exclaimed. "Those Persians or whatever they are will shoot us in the back!"

"Every weapon in this detachment will be covering us," Cruiser said. "We'll also take advantage of the cover and concealment given us by the rock formations and tall shrubs while we haul ass. The Skipper wanted me to emphasize that it's important that we keep running. However, if anyone is hit, we bring him back with us. Buddy up for that purpose and keep your eye on your partner during the withdrawal."

"What are we taking with us, sir?"

"We'll be lean and mean," Cruiser answered. "One bandolier of ammo each, two canteens, personal medical kits, rations for one meal, energy bars, and any other small items you prefer for this sort of operation. All that goes into your rucksacks. It won't be a heavy load. You'll wear your pistols and knives on your belts. The grenadiers will bring along their M-two-oh-threes with six rounds each. Benson will have three bandoliers for the SAW. And don't forget your NVGs. We'll use the One-twenty-sixes with LASH headsets for commo. Usual call signs." He looked at his watch. "Get your gear together. I'll check it when you're ready. Then we'll take it easy and store up some energy until twelve-forty-five hours. That's the time we'll head for headquarters to leave. Turn to, guys."

SEAL HEADQUARTERS
1255 HOURS

FRANK Gomez, the detachment RTO, had built a sturdy ladder from some lumber he pried off a supply crate. It made it easier to ascend the fifteen feet to the opening in the cavetop than having to climb up the rock ledges that led to the exit.

Now the nine men of the First Assault Section were lined up to ascend to the opening to begin the first leg of their patrol. Gutsy Olson led the way, with his Alpha Team members Pete Dawson and Rick Morales following. Lieutenant Jim Cruiser and the SAW gunner Tex Benson were aligned behind the Alphas. Monty Sturgis was the last man, with his rifleman Andy Malachenko and grenadier Wally Halonen just ahead of him. Everyone had his rucksack in his hand rather than on his back, since it was impossible to wear it and fit through the narrow opening above.

Lieutenant Wild Bill Brannigan stood beside the men. "We'll be keeping an eye out for you guys tomorrow morning. And don't worry. There'll be machine guns, grenade launchers, and M-sixteen rifles laying down covering fire while you rush across the valley back here. Good luck." He glanced up to where Gutsy stood. "Alright, Petty Officer Olson. Lead the way."

"Aye, sir!"

Gutsy went up the rungs until he reached the top. He pushed his rucksack through the opening and followed, rolling into a covering position with his rifle when he was through the hole. Pete Dawson quickly appeared, crawling a short distance down the rear slope before rising to a crouch to move farther from the top of the mountain. One by one, the others followed. When Monty Sturgis appeared, Gutsy teamed with him and the pair made their way to the spot where the rest of the team waited. Now everyone slung their rucksacks on their backs, and Cruiser gave the word to move out. The order of march was the same as used for climbing the ladder—the Alphas, Cruiser and Benson, then the Bravos.

Gutsy put Pete Dawson on point as they began their northerly trek. Everyone immediately settled into the rhythm of the movement, instinctively covering their area of fire with strict vigilance. The last man in the formation was Andy Malachenko, who would periodically turn completely to check the rear as they progressed toward the objective.

The most likely direction of an ambush was from the higher ground to their left, but if some of the bad guys were out on a patrol of their own and had managed to make their way around the SEAL positions, they might be lower down the hill. If the enemy was out for combat, they would not hesitate to fire upward at the section. The terrain made for a slightly uncomfortable walk because of the slant, but those SEALs who had tender ankles—a shared malady gotten from dozens of extremely hard parachute landing falls—had carefully applied Ace bandages to those sensitive lower joints to keep them from feeling too much of the strain.

This area they descended was already known to them. It was just a short time before that they had pursued a combined force of Pashtun rebels and Arabs up that same steep terrain until forced to break off contact because of tactical disadvantages.

1720 HOURS

THE section reached the first turning point ten minutes ahead of schedule in spite of taking a break to readjust their equipment. No matter how careful a man was, there was always a strap or two that somehow slipped or drew tauter during the first kilometers of a hike. It was also a good time to take a piss, enjoy a deep swallow or two from a canteen, and for the two smokers in the section to take a few drags off cigarettes.

When Cruiser saw that everyone had caught his breath and was ready to continue, he reversed the two fire teams' positions, and now the Bravos took the lead as they turned west.

1940 HOURS

WHEN the patrol came up to the second turning point, from where they were to change to a southerly route, Cruiser called another break. The SEALs had been on the move for two hours and ten minutes, and while not really stepping out, their hike had been steady. The terrain was flat with only gentle rises now, and they would be switching back in the opposite direction from the first leg of the trip. This meant the most physically demanding part of the operation—the ascent back up into the Gharawdara Highlands.

"This final stage is going to be the most difficult," Cruiser reminded them. "We should reach the ORP a bit before zero-one-hundred hours. Not only will we be negotiating steep terrain, but there'll also be security issues to deal with. That means flankers out as well as a point man and a Tail-End Charlie. Bravo Team will be in the front. Sturgis, your team takes the lead. Put out a point man and a flanker for the right side."

That was an easy request, since there were only two other men in the team; it was only a matter of who did what. "Andy will take the point and Wally goes on the flank."

Gutsy Olson spoke up before being asked. "I'll put Rick on the left side and let Pete bring up the rear."

"Then we're set," Cruiser said. "Take another ten minutes, guys, and I advise you to treat yourselves to an energy bar and some swallows of water. This is going to be a hard climb."

MIDNIGHT

THE fatigue had set in, but the superbly conditioned SEALs could deal with it through a combination of spiritual and physical conditioning. It was a matter of concentrating on the job to be done while letting the discomfort sink so deep into the subconscious that the conscious mind was not aware of it. The seeming chickenshit demands put on them in BUD/S back at Coronado had drilled this primeval instinct into their psyches without them having any awareness of acquiring this remarkable capacity.

In spite of the interruptions and several delays, the flankers kept their areas under ceaseless surveillance, as did the two men on point and rear guard. The movement across the rocky terrain was silent, with each step a measured, separate act of making sure the foot did not come down on a loose rock or dry vegetation to give off sounds.

They had to come to a complete stop half a dozen times to do some minor rock climbing as the ascent took them into higher country. The slopes of the Highlands looked like a moonscape except for the scrubby vegetation, but the effect given by the NVGs was eerie and surreal, an impression heightened by the dangerous environment they had entered.

Jim Cruiser, in the middle of the group with his SAW gunner, Tex Benson, kept a constant eye on the formation, making sure it stayed loose but organized. He had already worked out the details of the dawn attack in his mind, but he would wait until the objective was properly reconned before making a final plan.

ORP
0045 HOURS

THE two men chosen to recon the objective—Morales and Halonen—were out on their mission. The rest of the team were arrayed in their attack formation, with the Alphas to the right and the Bravos to the left. Cruiser and Benson with his SAW occupied a position in the center rear. The section was only fifty meters from the objective, but had plenty of cover in the scrub brush, boulders, and dips in the ground to keep them concealed.

It was in this risky location that Cruiser really appreciated the features of the LASH headsets. "Okay, guys," he whispered, "we've got about five hours to wait. As soon as Morales and Halonen get back, we'll go on fifty percent alert. Try and get some sleep. I'll sound reveille at oh-four-forty-five and we'll stay on watch until I give the word to move out."

The two scouts returned from their short patrol, and Morales joined his team while Halonen reported in to the team commander. "Sir, there's a fighting position straight ahead. There was only one guy manning it. We won't be able to get too close to it without a sharp climb. It seems to be facing this direction."

"Mmm," Cruiser mused. "Probably there to watch this flank." He thought a minute. "You guys heard Halonen. When the attack starts, I want both grenadiers to cut loose on that position with one grenade each. Benson, you give it a couple of good three- or four-round bursts. Then we rush them and shoot the place up. When I feel we've done enough, I'll give the word we've completed the mission. At that time, turn east for the run back to our own positions."

Now another voice came over the commo system. "Brigand One, this is Brigand Boss. Over." As soon as Cruiser replied, Lieutenant Bill Brannigan continued his call. "It sounds like you're in position. We'll be able to monitor all your transmissions, so as soon as you order the assault, we'll be ready to cover you. Over."

"Roger," Cruiser radioed back. "We'll get as close as we can, then start down the slope toward you. Over."

"Roger. Out."

0520 HOURS

THE battle started with one word of command from Lieutenant JG Jim Cruiser: "Go!"

Two M-203 grenade launchers barked, and as their projectiles arced across the thirty meters of ground toward the objective, Tex Benson pumped the trigger of his SAW, sending three short bursts of 5.56-millimeter rounds straight into the enemy fighting position. As soon as the two grenades struck their target and exploded, the entire section leaped to their feet and made a quick rush toward the objective. No fire was being returned, and Cruiser continued the attack completely up the slope without resistance. They reached the top and could see the ripped-up body of a Zaheya soldier sprawled in his own blood on the dirt inside his post.

Suddenly more enemy soldiers appeared from a bunker exit fifteen meters away. They jumped back as soon as the

SEALs opened up on them. Cruiser knew that he and his section had pressed their luck about as far as they could. It would be only moments before the whole enemy force responded to the assault.

"Haul ass!"

The First Assault Section now began racing down the slope, able to hear the firing from the Brigands on the east side of the valley. The three M-60s under Chief Matt Gunnarson's command were sending well-directed swarms of bullets crisscrossing across the enemy site above where Cruiser and his men now continued their withdrawal. As soon as they were into the brush, the section split into a wider, more spaced-out formation. They zigzagged through the natural cover, being exposed for only brief instances to view from above.

UP in the Zaheya positions, Captain Naser Khadid personally directed the fire of his Imperial Lions Special Forces detachment. Their FA-MAS bullpups pumped out short automatic bursts in the direction of the fleeing attackers. They had no real targets other than quick glimpses of the scampering Americans, and tried to guess in which direction and how far the enemy was moving. Now the incoming fire swept over them along with some M-203 grenades that exploded just below the location, sending up shards of shrapnel and jagged hunks of rocks. The Iranians ducked under the roaring volleys of rifle and machine-gun bullets directed at them.

A few moments later, the fusillades lessened and the Iranians leaped to their feet to renew the fight. But the only thing they saw was the sight of the attackers entering the cover of their own positions after scrambling up the eastern slopes of the valley.

"*Isteet shellik Kardaa!*" Khadid ordered. "Cease fire!" The first battle of the campaign was over, and one of their men had been killed.

CHAPTER 6

PO2C Pech Pecheur checked his watch, noting he was two hours and seventeen minutes into the midwatch. The SEAL sighed inaudibly about having an hour and forty-three minutes to go until relieved. He stood in his fighting position, gazing out into no-man's-land, alert for possible attackers or infiltrators, his attention goaded by his impatience. The concealment in the area was pretty good, but didn't offer a lot of effective cover. Thorn bushes did nothing to stop flying bullets, though a few of the boulders were large enough to offer protection from artillery or mortar shells. The Cajun grinned to himself, thinking it depended on which side of the big rock you were on, of course.

The flicker of movement was fleeting, but enough to snap him into a state of complete alertness.

"Watch it," he whispered over the LASH. "There's movement to the direct front of Two Sector." The assault teams were located by number from left to right, facing out in numerical

order. Two Sector was the Second Team's position, and everyone else on watch knew exactly where to look.

"Roger," came back Jim Duncan's voice in Sector Three.
"There's somebody out there."

Ensign Orlando Taylor was watch officer stationed just outside headquarters in a recently constructed OP. "Everybody
keep your eyes open," he said, hoping something exciting
would happen. Now and then fox and other animals scampered
through the area, and a small deer had caused a general call to
arms a couple of nights previously.

Suddenly a shot cracked from One Sector. "We got infiltrators!" Wally Halonen announced. He squeezed off a couple more rounds. "Two more of 'em!"

Now firing broke out from below the SEAL positions, the
incoming slugs slapping into sandbags and zinging off rocks.
The off-duty Brigands rushed from their section bunkers
with M-16s and bandoliers. The firefight now built up into a
crescendo of fusillades that raked across the entire defensive
line from no-man's-land. The Brigands returned fire, with
Chief Matt Gunnarson's three machine guns now joining in.
Sparks flew off boulders, and the vegetation shuddered vio-
lently as hundreds of 5.56- and 7.62-millimeter rounds
slapped rocks and buffeted the brush to the front of the
Brigands.

ARSALAAN Sikes rose from a prone position and
aimed his FA-MAS rifle upward at the American MLR. After kicking off a quick full-auto burst, he dropped back
down. His Arab Storm Trooper detachment was spread out
as skirmishers to his front, with Warrant Officer Shafaqat
Hashiri in charge of the left flank, while the Brit commanded the right.

"Kammal hajam ala adi," he ordered over his LASH.
"Continue the attack."

The Arabs used fire and maneuver as they advanced
across the valley floor, one group covering each short rapid
advance of another. Now that they had NVGs, they were
able to carry on night operations as often as they wished.
Most of the incoming fire from the American positions was

proving harmless, but now and then the bullet strikes came close, bringing parts of the assault lines to a halt. Since it is in the nature of Arabs to babble excitedly in stressful and dangerous situations, Sikes Pasha had issued strict orders that squad leaders were the only ones allowed to use the LASH headsets. That way instructions could be easily given as the battle unfolded without being lost in vocal yammering. The conversation was mostly from Sikes Pasha as he directed the operation with the help of Hashiri.

LIEUTENANT Bill Brannigan crawled through the hole at the top of the headquarters bunker and positioned himself among the shrubs around the opening. He peered down at no-man's-land through his ATN night vision binoculars, moving from one spot to another as he visually scanned the area. The 5X magnification gave him a clear view of each part of terrain he wished to peruse.

Now and then the Skipper caught a brief glimpse of one of the enemy soldiers as he scampered from one position of cover to another. They were professional and skillful, their faces darkened and carrying only the French bullpup rifles and bandoliers of ammo. The Skipper also noted their night vision capability. It was obvious they were under close control, and all their movements were coordinated by a commander and/or subcommanders.

Brannigan started to give some fire direction orders over the LASH when he noted that the enemy was now withdrawing. He waited a moment before sighting a couple heading rearward, toward their own position. "The attackers are pulling back," he said. "Adjust your fire accordingly."

The SEALs responded by moving their volleys farther out, in an effort to catch the unseen foe during their retrograde movement.

SIKES was pleased with his men. No casualties had been reported, and the retirement maneuver was working well. It was obvious the Americans had detected the withdrawal because the incoming rounds were now hitting closer to the slopes beneath the Zaheya positions. But they weren't able to spot any clear targets to zero in on.

"La ajal," Sikes ordered. *"Ala malak!"* The Storm Troopers obeyed his instructions by slowing down and adopting a calculated deliberation in their maneuvering.

As the Arabs continued heading back, they were slowed a few times when sweeping gunfire came close to them, but they were able to pick up the pace when the heavy impacts of bullets danced away. Finally Sikes was satisfied he was close enough to the Zaheya defensive positions to call in the support fire from the machine guns and grenade launchers. This part of the attack had been planned carefully, with much discussion among him, Brigadier Khohollah, Captain Naser Khadid, and Captain Jamshid Komard.

"This is Sikes Pasha," he said in stumbling Farsi over the LASH. *"Shuru kardeed shellikee.* Open fire!"

Immediately the rapid "pow-pow-pow" of the trio of MG-3 machine guns at a collective 3,300 rounds per minute and the "chunk-a-chunk" of the 645 rounds per minute from the three LAG-40 grenade launchers sent sweeping salvos across the American positions. It was a combined barrage of 55 bullets and 11 grenades a second.

OVER in the SEALs' Third Section, the incoming machine-gun rounds pounded hell out of the sandbags, while three rapid grenade detonations tore others apart. Chad Murchison and J. T. Snooker were stunned by the concussion of the explosions, but quickly reacted. They bailed out of their fighting positions and sprinted toward the bunker, diving over the sandbags into the interior. They quickly whipped around to cover their area of fire responsibility from this position, although their angle of fire was drastically cut. But with their cover blown away, they had no choice.

More pounding from the enemy worked its way from both north to south and south to north along the entire American front. The rapidity of the grenade strikes was a nasty surprise, as was the fact that three more fighting positions had been blown to hell in a very short time. Once again several SEALs had to abandon their posts and head for the safety of the bunkers.

The Skipper, still on top of the mountain observing the battle, watched in dismay as the attackers scurried up the slopes to their fortress and disappeared over the defenses to the protection of their trenches. The enemy's heavy covering fire had prevented the Brigands from turning the salvos onto the enemy as they clambered to safety.

The incoming enemy fire suddenly ceased, leaving an eerie silence over the scene.

Brannigan crawled back to the hole and slid in, quickly going down the ladder into the Headquarters bunker. He went outside to check the condition of the detachment personnel and defenses. He gazed around through his NVGs, noting where several fighting positions had been completely destroyed. The sandbags were split and scattered around the immediate area, and the stone walls had been blown apart or had collapsed.

Then Jim Cruiser's voice came over the LASH. "Skipper, we have a KIA here in the First Section. It's Halonen."

"And I have a WIA in the Second, sir," said Orlando Taylor, joining in. "MacTavish has taken some hits in the face with shrapnel. He's pretty dazed. I dispatched Bernardi to help him over to the corpsman."

"Okay," Brannigan said. "MacTavish is your SAW gunner, isn't he?"

"Affirmative, sir."

Doc Bradley came over the air. "I'm on my way back to headquarters to look after MacTavish."

"He and Bernardi are here now," the Skipper said. "They're just walking up." He turned to the two SEALs. "Go on to Doc Bradley's place. How're you feeling, Mac-Tavish?"

"I'm alright, sir," he replied in his North Carolina accent. "I just got some scratches, so I'll be fine directly."

"I'm sure you will," Brannigan said with an encouraging grin. But he noted MacTavish was pretty unsteady on his feet, even with Bernardi's help.

Doc Bradley and Frank Gomez came in together from

their shared fighting position. Brannigan nodded to Doc. "Bernardi took MacTavish into that clinic of yours."

"On my way, sir," the hospital corpsman said.

Frank Gomez said, "We had some direct hits on several of the fighting positions, sir. It looks like we'll be doing some rebuilding."

"That goes without saying," Brannigan said. "You might as well go back to your position until daylight. I want a hundred percent alert until the sun comes up. Then get back here—I'll have some transmissions ready for you. We'll have Halonen flown out. And we might have a medevac for MacTavish."

Bernardi reappeared from Doc Bradley's clinic, hurrying as he left the bunker to rejoin the Second Assault Section. Brannigan looked out over no-man's-land at the enemy positions. They seemed abandoned in the weird view provided by his NVGs. He took the binocular and made a slow sweep of the place. The Iranians and their Arab buddies were staying under cover. He replaced the device in its case, speaking into the LASH. "Section commanders, report!"

"First Section one man KIA, sir."

"Second Section one man WIA, sir."

"Third Section all present and accounted for, sir."

"Fire Support all present and accounted for, sir."

"Okay," Brannigan said. "Stay where you are. Make sure any of your guys who had their fighting positions blown to hell have good cover. Those bastards might start shooting again."

Doc Bradley appeared at his side. "Sir, MacTavish will be in pretty good shape in a couple of days, but we have to medevac him. He wasn't hit by shrapnel; it was by rocks and dirt. I cleaned him up the best I could, but if he doesn't get to more sophisticated treatment all that debris in his skin is going to result in tattooing. At first he didn't want to go, but I told him what he'd look like if he didn't get all that crap cleaned out of his face. That made him change his mind."

"I can't say that I blame him," the Skipper said.

"That's what most guys worry about," Doc commented. "They're more afraid of being blinded or disfigured than getting killed."

0700 HOURS

ALL the section commanders had reported to the Head-quarters bunker for the Skipper's conference, and now sat around drinking MRE coffee, waiting for the meeting to begin. Brannigan was with Gomez, tending to the commo chores; the morning watch was on duty as things returned to normal; and MacTavish sat quietly smoking a cigarette by the bunker entrance with his face completely covered courtesy of Doc Bradley's skillful bandaging.

Brannigan walked up and took a seat with the section commanders. "Hell of a thing, wasn't it?"

Senior Chief Buford Dawkins took a loud slurp from his canteen cup. "I sure as the devil hope we ain't facing a dead heat here."

"Mmm," Ensign Orlando Taylor said with a nod. "I am not as experienced as you gentlemen, but it seems to me we could well be entering a frustrating battle of attrition. This operation is going to be won by the side that lasts longer."

"Before we start considering further consequences, I want to discuss last night's fight," Brannigan said. "Besides having a man killed and another wounded, there is something else that's bugging the hell out of me. We had three of our positions completely blown away. We're fortunate we don't have half a dozen casualties."

"Lucky hits," Chief Matt Gunnarson remarked.

"What the hell were them grenade launchers they was firing at us?" the senior chief wondered. "It would be like having a belt-fed Two-oh-three that kept shooting out projectiles as long as the trigger was held down."

"That's true," Jim Cruiser said. "I saw one place where four or five grenades in a row hit close together. From the size of the detonations I'd say they were forty millimeters like the Two-oh-three."

Orlando Taylor spoke up again. "During my training I was exposed to two such weapons. One model was from Singapore and the other Spanish. They fired belts as Senior Chief Dawkins just mentioned, and were automatic."

Brannigan nodded. "It sounds like something to report to Commander Berringer. He and the rest of intelligence staff can probably figure out what we're up against. Meanwhile, we have to rebuild those damaged positions."

"It was only those old places that were blown apart," Cruiser said. "The ones we built came through the fight in fine fettle."

"That's strange," Brannigan commented. "The ones the Pashtuns made were well built. And camouflaged too." He was thoughtful for a moment, then exclaimed, "Just a goddamn minute! Weren't we told that the Arabs on the other side spent some time here?"

"Yes, sir," Cruiser said. "And also an Iranian SF officer."

"Those bastards!" Brannigan said. "They must've pointed out the exact locations of those old defensive sites to their fire support. They knew exactly where they were. Their weapons support people were already zeroed in on them before the attack even started."

"Jesus!" Chief Gunnarson exclaimed. "We should've thought of that."

"It's those kinds of little lapses and slips that cost lives," Brannigan said. He glanced at Taylor. "Chalk that up to lessons learned, mister."

"Aye, sir!"

The session was interrupted by Bruno Puglisi hollering down the hole in the top of the bunker. "Chopper coming in!" A couple of moments passed, then he yelled again. "Commander Carey and Commander Berringer are on it!"

Brannigan chuckled without humor. "Well, when those two show up you can be sure that our adventures in these parts are about to be kicked up another notch. Who's the petty officer of the watch?"

"Sturgis," Cruiser replied. "He'll act as escort for our visitors."

Hospital Corpsman Doc Bradley stepped in from his bailiwick, walking over to where Doug MacTavish sat. He took the wounded man by the arm. "That's your ticket out of here. C'mon, I'll take you to the LZ."

Cruiser spoke up. "We've got his gear ready in the First Section's area, Doc. Stop by on the way and have one of the guys carry it out for you."

"Aye, sir," Bradley said. "The Odd Couple took Halonen topside earlier." He led MacTavish outside.

"There's a damn good corpsman," Chief Gunnarson remarked. "We'll be losing him pretty soon."

"Is he getting out of the Navy?" Taylor asked.

"No, sir," Gunnarson answered. "He's signed up for NCP. He already had his premed studies completed before he enlisted. He'll be finishing up his education to be a doctor, and plans on serving in the Navy MC as a trauma surgeon."

"The injured and wounded will really be in good hands then," Cruiser commented.

PO Monty Sturgis led Carey and Berringer into the cave. The two staff officers toted their briefcases, as they usually did. Carey motioned everyone to remain seated as he and Berringer joined the group. "I read the report on last night's battle. Short and nasty, hey? Too bad about the casualties."

"Yes, sir," Brannigan said.

"Well, another situation has arisen," Carey said. "And if you're looking for some payback time, this may be it. I'll let Commander Berringer explain it all to you."

"We've heard from Aladdin again," Berringer said, pulling several maps from his briefcase. "It was a brief transmission but had a lot of information. On fifteen June, a detachment of twenty Arab volunteers will be on its way to join your neighbors on the other side of the valley. And they'll be coming by foot." He began passing out the maps. "These have been prepared for you. You'll notice the only markings are ones that deal with their arrival."

Brannigan looked at the chart. "Aren't those reinforcements coming in by chopper?"

"Negative," Berringer replied. "They don't want you alerted, so these guys are taking a fifty-kilometer walk from their jumping-off point to this area." He gave his audience a meaningful glance. "That means they're highly trained, well equipped, and in damn good physical condition."

"I hope you're here to get us ready to form a reception party," Senior Chief Dawkins said.

"That's it exactly," Carey replied. "As you see by their route, they're coming in through rugged territory to avoid detection. We'll be able to have the Air Force fly you to a convenient LZ in that area to make contact. The flight won't attract any undue attention, since they drop off recon teams there from time to time. And it won't take you long to unass the aircraft, since all you have to do is run down the ramp to the ground."

"You are to interrupt their journey and render them ineffective," Berringer said. "And try grabbing us an EPW or two as well. When the job is done, the Air Force will pick you up at either the same LZ, or another if your prefer."

"When do we leave?" Brannigan asked.

"Immediately if not sooner," Carey replied. "You'll fly out with us. So gather the guys you want, and we'll take you back to Shelor Field, where you can ready yourselves and firm up any OPORD you care to make."

Brannigan paused a moment, then said, "Alright. I'll be in command of the mission. I'm gonna take the Sneaky Petes. That's six of us. Oh, yeah. And Puglisi and Miskoski. That'll make eight. Mmm." He pondered a bit more than said, "And Ensign Taylor."

"Thank you, sir!" Taylor happily exclaimed.

"It's a good chance to enhance your experience," Brannigan remarked. He looked at Cruiser. "You'll stay back here in command. Turn the First Section over to your senior petty officer."

"Aye, sir!"

Brannigan's attention was now directed to Senior Chief Petty Officer Buford Dawkins. "You heard my choices of personnel, Senior Chief. Round 'em up and get 'em in here." As the senior chief rushed off to tend to the chore, Brannigan turned back to Cruiser. "Rebuild the fighting positions that were knocked down last night, but don't put 'em back in the same spot or they'll get pulverized again."

"Aye, sir!"

"What was that all about?" Carey asked. "Have your defenses been compromised?"

"I'll explain during the flight back to Shelor," Brannigan said. "Excuse me. I have to pack a few things."

CHAPTER 7

BRIGADIER Shahruz Khohollah was pleased. He smoked his Turkish cigarette almost gleefully as he looked across his desk at Sikes Pasha, Captain Khadid, and Captain Komard. "The attack of last night was a superb victory!"

Sikes wasn't so sure about a "superb victory," but it obviously was a tactical success in that the enemy's defensive system was damaged by concentrating fire on known positions to destroy them. This was accomplished as planned. "When them reinforcements arrive, we'll give the Yanks a what-for they ain't soon to forget, yeah?"

Komard was interested in the new men. "How many are we receiving, Sikes Pasha?"

"Twenty," he replied. "It doubles me force, that's wot it does." He glanced over at the Brigadier. "Things are a lot better than when we was at Chehaar Garrison, hey, Brigadier?"

"Absolutely correct, Major Sikes," the brigadier said. He

did not refer to Sikes by the title "Pasha," since he outranked the Brit. In fact, there were times when Khohollah was irritated by the arrogant manner in which Sikes conducted himself. It smacked of the old colonial attitudes of the British Empire. But the brigadier was convinced that the General Staff put great value on this deserter from the UK, and any undue complaints about him might prove most disadvantageous to the career of anyone who denigrated the man.

"Our situation improves daily," Captain Khadid said. He had never been at Chehaar Garrison during the situation with the armored cars. He had been in the Pashtun camp as a personal adviser to Yama Orakzai, the Pashtun rebel leader. This had been before and during the setbacks and humiliations that had been inflicted on Sikes by the Americans. The situation had infuriated the former British soldier.

"Yes," the brigadier said. "We are much better off." He was personally miffed as a general officer by the number of men he commanded. Even with the arrival of the Arab volunteers, he would have less than a hundred under his overall control. And no artillery. By proper military custom, Khohollah should have been leading two thousand to five thousand men into battle. However, in spite of the resentment, he showed enthusiasm and optimism for the sake of his subordinate officers and soldiers. He smiled at his loyal adjutant, Captain Jamshid Komard, whom he had given the command of the fire support unit. "Your men made superlative work of covering the withdrawal as well as knocking out the defensive positions."

"I shall pass on your compliments to the gunners, Excellency," Komard said. "They will be most happy about your approval." He hesitated, then asked, "Do you think there is a chance of us receiving mortars to replace the grenade launchers, Excellency?"

The brigadier shook his head. "Do not anticipate any such happening, dear Komard. To express the truth, I was greatly surprised by the reinforcements. I did not expect such a thing unless the *Amerikayizan* increased their strength in soldiers or weapons."

Captain Khadid lit a cigarette. "The political and diplomatic aspects of this operation truly test a soldier's patience, do they not?"

"You speak the absolute truth, Captain," Brigadier Khohollah agreed. "But we must keep in mind that the Iranian government is not run by the Army."

Sikes nodded. "I'm finding all that a bit too much to swallow meself. I'd just as soon give them Yanks a good whipping, then get the Pashtuns back in their place. Then we can get on with taking over Afghanistan."

"Be patient, Major Sikes," the brigadier advised him. He smiled, saying, "Could it be that you miss your little Pashtun wife?"

"I miss her, alright," Sikes admitted. "But we ain't married no more, since me and Cap'n Khadid was told to leave. That ended the marriage. It was a *muta* anyhow and supposed to be temporary by Islamic law." He paused hesitantly for a moment, then said, "I don't like to stick me nose in places where it ain't wanted, but I been wondering a bit if you have a wife or wives you miss."

"I only had one wife," the brigadier said. "She died five years ago. We were, alas, a childless couple; thus I have no descendants. Nor are there kin of any sort. And I cannot muster the desire for another woman. I believe, for whatever reason, that Allah in his mercy does not want me to remarry. I am now an old soldier alone in the world." He gestured around him. "And here I am in this strange situation, tied down by puzzling orders issued by my government."

"It ain't all bad, sir," Sikes said. "We do have some leeway in that we can carry on harassing tactics in any manner that suits us." He leaned forward. "I'm working on a couple o' plans, sir. When I get everything straight in me head, I'll bring 'em up." He was thoughtful for a moment, then spoke again. "I was wondering, Brigadier, that wot if we had some rotten luck and them Yanks kicked us out o' here, hey? Wot'd happen then?"

"I have heard no official word," Khohollah said. "However, in my personal opinion, almost the entire Iranian Army would be sent here to storm straight into Afghanistan and create a situation the Yanks—as you call them—would find most disturbing. We will stay low-key as long as they stay low-key. But we are eventually going to conquer Afghanistan, then the entirety of the Middle East."

Khadid smiled at Sikes. "The preliminary steps we take on this journey to glory must be careful and deliberate, Sikes Pasha. At least at this point in time."

"I understand," Sikes said. "But I don't like it one bluddy fucking bit."

"By the way, Excellency," Khadid said, "I am due to make a transmission back to Iran this evening. Do you have any messages for the high command?"

"Only that we are moving along according to plan," Brigadier Khohollah said. "There is nothing negative to report. By the way, will you be using the radio in the signals center, Captain?"

"No, Excellency," Khadid said. "That will not be necessary. I still have the one I took to Orakzai's fortress."

WESTERN AFGHANISTAN
14 JUNE
1600 HOURS

ENSIGN Orlando Taylor sat in the web seat aboard the Pave Low chopper, furtively studying the eight other SEALs who shared the aircraft with him. From their demeanors, anybody would think they were on their way to a peaceful picnic in the country instead of a violent confrontation in which men would be killed by other men.

Taylor had marveled about the fact that he had finally been under fire. Although he knew it wasn't a prolonged battle with many casualties, it was still combat. He had been scared, sure, but it didn't keep him from doing the job properly. He kept an eye on the situation, watched over his men, and coordinated everything through Petty Officers Paul Schreiner and Tony Valenzuela, who were his fire team leaders. When the SAW gunner Doug MacTavish had been hit, Taylor hadn't lost his head or flinched at the sight of the man's bloodied face. In fact, it had been he who pulled the wounded SEAL from the rubble of his blasted fighting position to safety. The best thing about the whole experience was that he had done nothing to shame himself or the Taylor family. He could openly and truthfully discuss the fighting with his father without fear of disapproval.

Taylor grinned to himself in a somewhat fierce manner as he thought of this latest experience in context with his three older brothers. As the youngest he had been the butt of jokes from those overachievers, who never accepted him as an equal. It seemed he would always be "the kid" in the family. The oldest sibling, now thirty-two years of age, was a vice president in a very prestigious bank in Atlanta; the second, at age twenty-nine, was an aerospace engineer with NASA in Houston in the Shuttle Program; and the twenty-seven-year-old was on the staff of a Georgia senator, and being groomed by the state's Democratic Party to run for Congress in the next election.

Damn fine accomplishments, Taylor thought, *but not a one of them has been in combat as a Navy SEAL.* He hoped his father would take notice of the fact and mention it at every opportunity during the next family reunion.

THE helicopter came in low and slow at an altitude of four feet AGL. The rear doors were open and the ramp down as Lieutenant Bill Brannigan stood at the head of the line of men making up the combat patrol. At a nod from the crew chief, the Skipper went down the ramp and leaped off to the ground. He was quickly followed by Connie Concord, the Odd Couple, and Matty Matsuno, who carried a five-gallon jerry can of potable water attached to a backpack. Then Garth Redhawk with an AN/PRC-112 radio unassed the aircraft; Ensign Orlando Taylor, Bruno Puglisi, and Joe Miskoski were the last out. Everyone was armed with M-16s, with two exceptions: Puglisi and Miskoski carried their AS-50 semiauto sniper rifles with two bandoliers of modified twenty-round magazines for the weapons.

The chopper immediately rose back into the sky as the ass end closed. Brannigan led his eight men over to the cover of a stand of boulders for an on-site confab. But before the session could begin, an angry cobra emerged from the rocks

with its hood flared as it assumed the standard upright pose
of aggression. The Skipper gazed at the poisonous reptile. "I
think we have a territorial issue here."

Puglisi, impetuous as always, made a slow approach toward the snake, evidently with the intention of trying to grasp
it. Redhawk, who was well acquainted with the rattlesnakes
of Oklahoma, did not think that a good idea. "Bruno," he said
calmly, "if that son of a bitch bites you, we won't have much
time to make our good-byes to you. So let us know when
you're going to make a serious move toward him, and we'll
bid you a fond farewell. With luck you'll last maybe five minutes after he sinks his fangs into you."

The snake darted its head at the SEAL, and Puglisi instinctively jumped back. "I thought you could charm these
motherfuckers."

Joe Miskoski laughed. "Bruno, you don't have a flute,
like snake charmers use, you dumb shit." Then he laughed
louder. "Besides, you're about as charming as a grumpy rhi-
noceros with gas and heartburn."

Brannigan grinned. "Let's try to be diplomatic like Dr.
Joplin where that snake is concerned, okay? We'll just politely get out of his bailiwick."

The patrol moved away from the natural rock pile toward
another. The cobra didn't follow, but he was plainly going to
stand his ground. Now the Skipper could concentrate on the
job ahead. "We're only a kilometer from the ambush site
here, but I want to have a little briefback before we go over
there." He pointed to Puglisi. "What's your job?"

"I'll be at the front of the ambush, and when the last man
passes me, I'll whack the son of a bitch," Puglisi said. "Then
knock off any of the bad guys who try to escape in my direction."

Brannigan turned to Miskoski. "What about you?"

"Well, we figured the enemy column isn't gonna be too
strung out, since this is a safe area for 'em," Miskoski said.
"So I'm gonna be down about thirty to forty meters from
Bruno to close up the front. When the first man comes up
even with me, I'll take him out."

Next it was Connie Concord's turn. "Ever'body is gonna

find a good place between Bruno and Joe. We'll space ourselves out as even as possible, depending on the terrain and
available cover. When the shooting starts, we'll go for targets of opportunity to our direct fronts."

"Right," Brannigan said. He nodded to Taylor. "Ensign,
describe the site."

"Aye, sir," Taylor said. "It's a narrow pass through these
hills with steep sides that go from ten to twelve meters deep.
We'll set up only on one side, since the enemy cannot escape
from the gully with any ease or speed. They, in fact, will
have walked into a natural trap."

"Okay," Brannigan said. "It's sweet and simple. Keep in
mind that we're also tasked with getting EPWs if possible. If
you see any guy that looks like he wants to quit or surrender,
ease up. Questions? Right then. Let's move out and settle
down. We won't have much to do until tomorrow morning.
So, to quote the first and oldest military order ever issued,
'Follow me.'" He started to move out, but stopped. "Oh!
One more thing."

"What's that, sir?" Dave Leibowitz asked.

"Watch out for snakes."

15 JUNE
0900 HOURS

THE SEAL patrol had good cover and concealment
from their position overlooking the narrow valley, but there
was no shade overhead. Bruno Puglisi, with a fresh magazine in the receiver of his AS-50 and half a dozen others lying out within reach, was uncomfortably warm. Each man
had brought along a couple of two-quart canteens, and there
was that jerry can of water being lugged around by Matty
Matsuno. However, the patrol drank sparingly because of
potential SNAFUs. Unexpected things happened continually
in warfare, and the enemy reinforcements could be delayed
by a glitch in their transportation arrangements, ammo issue, or dozens of other things. The Brigands could end up
spending two or three days at the location.

1015 HOURS

THE leading Arab showed up around the bend in the gully so quickly that Puglisi instinctively twitched. "Here they come," he whispered, recovering from the surprise. "They're kind of close together, so we don't have to stretch the ambush out any farther."

As the column came into view, the sight of the Arabs was impressive. All were well equipped, with the latest in assault rifles, rucksacks, canteens, bandoliers, and web gear. Their uniforms were in good shape, with excellent footwear, and they also sported the keffiyeh head coverings their people preferred. They were the red-checked style the SEALs had seen before.

Joe Miskoski, with his AS-50 locked and loaded, waited patiently, his eyes glued to the front man in the formation. The guy's face in the telescopic sight was that of a young and determined soldier, his beard and mustache well trimmed, as would be expected of someone just out of an elite training camp where the discipline was harsh and demanding. When he was in the right position, Miskoski's trigger finger tightened just enough to fire the powerful rifle.

The fifty-caliber round exploded the man's head, blowing it off in pieces.

The Arab just behind him stood still for an instant before a couple of .556 rounds from an M-16 kicked him sideways before he collapsed to the ground. Back on the other end of the line, Puglisi had already taken out the Tail-End Charlie a millisecond after he heard Miskoski's weapon fire. In ten seconds, the bursts of blazing M-16s suddenly quit. Seventeen men were down, and three stood with their hands up.

"Assad," Brannigan said. "Warn those guys not to move and do what you tell 'em."

"*Indak!*" Assad yelled. "*Isma minni!*"

"Redhawk and Matsuno!" Brannigan said. "Move down and take charge of those EPWs. Walk 'em down to where that slope is and bring 'em up on the far side toward the LZ. We'll meet you there. Ensign Taylor and Petty Officer Concord, go search the dead for documents or any other intelligence you find. Let's go, people!"

The four men assigned to go into the gully slid carefully down the steep sides until they reached the bottom. Redhawk and Matsuno moved over to the trio of men who still stood with their hands up. The SEALs used gestures to indicate the direction they were to go. Taylor looked at Connie Concord. "You go down to the end and start checking. I'll go up where the first guy is."

"Aye, sir."

Taylor had fired only one round during the short, violent action. He'd taken aim at an Arab directly to his front and squeezed the trigger. The guy had taken a jerky step, then fell to the ground. The young ensign stared at him in horrid fascination. He had killed a man. The shooting during the attack three nights before had been into vegetation in a reconnaissance-by-fire trying to locate the enemy. If he hit anyone, it was by sheer chance, and he didn't know about it. But this time he had deliberately shot another human being. He walked up toward the first man to die, doing his best not to look at the one he personally shot.

The Arab hit by Joe Miskoski was a mess. The entire top of his cranium from just below the ears and up was a splayed mass of brains and bloody meat. His eyes and nose were gone, leaving only the lower jaw. Taylor noticed the guy must have been seeing his dentist regularly; the teeth were white and even, without a cavity showing. The SEAL searched the pockets, finding nothing; not even an ID card. He supposed that was to be expected, since the dead man hadn't been a member of a regularly enlisted army.

After examining two more corpses, he came to the guy he had killed. He was a skinny kid, maybe eighteen or nineteen. His eyes were open, and his lips were in a sort of combination sneer and grin. Taylor suddenly looked directly at the dead face, almost stepping back when he noticed the victim seemed to be gazing at him. A quick search revealed empty pockets.

When Taylor and Concord met in the middle, they had nothing to show for their efforts. "I'm not surprised," Connie said. "These guys are not the usual raghead mujahideen. They're equipped good, carry them French rifles, got plenty of ammo, and are nourished good. This is gonna be a tough fight before it's all said and done, sir."

Taylor noted that if Petty Officer Concord had killed anybody—and there was no doubt he had—he wasn't going to lose any sleep over it. Taylor affected a grin. "Well, let's get back with the others. Good job, huh?"

"Yes, sir," Connie said. "We done good, alright."

THE LZ
1045 HOURS

GARTH Redhawk had turned on the homing beacon of the AN/PRC-112 to bring back the chopper, and the patrol was out in a loose defensive perimeter. Brannigan was inside the formation with Mike Assad, who guarded the three EPWs. The captives squatted unhappily on the ground, still stunned by the suddenness of the attack that had destroyed their unit. Assad had exchanged a few words with them, learning nothing new. They told him they were on their way from Iran to join the small force in the mountains.

Suddenly one of the Arabs leaped to his feet and dashed toward the perimeter, leaping over Bruno Puglisi. He ran wildly across the open ground, heading for the stand of boulders.

"I'll get him, sir!" Puglisi yelled, getting to his feet and going after the guy.

The Arab was fifteen meters ahead of the SEAL, not looking back as he instinctively sought the shelter of the rocky area. When he reached it, he went in between a couple of boulders. Then he shrieked and backed out, holding his hand.

When Puglisi arrived he saw what the trouble was. The cobra, still weaving back and forth in its attack stance, was ready to strike again. The Arab turned around, his hand and forearm black and swelling from the venom. Puglisi winced. "Jesus! You poor dumb bastard!"

The Arab knew the potency of the serpent's venom and realized that he was dying. He sank to his knees and began calling out in Arabic. Now Mike Assad joined them, having left the other two with the Skipper. Mike looked at the guy. "What the fuck happened to him?"

Puglisi answered by pointing over to the cobra.

Assad shook his head slowly. "We got nothing to give him for that."

"I know," Puglisi said. "He'll be dead before the chopper gets here."

"Shit, Bruno," Mike said, "he's only got another five minutes at the most to breathe."

Now the Arab was on the ground, almost delirious as he kept babbling.

"What's he saying, Mike?"

"He's praying for himself."

"We should shoot him and put him out of his misery, man!" Puglisi said.

"I'm not shooting him," Mike said. He turned and began walking back to the perimeter. He'd gone ten meters when he heard Bruno's AS-50 fire. Then the sniper caught up with him.

Neither SEAL spoke as they returned to the unit.

CHAPTER 8

IT had been a bad week for the two Arab EPWs brought back from the ambush site by Brannigan's Brigands. When they left their Iranian SF training camp, the fledgling insurgents thought they were on their way to their big opportunity to be conquerors in the name of Allah's glory. But they were only halfway to their first battle site when a bunch of crazy infidels suddenly appeared from nowhere and shot their unit to pieces. And if that wasn't bad enough, after surrendering, one of their buddies was bitten by a poisonous serpent and was put out of his misery with a bullet that turned his skull into something that looked like a shattered vase that had been filled with tomato paste and cottage cheese.

It was most definitely not a good experience.

Then, to make things slightly worse, immediately after the incident with the snake, they were blindfolded and had to sit with their hands bound by plastic strips and wait until an aircraft arrived. They were taken aboard with their captors to go for a flight—they didn't have enough experience to recognize they were in a helicopter—that ended when they landed at some unknown place. After being ushered off the aircraft still blindfolded, the two Arabs were taken into the interior of a large structure. When they were freed from their blinders and bonds, they discovered that their captors had put them behind some barbed wire in one corner of a building. For amenities the EPWs were provided with foam mattresses and a couple of chairs. At least they weren't mistreated, but being uncertain of what fate awaited them did not ease their emotional stress.

After a fitful night, the Arabs were given breakfast, then blindfolded again, and put back on an aircraft for a short flight that ended on a rocking airfield made of steel. From there the pair was led through a very narrow door and taken down steep steps until they were in the depths of some horrible place with engine noises. At that point the blinders were removed and they were separated and placed into small rooms with pipes and valves along the walls. A bright lightbulb that was never turned off glared from the ceiling, and from that point on they couldn't tell if it was night or day.

As time passed they became queasy as the floor where they sat rocked slowly back and forth. They also had moments when they felt this strange prison was actually moving.

0730 HOURS

THE name of the EPW sitting in the metal chair was Hamza Qazi. A brilliant light shined straight into his face, and he could not see the man who spoke to him, although he sensed that additional persons were present after he heard occasional coughs and someone clearing his throat. Qazi had been there for more than two hours, though he was unaware of exactly how much time had passed since he was fetched from his hard metal quarters.

The three men in the compartment with the prisoner were Dr. Carl Joplin; Edgar Watson, of the CIA's Iranian desk; and interrogator Fred Leighton, also a CIA operative. Leighton, who had spent much of his boyhood in the Middle East, where his father had been a field operations supervisor for an American oil company, spoke fluent Arabic with such a slight trace of accent that no Arab could determine his exact nationality. Between Leighton's language skills and the probing questions provided by Joplin and Watson, a lot of useful information was being dragged out of Qazi.

He was a Syrian, born and raised in the city of Deir Al Zor, not too far from the Iraqi border. His father was a shopkeeper who sold tobacco, candy, and magazines. The profits were small, but the family was comfortable enough, though frustrated from time to time from wanting better material things in their lives, such as an automobile and a larger TV set. Qazi left school at fourteen to help in the business. During his leisure time he hung out in the streets with a group of boys his own age and played in a local soccer league, where he was considered one of the better players. He was sixteen when he learned about the Jihad Abadi—the Eternal Holy War made up of Shiite mujahideen. Eventually he was recruited into the organization and learned that they disavowed suicide bombings, preferring to train their members in soldierly skills to fight the infidels of the West. This was much more effective in the holy struggle than blowing themselves up to inflict casualties on the enemy. Qazi and his buddies attended meetings and class sessions at the local mosque, where they were thoroughly indoctrinated in the group's philosophy. He was honored when his natural athletic abilities were noted, and he was sent for more advanced instruction at a training site in Iran. This choice of location confused the young Arab, who could not understand what interest the Iranians had in Arab insurgencies, except that those speakers of Farsi were also Shiites.

When he arrived in Tehran, he was put aboard a military bus with other Arabs from all over the Middle East. They went to an Army garrison in the north. It was a camp with training facilities and few amenities. The students lived in tents, used outdoor toilets, and drew their water from spigots around the area. There was no electricity, but this didn't matter to most of the Arabs, who were from the country or slum areas of places such as Baghdad, Amman, and Riyadh. At first Qazi was annoyed by having to use candles and camp lanterns, but he eventually got used to it as the first couple of weeks passed.

The orientation prior to moving into the hard-core phase of training taught the young men that Iran would be taking over all Shiite insurgencies and bring them into one large, effective army. The boys in the camp would be the cadre of that magnificent fighting force, destined by Allah to march into Europe as conquerors, then accept an unconditional surrender from the Great Satan, the United States of America. This fired up everybody's enthusiasm, and when the training began, they were ready to give it their all.

The first thing on the agenda was to toughen them up. The instructors, harsh and merciless, were all members of the newly organized Iranian Army Special Forces. They sent the Arab kids through obstacle courses, took them on long runs, and supervised prolonged periods of exhausting exercises. After a couple of weeks the candidates were considered properly conditioned for some real soldiering.

The Arab boys went into a program where they learned weapons, demolitions, map reading and orienteering, small-unit tactics, and other skills needed for the basics of combat. A crash course in acquiring a good working knowledge of Farsi was included. One pleasant part of the duty was that they were given an abundance of meat, vegetables, and fruit in their mess tents. Only when they were in the field did they go hungry as a preparation for long periods of tough, relentless campaigning.

After twelve weeks of hard work, they graduated and were assigned to permanent units. From that point on, they went on complicated and demanding FTXs to sharpen the skills taught them. Then Qazi and nineteen other young troopers were chosen for a special assignment in which they would go into a real war. They were issued French FA-MAS assault rifles, ammunition, rations, and brand-new field gear.

After being equipped, the rookies were taken by bus to a spot near the Iran-Afghanistan border, with maps showing their destination, where they would link with a battle group actively engaged in combat. They set off in high spirits, ready to fight and conquer.

Then they were ambushed.

Qazi's buddy, when questioned, gave the same story except that he was a country bumpkin from Yemen who had been recruited into the Jihad Abadi while working as a laborer in Saudi Arabia.

SEAL BASE CAMP
1200 HOURS

PO2C Bruno Puglisi was on Lieutenant Bill Brannigan's shit list.

The shooting of the snakebitten EPW may have been merciful, but Puglisi had taken it upon himself to perform the deed. He should have waited for orders from the Skipper before taking such a drastic step. Now the Skipper was between a rock and a hard place. The killing of a prisoner was a serious situation, and if the truth came out, Puglisi could be in bad trouble.

The Skipper had glared at him, speaking in a low tone of extreme anger. "You just better hope nobody gets real curious about this. If they do, you're gonna be in deep shit and I'll be having serious career problems of my own. As it is, I'm going to report that the guy was killed during an escape attempt."

"That's technically correct, sir," Puglisi happily agreed.

"Shut up!"

"Aye, sir!"

Brannigan then dropped the miscreant into the front-leaning rest, and chewed the SEAL's ass to pieces with loud bellowing. After venting his rage, the Skipper followed SOP and gave him the choice of administrative punishment or a court-martial. Puglisi had completed boot camp a long time ago, and he knew the better of that deal. He chose administrative punishment under Article 15 of the Uniform Code of Military Justice. That meant the incident wouldn't go in his personnel record. It also eased the Skipper's problem with keeping the snake-bite incident under wraps.

Now Brannigan could choose a punishment. If he was less than creative and did something like make Puglisi run up and down the mountain trails with a rucksack full of heavy rocks, it would make a hero out of the erring SEAL. In fact, some of the other Brigands might take on the task themselves to see how they could handle it. So the Skipper assigned the slightly miffed sniper to forty-eight hours of watch-and-watch. But rather than let him rest between stints of duty, he had him report to Senior Chief Buford Dawkins for extra "tasks." Consequently, rather than having four hours of sleep during his off-duty time, Puglisi sometimes got as little as one before having to report back to the watch officer for another tour of duty.

The senior chief was inspired, almost artistic, in the jobs he thought up for Puglisi to perform during his "free time." He had him count all the sandbags in One Sector and Two Sector, then report the percentage differences between the two areas. Another time he had him transfer a pile of rocks from one of the destroyed fighting positions to another location, twenty paces away. The rub was that Puglisi had to carry each rock over one at a time, place it down, then turn and go back to fetch another. Those chores and other things, such as using a toothbrush to scrub the deck of the Headquarters bunker and cleaning the Fire Support Section's machine guns, kept the struggling SEAL from getting much sleep between watches.

The rest of the detachment cringed at the chickenshit aspects of the ordeal. The collective feelings of the others were summed up by Joe Miskoski, who said, "You gotta be a real dumb sack of shit to get in a mess like that."

Bruno Puglisi would have agreed with him.

GARTH Redhawk and Matty Matsuno had become good buddies.

This friendship began during a quiet period after the ambush, when they were sitting in the Sneaky Petes' area, cleaning their weapons. The conversation had been the quiet sort common between young men busy at important tasks. Matty, who was wiping down his bolt, asked, "What's that little bag you wear around your neck, Garth?"

Garth explained the meaning behind the medicine bag and showed him the trident insignia, the piece of wood from the Oklahoma tree, and the small rock from South America. "I don't really go around looking for things," Garth said, "but if something is right for the bag, I know right away. And so far I only got these three things."

"It's Indian custom, huh?"

"Well, I prefer to call it Kiowa or Comanche custom," Garth said. "My dad isn't really into that stuff. He's a petroleum engineer and has a real logical and scientific mind. My grandfather on my mother's side taught me a lot about the old traditions."

"Is the way you put camouflage paint on your face an Indian, er—Kiowa or whatever—thing?"

Garth nodded. "My grandfather told me about the different patterns, and I designed the one I use myself. Once when I wrote him, I drew it down for him. He approved." He grinned. "Big medicine."

"Hell, I have the same situation at home you do," Matty said. "My granddad is into Bushido big time, but my dad couldn't care less. He's a software programmer down in the Silicon Valley. My parents are divorced, and my mom and I lived with my grandparents. My granddad belonged to a society that observed the philosophical and spiritual sides of Japanese martial culture. When I was about twelve or thirteen, he took me down to his club's dojo and signed me up for kendo lessons."

"Hey, man!" Garth said, laughing. "I know that *bushido* is the samurai code, but what's this dojo and kendo stuff?"

"Kendo means 'way of the sword,' and the dojo is the place where they practice and learn about martial arts," Matty said. "In other words, it's a sort of combination school and gym."

"My grandfather taught me the ways of the Plains Indians warriors with a couple of his old buddies," Garth said. "They even made bows and arrows the traditional way. They used to go down to a creek back home and get flint to make arrowheads. I really learned to respect those old guys. They were pretty good and taught me to hunt. They played up the stealth part, and I learned to move silently."

"That's like the ninjas, man!" Matty said. "I studied some of that too, but more of the spiritual side than anything else."

"You know what we ought to do," Garth said, "let's

exchange some of the lessons we learned as boys. It could be a lot of help out there on patrol."

"Yeah," Matty agreed. "It couldn't hurt." He began replacing the sling on his M-16.

USS *COMBS* 1800 HOURS

CARL Joplin and Commanders Thomas Carey and Ernest Berringer were alone in the wardroom. They had been served cups of coffee by a waiter, and they sat around the table in earnest conversation. The diplomat and the two staff officers had read transcripts of the interrogation of the two EPWs that had been completed an hour before.

"Well," Carey said, having finished perusing his copy, "once again Aladdin proved his worth when he told us about those Arab reinforcements."

Berringer, a trained intelligence officer, had a worried expression on his face. "Those EPWs said some things that scare the hell out of me. Evidently the Iranian Special Forces effort is stepping up. They must be running hundreds of Shiites through that training."

"Mmm," Carey nodded in agreement. "Those prisoners said there were fifty people in their group before twenty were pulled out to go to Afghanistan. And there were a lot more who seem to be stationed there and going through some rather sophisticated FTXs to get sharpened up." He was thoughtful for a moment. "I wonder why they didn't transfer some of their more experienced men instead of the bunch that included our EPWs."

"I think they're saving their best-trained people for the big push," Berringer said. "There's something sneaky going on with those fucking Iranians."

"There is one big bit of information lacking," Joplin commented. "We have no idea just how many Arabs are in the Iranians' program, and we need to know."

"We can't even make an estimate," Berringer said. "They might even have some additional training camps or programs that Aladdin doesn't know about."

"Damn it!" Carey said. "I wish there was some way we could contact him."

"Forget it," Berringer said. "He could be sitting right in the middle of the bad guys. He sure as hell doesn't want somebody to hear a transmission from us coming in on his commo equipment. I hate to think what they'd put him through to make him talk."

"I am certainly no expert in this sort of thing," Joplin said, "but it is obvious he is on his own."

"I don't mean to be disrespectful, Carl," Carey said, "but allow me to say that I've never been too keen on this mission we've forced Brannigan and his men to take on. I'm beginning to feel like we tossed them into a boiling cauldron."

"If things go wrong it will be all my fault," Joplin said. "I made a judgment based on my experiences in international diplomacy. It just seemed to me that the Iranians don't want to have a showdown at this time and in that place. In my estimation they want to keep it low-key so we won't make a big response to their presence there on the border. They also have the Israelis to contend with."

"Maybe you played into their hands, Carl," Berringer said. "I hate like hell to say that, but with time on their side, the Iranians could build up a big enough force to roll into Afghanistan and Pakistan both. That would give them a pretty strong foothold on the eastern side of the Persian and Oman gulfs as well as north of the Arabian Sea."

"Man!" Carey exclaimed. "The former Soviet Republics of Turkmenistan, Uzbekistan, and Tajikistan might throw in with 'em. They all have Islamic populations."

"Hell!" Carey exclaimed. "Even the Chinese Muslims in the west might join their cause."

Carl Joplin, PhD, sighed and stared into his coffee cup. "Such thoughts have also occurred to me." He raised his eyes to his companions. "Y'know, I've not been sleeping well lately."

CHAPTER 9

THE operational area had settled down to one of tense observation. The last shot fired had been by Bruno Puglisi on 17 June, when he and Joe Miskoski were in their snipers mode atop the hill over the Headquarters bunker. Joe was acting as spotter, using high-power binoculars to locate possible targets on the other side of the valley. He anxiously scanned the enemy position in hopes of locating a target for his partner. Puglisi rested his eyes by keeping them closed, and was ready to turn to the telescopic sight. He had spent a couple of hours seeing it had been properly mounted and zeroed in on his AS-50 sniper rifle.

After a quarter of an hour, Miskoski spotted a careless Zaheya soldier with the top half of his head exposed to view. The alert SEAL quickly pointed it out to Puglisi, who immediately sighted in on the man and pulled the trigger. The exact moment the firing pin hit the primer, the intended victim bent over to pick up a dropped pack of cigarettes. The heavy

.50-caliber bullet crashed into the side of the fighting position, then ricocheted off with a loud, buzzing whine.

A prayer of thanks must have been given to Allah that evening.

Now both sides were cautious and vigilant, keeping low profiles along their defenses both night and day. Off-duty hours in the safety of the bunkers offered the only real security when meals could be consumed, reading materials scanned, and slumber enjoyed. The only thing that kept the combatants from sinking into a state of deep lethargy was the constant danger they faced. Those on watch in hours of darkness peered expectantly through the NVGs, while the watch commanders used night vision binoculars to search out movement within the flora and boulders strewn across the expanse of no-man's-land.

This was the tedious anxiety of trench warfare exactly as it had been from 1914 to 1918, during World War One.

WASHINGTON, D.C.
6 JULY
1000 HOURS

WHEN Dirk Wallenger returned from the three-day Fourth of July weekend, he had a special message on the answering machine in the den of his home. The communication, delivered in an Arabic accent, was short but important. "This is Ali. Please meet me tomorrow at the regular time. However, please go to the alternate place. Thank you."

THE next morning following the call, Wallenger walked up to the taxi stand where Constitution Avenue, Second Street, and Maryland Avenue converge. He was a short, dumpy man in his early thirties with a cherubic face that exhibited childlike qualities. This effect was belied somewhat by a pair of eyes that exhibited glints of aggression. Wallenger quickly spotted the driver he was looking for and got into his vehicle. The man, not bothering to ask for a destination, wasted no time in pulling out into traffic. He turned south on Third Street, going down to Independence Avenue, where he made a right turn. Now they were settled into stop-and-go traffic, where it was possible to move along slowly while conversing. The cabbie looked into his rearview mirror at his fare. "How have you been, Mr. Wallenger?"

"Fine, Ali," he replied. "I take it you have some news for me."

"Yes, Mr. Wallenger," Ali replied. "Some most interesting information was sent to my mosque. It is saying that a mujahideen taken prisoner by American Special Forces was shot dead. Executed without provocation."

Wallenger had already taken his notebook out and was poised to scribble. "May I have some details?"

"Of course," Ali said. "This has happened in the western part of Afghanistan. There was a fight and the Americans were hidden. They shoot and kill everybody but three mujahideen, who are surrendering and begging for mercy."

"Can you be more specific than just the 'western part' of Afghanistan?"

"It was most close to the Iran border, sir," Ali said. "It was part of the mountains called Gharawdara Highlands. I am told that is the correct manner in which to be pronouncing it."

"Can you spell that?"

"Alas, I am unable to do so in either the Arabic or English alphabet, Mr. Wallenger."

"Never mind, I can look it up on a map," Wallenger said. "Where did this news come from?"

"It is coming from Bahrain, sir."

"Ah, yes!" Wallenger exclaimed. "It must be out of the prison at Station Bravo."

"Yes, sir."

"What was the date of the incident, Ali?"

"It was on fifteen of June, sir, in the morning when the battle is taking place," Ali said.

"Mmm," Wallenger mused. "Okay. Tell me the circumstances in which this information was discovered by the person who reported it."

"He is talking to one of the men in one part of the prison and he tells him about the shooting," Ali explained. "Then the man in prison is saying his friend who was with him is also in the prison." He reached into his shirt pocket and pulled out a piece of paper, slipping it through the slot in the shield behind him.

Wallenger took the scrap and read the names printed in block letters. "Let's see. We have Hamza Qazi and Rahmat Nahayan. And they are both confined in the prison at the American base in Bahrain, true?"

"Yes," Ali answered. "That is true. At Station Bravo."

"Very good," Wallenger said. "Did this person making the report talk to both these men?"

"Yes. And they are telling the same story, Mr. Wallenger."

"Do they know the reason the one man was shot?"

"Yes, Mr. Wallenger. He was hurt and the Americans did not want to carry him. So they killed him."

"Alright," Wallenger said. "Are there any more details?"

"No," Ali replied. "I am assured that this is the whole story."

"Very well," Wallenger said. "I guess that's everything I need. If you get any more information about this, please let me know." He settled back in his seat, feeling very good about the revelation. "You can take me back to the cab stand."

"Yes, sir, Mr. Wallenger."

Ali pulled into the parking lot driveway of the Department of Agriculture and turned around, going back to Independence Avenue for the return trip. Twenty minutes later he pulled up to the cab stand and stopped. Wallenger leaned forward. "I appreciate this information very much, Ali, and I know what to do with it."

"I am most pleased, Mr. Wallenger," Ali said. "We at the mosque know you will use it to be proving the Muslims are innocent victims of American military aggression."

"I certainly will," Wallenger said. "You can depend on me." He pulled five hundred dollars out of his wallet and passed it over to the driver, then got out to return to his office.

* * *

DIRK Wallenger worked for GNB—Global News Broadcasting—a cable TV network headquartered in the nation's capital. It was carried by some three hundred independent stations around the country, with a total viewing public of several millions. GNB was known for its antiwar, anti-American government agenda, and Wallenger was its prize commentator. He gained the confidence and admiration of the network's staff on a story he brought out of South America about American Green Berets massacring innocent villagers in the Gran Chaco territory in Bolivia. Demonstrations of rage broke out in all the major urban areas of Latin America as condemnations of the crime were voiced in the United Nations. Even some elements in the U.S. Congress called for special hearings. The usual group of shock jocks, Hollywood stars, and television personalities and journalists with agendas voiced their opinions and assessments of the situation, both pro and con in loudly argumentative segments on special news programs. And, of course, the usual bevy of pundits made up of retired lieutenant colonels from the U.S. Army and Air Force were also on hand to expound on their opinions and assessments of the incident.

Wallenger's moment of glory came at a White House news conference when he confronted Press Secretary Owen Peckham with accusations about the massacre. Although the reporter was more or less blown off by Peckham, he had made a big impression, managing to keep the story going for weeks, even though no proof of its veracity was ever presented.

WHEN Wallenger reached the GNB offices, he went straight to the network president, Don Allen, with the scoop. He couldn't wait to tell Allen about this latest coup, and he was looking forward to the next White House news conference with fierce glee.

AL-BAHRSHATT, KUWAIT
7 JULY
1430 HOURS

KHALIL Farouk was the agent-at-large of the Jihad Abadi terrorist group controlled by the Iranian government. The man had been instrumental in recruiting the Englishman Arsalaan Sikes—né Archibald Sikes—into the organization after talking him into deserting from his British Army unit stationed in Iraq. At the moment Farouk was in this seaside town on the Persian Gulf to recruit mujahideen for a special operation.

The terrorist agent's point of contact was Kaif Jamil, who was coordinator for several insurgent groups scattered throughout the Middle East. Jamil's specialty was the recruitment, training, and placement of suicide bombers. He did his work under the noses of the American forces stationed in the vicinity, and had even sent supernumeraries into Palestine to help out Hamas from time to time. The cover story he used to conceal his true activities from his neighbors was that he managed a labor-hiring contract firm that filled requests for semiskilled workers needed in both industry and agriculture.

At this point in time, Farouk and Jamil were seated in the back room of the latter's place of business, and Jamil stared in unabashed disbelief at Farouk. "How many men did you say you wanted, Brother Farouk?"

"Fifty."

Jamil stared at him open-mouthed for an instant. "Uh . . . you said *kham*stash, correct?"

"No," Farouk replied. "I said *kham*sin. Fifty, not fifteen."

"I never inquire into actual locales or purposes in these operations of martyrdom for obvious reasons of security," Jamil said. "But my curiosity is piqued to the extent I almost feel like asking." He cleared his throat. "Ahem. But I shall not."

"How long will it take you to gather the martyrs, and where may I collect them?"

Jamil stroked his beard. "Let me think . . . two weeks, I believe. There are several of our *jihaden* who are now planning attacks. I am sure they will gladly relinquish some of their *shahiden* if the cause is great enough."

"I assure you it is a most vital and auspicious sacrifice the *shahiden* will make," Farouk said. "It will aid in the liberation of an entire Islamic nation from the cruel grip of the infidels."

"I am not surprised, Brother," Jamil said. "The fact that you require fifty sacrificial bombers is most impressive." He leaned back and let out a deep sigh. "Where do you wish these martyrs to assemble for you?"

"In Pakistan," Farouk said. "They are to arrive at Ali Jinnah International Terminal in Karachi. They will fly PIA from two Saudi cities—Al Hadidah and Riyadh—as well as Qatar and the United Arab Emirates. Divide them any way you wish, but the sponsor feels that if they arrive from at least four different locales, it will assure complete security and secrecy."

"That can be arranged," Jamil said. "However, there will be expenses—plane tickets, passports, logistics, rations, and other items. I estimate ninety thousand U.S. dollars."

"The funds will go to your bank in Saudi Arabia, Brother Jamil," Farouk said. "Am I to assume your estimate of the price includes the explosive materials?"

"Of course," Jamil said. "I will see that all of that is dispatched to you in our usual manner. Now let us turn our attention to the *shahiden*. What day do you desire their arrival in Karachi?"

"You say you need two weeks, so let us allow a bit of extra time," Farouk said. "Is it possible for them to arrive on the twenty-fifth of July?"

"I see no problem with that."

Farouk stood up. "Excellent. If you have any questions or information, I can be reached the same as always. *Ma'al salama*, Brother."

"And good-bye to you, Brother."

ZAHEYA POSITIONS
9 JULY
1030 HOURS

SIKES Pasha was in a bothersome mood. "I didn't think you blokes would ever do anything like that." He was seated in Brigadier Shahruz Khohollah's bunker with Captain Naser Khadid.

"May I give you a bit of advice, Major Sikes?" the brigadier said. "And please accept it as friendly counsel given from an older soldier to a younger."

"Yes, sir," Sikes said.

"Never commit yourself to one course of action in a strict style," the brigadier said. "It limits your options terribly. There are times when circumstances dictate changes in tactics and strategy."

"But I thought one of the important decisions behind Iran taking over all Middle East insurgencies was to put a stop to the waste of people in suicide bombings," the Brit said. "It was even said wot a shame it was that them suicide blokes wouldn't be able to make no more babies to grow up for Islam's struggle."

"The individuals who are going to be employed would martyr themselves within a few months at any rate," Khohollah argued. "If it will serve our cause to have them do it here in this valley to our front, then look upon it as Allah's will."

"To tell you the truth, I ain't all that religious," Sikes said.

"Well," Khohollah said, "at the present time we have much more to worry us than the fate of suicide-prone martyrs. We should turn our attention to how the arrival of the twenty reinforcements was discovered by the Americans."

"And soon enough to do something about it," Sikes added. "It's a bit o' bother, alright. Those were twenty damn good blokes wot was wiped out."

Khadid, who had been content to simply listen to the conversation, now joined in. "There is a leak, no doubt. A turncoat somewhere within our organization, and I would think the traitor is back in Iran somewhere. Perhaps he's serving on or near the General Staff."

"Whoever he is or whatever his position, it is baffling how he managed to get the information out," Khohollah said.

"I'll leave them intelligence blokes to work on that," Sikes said. "It ain't my cup o' tea worrying about spies and the like. I'll put me mind on keeping me defenses proper and manned. I can you tell you one thing for sure, gents. This next attack against them Amercians is gonna be a sight to behold, hey?"

CHAPTER 10

OWEN Peckham, the White House Press Secretary, sat at his desk slowly sipping a cup of coffee. He was tired, but not so much physically as one would be from overexercise or hard work. His fatigue was mental and spiritual, and the man was emotionally beaten down. The problems of disaster relief, border security, crooked lobbyists, the war against terrorism, and a myriad of other unpleasantness he had to deal with were draining him of all enthusiasm for his job. He wondered what else would pop up to plague him.

Peckham checked his watch, noting that within a quarter of an hour he would have to go out into the press room, where eager denizens of the media were ready to fire salvos of provocative questions at him—each journalist able to gain prestige, pay raises, and career advancement from beating up on the poor White House Press Secretary.

His attention was diverted when Arlene Entienne stepped

into his office after a couple of raps on the door. Peckham gave her a nod and a smile. "How're you doing, Arlene?"

"Pretty well under the circumstances," the White House chief of staff answered, giving him a close look. "Are you coming down with a cold?"

He shook his head. "I'm just way down—period."

"Dear Owen," she said, sitting down in the chair to his direct front. "You've been through a hell of a lot."

"Oh, it's no more than you do, except I have to deal with those birds of prey out in that press room."

"And for that you have my sincerest sympathies," Arlene said. "But I think today they'll be beating a herd of dead horses. We've been through the same issues for several weeks now. The troubles in the Middle East are down to some suicide bombings, and that happens so often it doesn't attract much attention anymore. Those cold-blooded reporters are in a constant need of bad news to keep themselves in the limelight."

"Yeah," Peckham said, "you're right. They'll even reveal classified information if they run across any they think is newsworthy. Today I'm going to disarm them with a string of terse announcements. Maybe I'll create a vacuum they can suffocate in."

"I think you've got everything under control," Arlene said, standing up. "I just dropped by to see how you were doing. I've been worried about you."

"Your concern is much appreciated," Peckham said.

WHITE HOUSE PRESS ROOM
1000 HOURS

OWEN Peckham stood at the end of the short hall leading into the press room, with his hand on the doorknob. After three deep, steadying breaths, he opened the portal and stepped inside the room.

Now showing a confident and cheerful grin, he strode up to his podium and set his notes down on it. "Good morning, ladies and gentlemen! So nice to see you today." He nodded to several people he knew personally and had hobnobbed with at various social functions around Washington. "Hello, David. How are you, Betty? Jim, you're looking quite chipper today."

The crowd of journalists, all well known to the American public, sat in anticipation of the coming press conference, hoping something would happen, such as Peckham making a glaring slip in which some phenomenal misconduct by a member of the White House staff would be revealed.

"First I have some announcements to make," Peckham said. "As you know, indictments have gone out this week regarding the lobbying scandal. At this point I have no statements to make regarding that unhappy situation until the accused have shown up in court to plead their innocence or guilt. That's the American way; at least as long as we follow the principle of those under indictment being innocent until proven otherwise."

But that did not deter Joyce Bennington of the *Boston World Journal*. "How far into the White House has this situation penetrated?"

"As I said, Joyce," Peckham replied, "no statements will be issued at this time." He turned to his notebook. "The border security question is firmly resolved with the approval of not only National Guard but also active duty military units bolstering the Border Patrol until all the safeguards such as fences—both physical and electronic—are installed."

Brian Mackenzie of the *Ontario People's Advocate* spoke up. "Does the President really feel these drastic steps are necessary?"

"I wouldn't employ the adjective 'drastic,'" Peckham said, smiling at the Canadian. "I believe 'necessary' would be a more appropriate description. Anyhow, I'm surprised you're not up there in Canada looking into your own immigration procedures." He shifted into an impersonator, speaking in a contrived Canadian accent. "And I believe they've proved somewhat inadequate, hey?"

Some chuckles showed appreciation for his mimicry, and a wag in the back of the room spoke to the Canadian journalist, also out to hassle the guy, "You Canucks better start being more careful about all them foreign hosers getting visas to come to your snow pile, hey? There's probably more terrorists in Toronto than Baghdad, hey?"

"Now, now," Peckham said, "let's not make light of our neighbors to the north." But he couldn't suppress a grin at that one; Mackenzie was a royal pain in the ass. "And to change the subject, all the misspent money on hurricane relief has been identified and the people responsible for this mismanagement face penalties for these oversights and mismanagement. I'm sorry, but I have no names to give you right at this time." He paused and surveyed the crowd. "Now I'm ready for more of your questions."

A short, pudgy man quickly got to his feet, quickly identifying himself. "Dirk Wallenger, Global News Broadcasting."

Peckham flinched inwardly in spite of the friendly smile he showed to Wallenger. "How are you, Dirk?"

"Fine, thank you, Owen," Wallenger said. "I am wondering if you have any comment or news regarding the wounded Arab prisoner who was summarily executed by an American Special Forces group in western Afghanistan on the seventeenth of June."

"I know nothing of the incident," Peckham stated, truly puzzled. "May I inquire as to your sources?"

"I'm afraid not," Wallenger said. "But I can ensure you that they are impeccable and accurate."

"I'll have to investigate the incident and get back to you on that," Peckham said. "But I can tell you now that the White House has not received word from the Pentagon about any prisoners being executed."

"Maybe not," Wallenger said, "but would the people in the Department of Defense inform the President of such an incident?"

"Of course they would," Peckham said.

"Does that mean you deny it?"

"Dirk, I can neither deny nor confirm it until inquiries have been made." He pointed to another journalist, knowing that the opening rounds in a new slant of the antiwar campaign had just been introduced.

OVAL OFFICE
WHITE HOUSE
1400 HOURS

"I just wish I knew where that tubby little son of a bitch gets his news tips."

The President's voice was edged in anger as he sat at his desk looking across at Owen Peckham, Arlene Entienne, and Colonel John Turnbull of SOLS.

"If he's been given the correct location it has to come from somewhere within the Persian Empire caper," Arlene said.

"That's what I was afraid of," the President said. "Evidently something critical has occurred in one of our most sensitive areas." He glanced at Turnbull. "Isn't that where we're having a standoff with an Iranian Special Forces team?"

Turnbull nodded. "Yes, Mr. President. It's been dubbed Operation Battleline." He shifted in his chair. "Maybe this Wallenger punk is blowing smoke. The screeching leftists haven't had a chance to raise hell for a few months now."

"He's a radical, alright," Peckham said, "but he would never make a statement at a White House press briefing unless he knew it to be true." He quickly added, "Or had some evidence that made it *seem* to be true."

The President had to admit that Peckham was right. "I believe Carl Joplin and Edgar Watson are in the vicinity of Persian Empire, are they not?"

"Yes, sir," Arlene said. "They're the other half of the Lamp Committee." She was referring to a small group including her, Colonel Turnbull, Joplin, and Watson, that had been set up to deal with the mysterious intelligence informant who had been code-named Aladdin. "We thought it best to have them handy in case this situation with Aladdin broke wide open."

"It's hard to believe that such a thing could happen," Turnbull said. "I've become extremely familiar with that SEAL officer Brannigan over the past year. His men are considered wild and almost unpredictable, but I doubt if they would kill a wounded EPW in cold blood. If such a thing happened, they must have had a reason." He paused for a moment. "But it could have happened in the heat of battle or if something awry threw a desperate situation further out of kilter."

"God!" the President said. "I hope not. But we have to make a thorough investigation of this thing. Arlene, send word to Carl and Edgar to look into this and get a report back to me ASAP."

"Yes, Mr. President."

**GNB STUDIOS
WASHINGTON, D.C.
15 JULY
2258 HOURS**

THE broadcast area was quiet as Dirk Wallenger settled down at the desk on the set. His notes were arranged in front of him, and the teleprompter was keyed up and ready to go. He was eager for the night's program to begin, and everyone in the studio realized the importance of the news about to be broadcast. Even the network president, Don Allen, stood behind the cameras to witness the event. The credits began rolling at 11 P.M., announcing the *Wallenger Report with Dirk Wallenger*. At exactly the right moment the floor director looked at the commentator and counted, "Five, four, three, two, one, go!"

"Good evening, ladies and gentlemen," Wallenger said the instant the red light glowed on the camera to his direct front. "This is Dirk Wallenger with breaking news from the war in the Middle East. And do not expect to see anything of this story for a few days on other broadcasts. This information came to me through my network of concerned informers. My exposé of the incident will force the other TV news organizations to acknowledge it happened and they will have to report it to the public in spite of government censorship." He paused for effect. "I regret to say that there has been yet another heinous crime committed by members of the American armed forces in the Middle East. This sad event occurred in the west of Afghanistan, up in the Gharawdara

Highlands, where a group of Special Forces Green Berets
sneaked up on an international aid group from several Arab
countries and attacked them. The result of this armed assault
was the massacre of all with the exception of three who
managed to surrender and save their lives despite the hail of
gunfire directed at them.

"Did I say 'saved their lives'? Well, two of them did; the
third, who had been badly wounded, was not destined to receive mercy from his war-mad captors. You see, ladies and
gentlemen, this unfortunate man who had come to offer suc-
cor and aid to suffering Afghanistan people who are being
smashed under the boot heels of the American occupiers
turned out to be a burden to the murderers. Imagine! They
would have to actually carry him—or have his unhurt companions do the job—but it was an inconvenience either way
because it slowed them down. And what was their solution to
this bother? I imagine many of you have already guessed the
answer to that question. For those of you who are in sus-
pense, I shall tell you what these brave Green Berets did.
They shot him in cold blood. Yes! As he lay there in agony,
unable to defend himself, they fired a bullet into his head."
He paused again to let his words be contemplated by the
viewers. "And when I return, I will provide more grisly details of this wanton criminal act."

The floor director signaled that the commercials were
running. Don Allen gave Wallenger a thumbs-up. "That's the
way, Dirk! Give 'em hell!"

Wallenger winked back at him, arranging his notes for
the continuance of the program.

USS *COMBS*
PERSIAN GULF
16 JULY
0830 HOURS

THE MH-60G chopper came down onto the helipad on
the aft end of the ship, landing softly. Lieutenant Bill Brannigan stepped out and was met by Commanders Tom Carey and

Ernest Berringer. There were no vocal greetings because of
the noise of the aircraft's engine, only an exchange of salutes.
Brannigan, carrying his M-16 and a bandolier of ammo, followed the other two officers off the landing area into the
ship's superstructure.

They could speak in the passageway as they hurried farther into the vessel's interior. Brannigan, who was between
the two, was not in a good mood about being pulled out of the
SEAL base camp. He spoke angrily to Carey, to his front.
"What the fuck's going on—sir?"

"You have an appointment with General Leroux," Carey
answered over his shoulder.

"Who the hell is he?"

Berringer replied, "He's Army and the CG of the SFOB
aboard the *Combs*. He's also a representative of the JCOS
and has direct access to other command levels at the snap of
one of his impatient fingers."

"Shit!" Brannigan blurted, thinking, *What the fuck did I
do now?*

A marine stood at the entrance to Leroux's compartment
and immediately opened the door as the three men walked
up. Carey led the way in, where another door was opened for
them by a Special Forces sergeant, who was obviously part
of the SFOB staff. At that point Carey indicated that Brannigan was to step in first.

When he entered he found himself facing a grizzled U.S.
Army brigadier general who had the look of someone who
was more at home in the field than in an office aboard a naval
destroyer. Leroux leaned back in his chair and returned Brannigan's salute. He didn't say anything for a few moments,
then growled. "So *you're* Brannigan, are you?"

"Yes, sir."

"There's a chair in the corner," Leroux said. "Grab it and
drag it over here, then plop your ass down on it." He waited
until the order was obeyed. "Alright, Brannigan, what's this
shit about you shooting a wounded EPW?"

Brannigan, now aware that both Carey and Berringer were
standing behind him, took a deep breath. It was all coming
home now. "It's true, sir."

"Well now, ain't that some shit," Leroux said. "One of them pansy journalists at a White House press conference brought up the situation and it went out on the eleven-o'clock news. Real nasty, Brannigan! So you just tell me what happened. And I don't want any bullshit."

"Aye, sir."

"Goddamn! I'm getting real tired of all this sailor shit and this fucking boat and everything else," Leroux spat. "With me it's 'yes, sir' and 'no, sir,' not this 'aye' and 'nay' or whatever else y'all use. Got it?"

"Yes, sir," Brannigan said.

"Now, I know all about your Operation Battleline, so you can leave that out," Leroux said. "Tell me what happened at the ambush that led up to this wounded raghead getting killed."

"Yes, sir," Brannigan said. "We were back at the LZ waiting for the chopper to begin the exfiltration with the three EPWs we'd captured. One of them suddenly jumped up and made a run for it."

"Ha!" Leroux exclaimed. "So you shot him trying to escape, huh?"

"No, sir," Brannigan said. "He tried to get into a bunch of boulders when a cobra bit him."

"Jesus!" Leroux said with a laugh. "The son of a bitch was snake-bit?"

"Yes, sir," Brannigan said. "Two of my men had chased him up to the spot and saw that the poison was spreading fast. There was nothing any of us could do to save him. So one of my men shot him in the head to put him out of his misery."

"Was he following your orders when he killed the guy?"

"Negative, sir. I was still back with the main group, and he did it on his own," the SEAL explained. "The guy is one of my best men, but he's impetuous as hell."

"How did you handle the shooter?" Leroux asked.

"I gave him the choice of a court-martial or administrative punishment," Brannigan explained. "He chose Article Fifteen, so I put him on watch-and-watch with plenty of chores to tend to between his stints of duty."

"Okay, Brannigan," Leroux said. "We're going to have to do some fudging on this, understand? When the guy made his escape attempt, he was not wounded or injured at that time, right?"

"That's right, sir."

"Good," Leroux said. "The other two EPWs are confined at the Barri Prison in Bahrain. The source of the information might have come from one of them or maybe one of your guys. Have any of them been out of your OA since the incident?"

"No, sir."

Berringer, the intelligence officer, interjected, "I've spoken with the S-Two at Station Bravo, and we've come to the conclusion the leak came from inside the prison. We're prepared to start a probe."

"Do it!" Leroux said. He turned back to Brannigan. "Okay, here's how it's gonna be. The official report of the investigation—which we just had right here in this office, by the way—is that a healthy, uninjured EPW was shot while trying to escape. I want you to make sure all your men understand this. It's not an outright falsehood, but the truth of the matter is that the guy got killed during an escape attempt. Now, if somebody pops up and happens to ask if he was bitten by a snake, we'll have to handle that a different way. But that's not much of a possibility. Hell! It's not even a probability."

"Alright, sir. I understand."

Leroux's demeanor relaxed, and he actually smiled. "So how's everything going in Operation Battleline?"

"We're just sitting tight, sir," Brannigan said, "waiting for the worst-case scenario to unfold."

"Do you need anything?"

"No, sir. We're loaded for bear. This has been first-rate as far as supplies go."

Leroux stood up and offered his hand. "You've done a fine job out here, Lieutenant Brannigan. Well appreciated."

"I'll pass the word to my men."

"Now keep in mind what I've said about this dead EPW," the general reiterated. "I don't want to see any American serviceman getting into trouble over this incident. And, believe me, there are some real bastards back home who love it when they can stick it to one of our ladies or gentlemen."

"I understand, sir."

Another exchange of salutes and Brannigan left the general's presence.

CHAPTER 11

FRED Leighton stood at his office window, looking down on the compound. Barri Prison had a stark, antiseptic appearance behind the razor wire and guard towers that rose off the desert floor. The white buildings with yellow trim were square, monotonous, and bland to the senses. But it wasn't designed to be an architectural masterpiece; this was a place of confinement for two-hundred-plus Arab prisoners swept up in various operations, not only throughout the Middle East but in other parts of the world as well. A few had been yanked off various airline flights after their names were discovered on lists of terrorist suspects; others had been policed up for some deadly mischief in Europe. Like those captured in places such as Afghanistan and Iraq, these were brought to this place of confinement at the far western end of Station Bravo. The facility, fast taking the place of Guantánamo Bay, was isolated from the rest of the garrison by continual motor patrols keeping a 24/7 surveillance on the immediate area.

This was Leighton's base of operations—not only because he was the area's principal CIA operative, but also because his fluency in Arabic put him on call for various interrogation tasks that popped up. His language skills gave him a psychological edge over the detainees during periods of intense questioning. Leighton had only the slightest trace of accent, and his complete knowledge of the Arabic tongue included not only the academic, technical, scientific, and military aspects, but also the latest slang and political rhetoric. As a boy growing up in several Middle East countries where his father worked as an oil field operations supervisor, Leighton spoke to every social class of Arab that existed, from intellectuals right down the social gamut to the rough-tough guys who did the muscle-work out on the derricks.

His phone rang, and he turned around to answer it. The few words spoken informed him that the prisoner he requested had been taken to interrogation and was waiting for him.

"Right," he responded, then hung up.

HAMZA Qazi was alone in the room, sitting at a table with an empty chair on the other side. He could tell this place was for informal or even friendly interrogations, in contrast to other areas where he had been taken. For the first few times when he faced questioning after he arrived at the prison, there was nothing in the stark chambers except for the inevitable bright light in the ceiling. At those times Hamza would be wearing clothing much too large for him. This put him at a serious psychological disadvantage, since he had to make an effort to keep his pants from falling down. Additionally, he was forced to stand and wait for hours until a visitor appeared. The man usually brought a chair with him, and the man made himself comfortable while conducting the interrogation. Then another man would appear—sometimes friendlier and sometimes much more hostile—and take over the procedure as Hamza's legs trembled with fatigue and he struggled with his baggy attire. Eventually this second interrogator's place would be taken by the first or perhaps a third in a rotation that seemed endless.

The door opened slowly, almost gently, and a man entered whom Hamza recognized, although he didn't know his name. The visitor smiled, saying, *"Kaeyfae haelik?"*

"I am fine, *shokran*," Hamza replied.

Fred Leighton sat down. "Would you like some coffee? I can have some brought in."

"That would be nice," Hamza said, relaxing now.

Leighton got up and went to the door, opening it and speaking some words in English, then came back and sat down again. "It's been a while since we've chatted, Hamza."

"Yes, *effendi*."

"How have you been? Are you getting enough to eat?"

Hamza nodded, feeling more encouraged by the considerate questions. "Please, effendi, how long will I be here?"

"I cannot say, Hamza," Leighton replied, noting that the prisoner did not include his friend Rahmat Nahayan in the question. "It depends on how you behave and cooperate."

They were interrupted when an MP guard rapped on the door, then stepped into the room. He sat a thermos pitcher of coffee on the table with a tray holding cups, sugar, and milk, then made a silent exit.

Leighton poured the coffee and gestured to Hamza to help himself to the sugar and milk. "Some of those guards are nice fellows, aren't they?"

"Yes, effendi," Hamza said. "And some are very strict and unpleasant." After dumping in three servings of sugar and a generous pouring of milk, he stirred his coffee.

"Yes, you are right," Leighton said. "Have you found any who are particularly friendly and helpful to you?"

"Only one I can truthfully say I like," Hamza said.

"Oh? And who might that be?"

"Arjumand Allawi," Qazi answered. "He is a sergeant."

"I see," Leighton said. "Do you and Arjumand talk a lot?"

"Yes," Hamza said. "He was born in America but he speaks Arabic just like I do. His parents are from Syria."

"What do you talk about?"

Hamza shrugged. "Many things, effendi. He tells me about his home and I tell him about mine. Or sometimes we talk about football. Arjumand likes to play as much as I." He smiled modestly. "I was quite good back in my hometown league."

Leighton knew he was talking about soccer, not the American brand of football. "I guess you miss the excitement of the games, *lae*?"

Hamza grinned, saying, "It was my fondest dream to play in the World Cup."

Leighton smiled back. "Perhaps someday you will." He let a moment of silence slip by as they both sipped their coffee. "Did Sergeant Allawi ever ask you about the circumstances when you were captured?"

"Oh, yes," Hamza said. "He was very interested in that."

"What did you tell him?"

"I told him what happened," Hamza said. "I told him how my friend Taqqee tried to run away and escape but was bitten by a snake."

"Really?" Leighton said, feigning surprise. "How unusual. What happened?"

"The Americans that captured us could not save him," Hamza said. "Taqqee was in great pain and dying. He said his prayers as loudly as possible as if he would have to shout for Allah to hear him. So one of the Americans had to shoot him so he would not suffer more."

"It must have been a very large snake," Leighton said.

"Oh, yes, effendi," Hamza said. "It was a cobra. People cannot survive such a serpent's poison. It is a sure awful death."

"How terrible for Taqqee," Leighton said. He poured them each another cup of coffee. "Tell me more about your friend Sergeant Allawi. He seems a very nice fellow."

The conversation settled into a pleasant chat, and Leighton paused after a while to go back to the door and request some pastries to go with the coffee.

SEAL BASE CAMP
THIRD SECTION BUNKER
21 JULY
2010 HOURS

PO3C Chad Murchison came in from his stint on the second dog watch, going over to his living area. After setting down his M-16 and bandolier of ammunition, he knelt to pull some MREs out of his rucksack.

Guy Devereaux, lounging on his foam mattress with a paperback Western, looked over at him. "You got a letter, Chad. It's over in Greene's area. He said he left it out where you could find it."

"Thanks," Chad said. He walked over to his team leader's sleeping place and found it with some other letters for members of Foxtrot Fire Team. It was from his girlfriend, Penny Brubaker. "Ah, shit," he said.

Guy chuckled. "What do you have there? Something from a bill collector?"

"Naw," Chad said. "I don't know why I said that. It's from Penny."

"That should put you in a good mood," Guy said. All the men in the detachment knew Penny Brubaker, having met her in Afghanistan when she worked for UNREO in a relief effort for the indigenous people. "I heard she's taken a house in Coronado and is waiting for you to finish your tour over here. She's a nice girl, man."

Chad walked over and settled down on the bunker floor next to Guy. "Yeah. She's a nice girl, alright."

Guy put his book down and sat up. "She must be lonely there."

Chad shook his head. "She's got her cousin and her cousin's husband staying with her. So she's got company."

"Are you two getting married when you get back?"

"I don't know," Chad said. He looked at his buddy. "I'm really confused about how I feel about her."

Guy raised his eyebrows. "What's the problem, man? She's a real doll. You must be a babe magnet to get a girl like her. She could be one of them supermodels."

"I've known her all my life," Chad said. "I always had a big crush on her when we were kids, and we started going steady in prep school."

"Oh, yeah," Guy said. "You didn't go to a regular high school, did you?"

Chad shook his head. "It was a private high school. She and I were day students because we lived close. That was when I became quite fond of her in a romantic way."

Guy chuckled. "You really express yourself funny at times."

Chad grinned. "I know. At any rate, I was a year ahead of her and went to Yale while she finished her senior year. Well, to make a long story short, she threw me over for a jock. It shook me up bad, so I joined the Navy."

"That's right!" Guy said. "When you ran into her over here you two hadn't seen each other for a long time." He showed an expression of puzzlement. "Wait a minute! You two was getting along great, as I recall. And in a 'romantic way,' as you would say with such sophistication."

"She had dumped the guy and decided I was the one she wanted all along."

"What the hell's the problem, buddy?" Guy exclaimed. "You turned out to be the best man after all."

"Yeah," Chad said, getting to his feet. "But . . ." He stopped speaking for a moment. "I guess I'm emotionally flummoxed about the whole affair."

"I'm not sure I know what you're talking about," Guy said. "You sound like you're uncertain about how you feel about her."

"Yeah."

Chad walked over to his own area and sat down on the mattress, staring out the bunker entrance. Guy noticed he hadn't opened the letter; it was almost as if he dreaded reading it. Chad didn't seem to be exactly disturbed, but he wasn't relaxed and at ease either.

It's gonna be real interesting to see how all that works out when we get back to Coronado, Guy thought. He settled down and turned his attention back to his Western.

STATION BRAVO, BAHRAIN
BARRI PRISON
23 JULY
1000 HOURS

SERGEANT Arjumand Allawi sat in a chair outside the office door, working hard at trying to appear nonchalant. He was from an Army Reserve Military Police unit in Buffalo, New York, and had been in his present position as a guard at Barri Prison for nine months.

He had grown up bilingual, speaking both Arabic and English, acquiring fluency in both languages with the ease of all youngsters exposed to a multicultural environment. Both his parents were from Syria and were well established in the local Islamic community in Buffalo. The family had an ethnic grocery store that sold all sorts of canned and packaged foods from the Middle East. They even stocked soft drinks and fruit juice that most customers purchased for sentimental reasons rather than for any superiority over American products.

The door next to him opened, and Allawi turned to see Fred Leighton looking out at him. Allawi always thought there was something weird about the guy; he wore BDUs like everybody else, but he sported no unit or rank insignia on the uniform. Rumors abounded about who he might really be, the suppositions ranging from a CIA agent to an operative of the Saudi Arabian intelligence service. Those who heard him speak Arabic noted it was flawless, with an exotic sort of accent.

Leighton finally spoke after a moment of staring at Allawi. "Come in."

Allawi walked into the office, noting there was a desk in the center rear of the room, and a table and chairs off to the side. That was where he was directed with curt gestures. Leighton walked around and sat down. He didn't say anything for almost a full minute. Allawi was annoyed. "I'm not gonna stand here all fucking day, dude."

"You'll do what I tell you," Leighton said.

"You don't show any rank, pal," Allawi said. "So unless you produce a fucking ID card that shows you're an E-Six or above, I'm not taking any shit off you."

"Sit down."

Allawi obeyed, noting there was something about Leighton that was far, far out of the ordinary. "So what do you want?"

"You're a reservist from Buffalo, New York, right?"

"Right," Allawi said.

"And you attend Nijmi-min-Islam mosque in that city, do you not?"

"Well," Allawi said, "I've attended services there, but I'm really not religious. I went because my father insisted. You know how old folks can be about stuff like that. I haven't been inside the place in a couple of years."

"You were there about six times last year in the week of the second to the eighth of May," Leighton said.

Cold fear gripped Allawi like ice water thrown over him.

"And you've been present at the house of Askary Shareef on many occasions," Leighton stated in a matter-of-fact tone. "Why?"

"Well, y'know, I went there, y'know, with friends," Allawi said. "Some guys I knew were invited, and they asked me to come along. It was social. Just sitting around and talking."

"What were you talking about?"

"Hey, am I in some kind of trouble here?" Allawi said in nervous anger. "Just in case, I want a lawyer. Understand? I'm not going to sit here and go through a third degree."

"Yeah, you will."

The tone in Leighton's voice was one of finality, clout, and power. Here was a man who, for whatever reason or authority, could go far beyond the norm of legality and not have to worry about it.

"Let's just wait a minute," Allawi said. "This is getting too weird."

"You like to talk to the prisoners, don't you?" Leighton asked, ignoring his statement.

"Well, yeah, it's always in the line of duty," Allawi said. "Well, sometimes I do some chitchat, y'know. It's a normal thing." He cleared his throat and sat up straighter. "I believe it's called communication."

"Who do you talk to after your chitchats with the prisoners?"

"I don't know what you mean," Allawi said.

"I'll be more explicit," Leighton said. "When you pick up information from the prisoners, who do you pass it on to?"

"I have no idea where this is leading."

"I'll be even *more* explicit," Leighton said. "Who did you tell about the two prisoners Hamza Qazi and Rahmat Nahayan and their buddy who was bitten by a cobra? I'm really interested in hearing about the guy who was snake-bit while he was an EPW. Now, who was it you passed that information on to? And why?"

"Look, whoever you are, I'm not putting up with this shit, understand?"

"Now let me explain something to you, Sergeant Allawi," Leighton said in a very calm tone of voice. "You can either be cooperative here or somewhere a lot worse. If you're not careful you're gonna end up so deep in the federal prison system they'll have to pump fresh air and sunshine in to you."

Allawi glared back defiantly.

CHAPTER 12

ALL hands, or as SCPO Buford Dawkins would have said, "every swinging dick" of Brannigan's Brigands was standing-to at their posts. Those who had been off-duty had been summoned from their billets by the noise of several helicopters on the Zaheya side of the valley. The disturbance brought the SEALs rushing to the MLR with weapons and bandoliers, expecting the worst-case scenario. The aircraft, out of sight behind the western mountain range, could be heard settling down on the LZ to the rear of the enemy's fortified area. The telltale remnants of dust clouds drifted into the SEALs' collective view on the southern portion of the OA.

Lieutenant Bill Brannigan dispatched the RTO, Frank Gomez, to make a transmission to the USS *Combs* for a quick surveillance flight over the area. Gomez returned a little less than a couple of minutes later with a scribbled message, and handed the note to the Skipper. He read the missive, wadded it up, and threw it over the parapet, to be buffeted by the wind along the mountainside.

Brannigan spoke into his LASH. "We're gonna stay on a hundred percent alert until further notice. SFOB isn't able to provide any aerial recon right now, since all available aircraft at Shelor Field are committed to other missions."

The Odd Couple occupied the OP just above headquarters, and they both peered over no-man's-land, carefully looking for some indication of activity. Dave Leibowitz shook his head. "I don't see anything unusual."

"Me neither," Mike Assad said. "Them guys are out of sight in their positions, and nobody's scurrying around. Everything seems laid back over there."

"That doesn't mean the shit isn't about to hit the fan," Leibowitz said.

They heard some scuffling below, and a few moments later the Skipper came through the hole, keeping low as he crawled over to join them. "We couldn't see anything from the MLR. Have you guys picked up on any activity?"

"Negative, sir," Assad replied. "There hasn't been a thing going on over there. As usual, we can't see any coming or going. But it's obvious some choppers have come in to visit the bad guys. I'd give my next payday to find out what's going on."

Brannigan had his own binoculars trained on the site. "Maybe it's just a supply delivery or something like that. But you never know." After a quarter hour of observation, he was ready to leave. "Keep your eyes peeled, guys. The whole detachment is going to be on watch for a while. When I decide we can stand down I'll send somebody up here to relieve you. It'll probably be Miskoski and Puglisi and their sniper rifles. Stay alert!"

"Aye, sir!"

Brannigan wiggled back through the hole and made his way down into the bunker.

MAJOR Arsalaan Sikes Pasha watched the fifty newcomers unass the pair of Iranian Army French-manufactured Aérospatiale helicopters. The newly arrived Arabs wore nondescript fatigue uniforms that had evidently been culled from supply quartermaster warehouses of at least a trio of nations. Now that they were on the ground, the group milled around in confusion amid a trio of large bundles they had brought with them. Then Sikes spotted a familiar figure emerging from the nearest aircraft, stepping gingerly to the ground. The Brit instantly recognized him as his former mentor in the Jihad Abadi.

"Hey there, Khalil!" Sikes called out. "Wot the bluddy hell are you doing here?"

Khalil Farouk showed a smile of genuine pleasure at the sight of his English friend. He waved and hurried over. "Arsalaan! It gives me much pleasure to look upon you again." They embraced in the manner of Islamic males. "You are looking most soldierly, my friend."

"I been doing more'n just a bit o' soljering, you can believe that," Sikes said. He gestured to the crowd of young Arab men. "Are them the poor buggers wot's gonna blow themselves up then?"

Farouk nodded. "Yes. It was deemed necessary that drastic steps be taken to loosen the Americans' grip on this area."

"I ain't very pleased with this, Khalil," Sikes said glumly, giving the volunteer suicide bombers a somber gaze. "Most o' them blokes look like they ain't got the sense to come in out o' the bluddy rain."

"You must look upon this with cold logic, Arsalaan," Farouk said. "Their deaths will be a great help to our cause and will save having trained soldiers killed."

"Well," Sikes conceded, "I suppose you're right, but I ain't too keen on it; not by a long shot."

The helicopters revved up and climbed back into the sky, the rotors kicking up clouds of blinding, stinging dust that swept over the scene, causing everyone to duck and turn away. When the disturbance dissipated, Khalil looked up at the mountain next to the LZ. "I see no fortress, Arsalaan."

"Oh, it's there, don't you worry none about that," Sikes replied. He looked around, then barked at his warrant officer. "Mr. Hashiri! Get over there and get them blowsy bastards organized! And detail a few of 'em to carry that gear with

'em." Just as Hashiri trotted off to take care of the task, the
Brit added, "And be careful of them bundles. They're bluddy
bombs!"

Hashiri organized the crowd of Arabs into a reasonable
semblance of orderliness and got them to pick up everything
they had brought with them. When he was satisfied they
were under control, he led them off the LZ toward the
ingress that would give them access to the interior of the fortified mountain.

Sikes Pasha and his friend Khalil Farouk followed, re-
newing their friendship with animated conversation.

STATION BRAVO, BAHRAIN
BARRI PRISON
26 JULY
1320 HOURS

PO2C Mike Assad and the CIA operative Fred
Leighton were not in the main building of the prison. The
two had just entered a small cell block under the escort of
a taciturn guard. The lockup was a square cement structure
with three rows of cells that were connected by short hall-
ways. No windows offered outside views or natural illumi-
nation for the foreboding interior of the structure. The lights
in the ceiling were extremely bright, giving the place an aura
of brilliant, stark hopelessness. And that was exactly the intent of the architects who designed the place.

When the trio reached the end of the first hallway, they
halted. The guard turned to a steel door, pausing only long
enough to open a viewing port. After a quick glance, he inserted a key into the heavy portal and pulled it open. Mike
and Leighton stepped inside. A single prisoner sat on his
bunk, looking at them. He wore an orange jumpsuit in the
stark atmosphere of his cell, and he was listless to the point
of appearing to have no interest in his surroundings.

Leighton, turning to the SEAL, pointed at the inmate.
"Do you know this guy?"

Mike, his BDUs still smelling of wood smoke and sweat
after his quick departure from the SEAL base camp, walked

in front of the man and looked down at him. "Yeah. I know him. I'm not sure of his first name, but his last is Allawi."

Sergeant Arjumand Allawi studied his visitor for a moment, noting he was an Arab-American. Then he shrugged. "I never saw this guy before in my life."

"Nobody's asking you questions about our guest, Allawi," Leighton said. He turned his attention to Mike. "Where do you know him from?"

"Buffalo, New York," Mike said. "The Ninji-min-Islam mosque."

Allawi sneered. "You was never there."

Mike, in accordance with previous instructions from Leighton, remained silent, stepping back toward the cell door.

Leighton walked to a point in front of Allawi, standing with his feet apart and arms crossed over his chest. "This man with me is a SEAL in the United States Navy, Allawi."

"Whoopee," Allawi said sarcastically.

"He was undercover at that mosque as an operative," Leighton said. "He took all the classes of indoctrination and showed the right attitude. When they figured he was ready, he was shipped off to Pakistan to join the al-Mimkhalif terrorist group." He paused. "I should have said the *defunct* al-Mimkhalif terrorist group."

Allawi glanced at Mike again. "I still don't know him."

"Let's not say you don't *know* him," Leighton said. "Let's say you don't *remember* him or maybe you don't *recognize* him. But he knows you, and that's what's important."

Allawi shrugged. "He's bullshitting you, Leighton."

Leighton glanced over at Mike. "Tell us what you recall about the prisoner here, Petty Officer Assad."

"When the other guys in my group and I first arrived at the mosque to get with the terrorist program, he gave us an indoctrination and explained the setup," Mike said. "He also taught a couple of classes on the Arabic language and alphabet."

"Sure," Allawi said. "I gave classes on Arabic because there were lots of guys who had been born in America. Some of 'em were second- and third-generation and hadn't been exposed much to written Arabic. The mullahs taught religious stuff because some of the guys hadn't had much of an Islamic environment in their homes. Hell, there's nothing wrong with that, is there? It's called going back to your roots; very hip and trendy."

Mike said, "What I recall most vividly about this guy is that he was the organizer of a program to get some of the students to enlist in the reserve components of the armed forces. I'm talking about the National Guard, reserves, and outfits like that to get military training, and learn the SOPs of the various units. He led the way when he joined the Army Reserves. They made a big deal out of it at the mosque."

"See?" Allawi said. "I was a patriot and wanted to serve my country."

"Bullshit," Mike said. "I remember your hate-America talks and all that death-to-the-infidels crap you preached."

"I'm not talking to you two fucking guys anymore," Allawi said.

Leighton walked over and banged on the door. When it opened he motioned Mike to follow him out into the hall. Mike walked over to the exit, then turned and looked back at Allawi.

"Dude, you are *so* compromised."

OVAL OFFICE
WHITE HOUSE
28 JULY
1430 HOURS

WHEN Liam Bentley walked into the Oval Office he was surprised to see not only the President standing at the front of the desk, but also the woman and two men sitting in nearby chairs, like it was a casual visit among neighbors. The Chief Executive stepped toward the visitor with his hand extended. "Welcome to the Oval Office, Mr. Bentley."

"Thank you, Mr. President," Bentley said, holding on to his briefcase as he shook hands.

"This is somewhat of a historical moment," the President said. "The newly created post of FBI White House Liaison Officer goes into effect at this time and date. This is something entirely fresh and innovative."

"Yes, sir," Bentley said. "I'm honored to be the first."

"Let me introduce you to my White House chief of staff, Ms. Arlene Entienne; the press secretary, Owen Peckham; and Colonel John Turnbull of the Special Operations Liaison Staff." He chuckled. "We seem to have our full share of liaison today."

Bentley took an empty chair as directed, putting his briefcase in his lap. "I'm most happy to join this group, and I'm looking forward to all the coordinating and information-sharing aspects of the arrangement. I'm sure we'll be able to accomplish many meaningful tasks that will increase the effectiveness of the homeland security program."

Colonel Turnbull decided the guy was probably a damn good agent, but he had way too much urbanity to be a soldier. Probably too much to be a field operative for the bureau either, but well suited for a supervisory or administrative position.

The President took another chair with the group, looking directly at Bentley. "I have been told you can bring us up to date on this matter in which a member of the press made inquiries involving the shooting death of a wounded enemy prisoner of war."

"Yes, sir," Bentley said. "And speaking of briefings and the like, the CIA brought me up to date, since their representative to the White House is in the Middle East."

"Yes," Arlene said. "That would be Edgar Watson. He's another member of our group, as is Dr. Carl Joplin, who is also in the war area."

"Well, to get started," Bentley said, retrieving a report from his briefcase, "the journalist in question—Dirk Wallenger of Global News Broadcasting—didn't seem to have all the facts straight, or he changed them to suit his own purposes. The prisoner was not wounded. As a matter of fact, he had been bitten by a deadly, poisonous snake. It was a cobra."

"Whew!" Owen Peckham said. "That doesn't make it much better. He was incapacitated, at any rate."

"He received the bite during an escape attempt," Bentley explained. "But, sadly, he was indeed shot afterward as he lay helpless on the ground."

"Oh, shit!" Colonel Turnbull exclaimed.

"It was a mercy killing," Bentley said. "The SEALs who had captured the man had no means of treating him, and one took it upon himself to keep the poor fellow from suffering an agonizing death. Several witnesses have been questioned about this since those facts were revealed to Brigadier General Leroux at his headquarters aboard the USS *Combs*." He gave the report a further perusal. "The man who fired the shot was evidently punished for taking the action without his commanding officer's permission."

"Mmf!" Turnbull snorted. "And that's as it should be."

"But what worries me," the President said, "is how the hell did this guy Wallenger hear about it?"

"That's being worked from two angles, Mr. President," Bentley said. "The first is from Barri Prison in Bahrain, and the second from right here in Washington. As we build the facts from both ends, everything will eventually meet in the middle and we'll all know the exact truth of the matter."

"Then tell us what you know now, Liam," the President said, putting himself on a first-name basis with the FBI agent.

"I'll start in Barri Prison," Bentley said. "There were two other prisoners with the one who was bitten by the cobra. They are both confined in that facility, where there is a guard by the name of Arjumand Allawi. He is an American citizen and a sergeant in an Army Reserves military police battalion assigned as custodians. He has been observed in countless friendly conversations with various prisoners, including the pair who were captured by the SEALs. Both the inmates, when questioned, stated they had told Allawi about the incident. He was the only one they informed of the snake bite, and we are now convinced he passed on the story to somebody else outside the prison."

"Fine," the President said. "That's one end. What's the other?"

"There is a cabdriver here in Washington named Daleel Guellah, who is known by the code name of 'Ali.' He has been under surveillance for close to a year now. One of his regular customers is Dirk Wallenger. Wallenger most likely learned of the incident of the dead prisoner from him. And 'Ali' had the information from someone in their net between him and Allawi at Barri Prison. Either 'Ali' or Wallenger himself changed the story to make it come out as the murder of a wounded prisoner of war."

Owen Peckham chuckled with delight. "Oh, how I would love to see that pudgy son of a bitch go to jail!"

Arlene Entienne smiled too. "I'll go along with you on that, Owen. I know he's been a bane to you during press conferences."

"I appreciate your support, Arlene," Peckham said. He looked over at Bentley. "Have you questioned Wallenger yet?"

"No," Bentley answered. "But there are plans to not only interview Mr. Wallenger, but also Don Allen, the president of GNB."

Turnbull leaned forward with a grin. "Do you think that whole GNB group might be working for the terrorists?"

Bentley shrugged. "All we are certain of at this moment is what everybody already knows, Colonel. Their newscasts go in a leftist direction as a matter of practice. There have been times when they've put an extra-strong slant on certain types of reports to support their agenda. The GNB has this reputation even among other journalists."

The President leaned back in his chair. "I want the FBI to go to the very heart of this matter, Liam. Consider that an executive order."

"Yes, Mr. President."

CHAPTER 13

NUMEROUS dark shapes slipping over the Zaheya defenses and heading down into no-man's-land were suddenly discerned by the SEALs standing-to on their MLR. Lieutenant JG Jim Cruiser was the officer of the watch, and he responded immediately to the excited whisperings coming over his LASH headset.

"All hands!" he said in a businesslike tone of voice. "Turn out! We've got 'em coming over here at us big time."

The SEALs off duty responded quickly, rushing from their bunkers to fighting positions, having grabbed weapons and ammo kept next to their bedrolls. Chief Matt Gunnarson's trio of machine-gun crews were up and ready within sixty seconds. In spite of the frantic activity in the American lines, no careless noise was made that would alert the attackers that preparations had been made to meet the assault.

Bill Brannigan joined Cruiser, studying the scene through his NVBs. "I don't see anything."

"They've already dropped out of sight into the cover down in the valley," Cruiser explained. "I counted thirty, but there was more than that."

Bruno Puglisi's voice came over the net. "Skipper, d'you want me and Joe to go topside with our AS-fifties?"

"Negative," Brannigan replied. "Get on line. We're going to need all the firepower we can muster up here."

"Aye, sir," Puglisi replied. "We'll grab a couple of the extry M-sixteens."

Over in One Section, Tex Benson, the SAW gunner, caught sight of an individual diving into the cover of a thicket. He aimed the automatic weapon into the vegetation and sent in a short burst of fire. An explosion immediately followed that sent rocks and other natural debris hurtling through the air.

"What the fuck was that?" somebody remarked.

"Maybe one of them assholes stepped on a mine," another somebody replied.

"Keep the chatter down!" SCPO Buford Dawkins said. "Nobody yaks over the LASHes except to give orders or warnings. Anyhow, nobody's laid any mines out there that I know of."

Some additional single shots from the American side of the valley sounded as the SEALs did some search by fire, and after half a dozen rounds were fired, there was another explosion. Chad Murchison's voice could be heard right after the fusillades. "The raghead I shot exploded!"

Suddenly some enfilading fire from the SEAL machine guns swept a portion of no-man's-land where some more ragheads were spotted as they dashed from one thicket to another. The results were two more explosions.

"What the fuck is blowing up down there?" came the senior chief's voice as he ignored his own orders to can the excessive chatter.

ZAHEYA BATTLELINE

LESS than half an hour had passed since Brigadier Shahruz Khohollah gave the attack order via his communications system, sending the suicide bombers over the barricades and down into the valley. Five minutes later, Sikes Pasha and the Arab Storm Troopers, along with Captain Naser Khadid and the Iranian Imperial Lions, scrambled from their fighting positions and rushed downward to the valley floor to trail after the human bombs. The young Arab zealots followed previous instructions by taking advantage of the cover and concealment in no-man's-land. They scampered awkwardly forward to get nearer to the American MLR. The mandates given them were simple: Get as close as possible to the infidels, then blow themselves up.

The Arab and Iranian rifle units behind the martyrs were spread out in skirmish formations, firing upward at the enemy. This tactic would most certainly attract attention and bullets their way, but it also would give the bombers a better chance to get close enough to detonate their explosives and take out a greater number of Americans.

Sikes Pasha saw yet another explosion erupt, spreading a brilliant millisecond of light over the scene. "Poor bluddy sod," he muttered to himself, then he spoke into his LASH. *"Amkammal rimaya*—keep firing!"

As the Storm Troopers continued to send up their fusillades, the Imperial Lions followed suit. The suicide bombers, now at the base of the slope leading to the SEAL positions, were just about in position to begin the ascent under the cover of the sweeping gunfire from their Islamic brethren behind them.

THE BATTLE

THE sun was nearing the apex of the eastern mountains, and the light of day was increasing measurably. Along the line in Three Section, SCPO Dawkins and his SAW gunner, James Duncan, kept busy going after targets of opportunity, sometimes making guesstimates as to where some individuals might come back into view after rolling or diving into the covering vegetation.

Dawkins spotted one guy emerging from between a stand of boulders and fired quickly at him, scoring a direct hit. He watched in amazement as the guy exploded, a small, dark object flying straight into the air from the center of the detonation. Both Dawkins and Duncan watched the thing, worried it might be a large grenade or a mortar shell. It arced toward their position, then began a downward plummet. The two SEALs dived for cover as it hit the ground near them, rolling along the ground until coming to a halt. They looked at it, then each other, then back at the gruesome object.

The head of a young Arab, his eyes open wide and his mouth grinning eerily, lay against a sandbag a couple of yards away.

Dawkins rose to a crouch and went to it, grabbing the severed cranium by the hair. He heaved it over the side of the fighting position toward the ground below. Duncan shuddered. "That's the damndest thing I've ever seen! I'll be having nightmares about that son of a bitch for the rest of my life."

"Well," Dawkins allowed, "it was kind of weird, alright."

ONE of the bombers, a sixteen-year-old who had left school to martyr himself for Islam, had done a good job of getting close to the American positions. He was a skinny little Saudi Arabian, and he used his slight physique to remain out of sight in the scrub brush as he scrambled across the valley of no-man's-land. His mind-set was such that he scarcely noticed all the firing, with bullets clipping the air around him and zinging off rocks. The kid's entire concentration was on staying alive long enough to get up the slopes right under the infidels and yank the firing cord of his explosive vest. When he reached the far edge of the natural growth of thorn bushes, the determined boy stopped and flung himself to the ground.

The sun hadn't cleared the high country to the east, but it had risen enough that the dark orange of dawn had disappeared from the sky. The kid thought of how proud his parents would be, especially his father when they told all the men at the mosque of this great sacrifice made in the name of Allah the Beneficent. Now the night's coolness was gone, and as the day grew brighter, it seemed like the lights of Paradise shined down on the scene. The lad felt a fierce joy grip his heart, and he hollered, "*Allah akbar*—God is great!"

He leaped to his feet and rushed into the open toward the slope. When he reached it, he clambered upward, tears of joy in his eyes. He managed to go only five yards before the bullet struck his shoulder, twisting him around and causing him to fall face first into a painful slide down the rugged slope to the base of the mountain. An instinctive realization that he had received a mortal blow swept through his fading consciousness. Blood was in his mouth, and he could barely breathe. His life and the time to end it gloriously were fast running out. It took all his waning strength to grab the detonation cord and give it a weak pull. The battery-powered detonator sparked, the cap flashed, and five pounds of C-4 plastic explosive were set off.

The kid's upper torso was vaporized, and the concussion of the blast killed a rabbit in a nearby thicket.

THE SEALs were now fully aware that the attackers—at least those in the direct front of the assault formation—were suicide bombers wearing explosive vests. Everyone concentrated on singling out the crazy bastards, and shooting them down as they charged out into view. Those who escaped the initial incoming rounds ducked back when the volleys of fire from the Americans built up. Occasional explosions still occurred, sending natural and human debris flying upward, along with shock waves that bounced off the hard ground.

Brannigan now issued instructions that all machine gunners, grenadiers, and SAW gunners were to fire hot and heavy, sweeping the areas near the base of the slopes. It was obvious that the bombers' forward momentum had stopped there, and the fanatics were only waiting for half a chance to rush upward toward the SEAL positions. Meanwhile, the enemy backup force of riflemen had been discovered just past the midpoint of the valley. They were undoubtedly waiting for the bombers to disrupt the defenses enough to allow a decisive charge that would carry them to where they could close in for the kill. If they accomplished that, it would pretty much bring Operation Battleline to a halt, with the Iranians being the big winners.

The combined fire from machine guns, SAWs, and grenade launchers was an awesome, rolling thunder of continual destruction. Both human beings and vegetation in the area were smashed and sliced by the incoming slugs, which cleared them away as if some roaring giant weed whacker were being swung through the area.

CAPTAIN Naser Khadid both crawled and rushed from squad to squad among his Iranian Special Forces troops, checking them out. The Imperial Lions had a couple of men lightly wounded, but Khadid knew that when the Americans were satisfied all the suicide bombers had been blown up, they would begin turning 100 percent of their firepower onto his unit and Sikes Pasha's Arabs.

"This is Khadid," the captain said in English over the LASH to Sikes. He spoke in that language so none of the Arabs or Iranians could understand him. "I have lost track of how many of the martyrs have exploded, but I am beginning to feel they may be all dead."

"Right," came back Sikes. "Poor stupid bastards! It looks like they sent themselves to hell without accomplishing a single fucking bluddy thing."

"They did not go to hell, Sikes Pasha," Khadid said. "They are in Paradise this very moment."

"Right, mate," Sikes said. "But it looks to me like all that's melted away to our front. We're gonna end up being out here on our own with them Yanks having a jolly good time shooting the hell out of us."

"I am in total agreement," Khadid said. "It is time to withdraw. And we must do it fast."

"Right," Sikes said. "Are you listening to this, Brigadier?"

Now Khohollah's voice could be heard. "Yes, Major Sikes. I shall order the support section to begin heavy fire with the grenade launchers and machine guns. As soon as they start,

I urge you and Captain Khadid to withdraw from the valley
with all haste."

Khadid responded, saying, "I am ready, Brigadier!"

Within half a minute the German machine guns and Spanish automatic grenade launchers employed by Iranian soldiers
began laying down covering fire that pounded into the American line.

AT the same moment that the incoming barrage plas-
tered the SEAL positions, Brannigan noted that the Zaheya
infantry units were pulling out of the valley. That left him
two choices; one, duck down and avoid casualties; or two,
mount a rapid attack and stream down into the valley and rush
across to close with the retreating enemy before they could
reach safety. It took him one immeasurably short spark of time
to reach a decision.

"All sections, counterattack! Chief Gunnarson, whip those
M-sixties up on the enemy support fire elements!"

The SEALs, grabbing extra bandoliers at their feet, slung
them across their shoulders and climbed over the positions
to scramble down the incline into no-man's-land. The SAW
gunners and grenadiers continued to coordinate their efforts,
firing across the two hundred meters of space to where the
Zaheya riflemen were making a disciplined withdrawal from
the battlefield.

NOW both sides were locked in a massive firefight. A
couple of Iranians and an Arab dropped to the ground as the
exchange of gunfire built up in intensity. Two SEALs—Paul
Schreiner of the Second Assault Section and Paulo Garcia of
the Third—went down under incoming slugs from FA-MAS
rifles.

Sikes and Khadid practiced fire-and-maneuver smoothly,
keeping their battlefield formations moving slowly, albeit
effectively, toward the slope leading to their fortification.
They and the SEALs began to catch glimpses of each other,
exchanging bursts of fire. The Americans' initial headlong
rush toward the enemy had now slowed to their own careful,

coordinated efforts as they continued keeping pressure on the Zaheya riflemen, who resisted with fierce determination and skill. The covering fire from the M-60 machine guns back at the base camp whipped over the SEALs' heads as Gunnarson's men ignored the heavy fire from the other side's support weapons.

The fluid movement of the fighting now came to a standstill as both sides found cover and concealment on their particular side of the valley. The fighting men locked into the battle, settling down to take potshots at each other that were punctuated occasionally with grenade bursts. Out of sheer desperation, everyone was ready to slug it out in the wild hope of victory. Above, on both sides of the valley, the fire support elements had all but neutralized each other. They could not exchange fire without getting into a no-win situation of eventually being blasted out of their fighting positions, and that also meant they could no longer cover their comrades-in-arms below, in the valley. All machine gunners and grenadiers were hunkered down, having thoughts about damning convention and logic to battle it out and destroy each other.

Stalemate.

Unknown to each other, the field commanders of the combatants in no-man's-land reached a mutual decision that the battle had now turned to one of attrition in which there would be no winners. At almost the same instant, Sikes Pasha and Lieutenant Bill Brannigan decided it was time to break it off, and each ordered a withdrawal to their own positions. The two sides put out fusillades of gunfire as they made their retrograde movements, not really trying to hit each other but concentrating on keeping the other guy from showing any tendencies toward aggressive behavior.

The battle that had begun at begun at dawn came to an anticlimactic finish at midmorning as the participants hurriedly ascended the slopes and disappeared over their parapets, carrying their KIAs with them.

CHAPTER 14

DIRK Wallenger's spacious home was on fashionable R Street Northwest, and was an old two-story brick edifice with four bedrooms, three baths, living room, family room, dining room, kitchen, den, office, breakfast nook, gym, and solarium, all conveniently arranged in eight thousand square feet.

Wallenger sat behind the desk in his den after deciding that particular spot would give him a psychological advantage as he gazed across its teakwood expanse at his two visitors. One was Liam Bentley, the Federal Bureau of Investigation's White House Liaison Officer, and the other was also an agent from the FBI. He was John Wright, who worked in both domestic and foreign intelligence, and was a profiler, specializing in the shadowy world of operatives, informants, and wannabe spies. After his introduction to Wallenger he had remained silent while his partner did most of the talking.

While Bentley carried on the preliminary steps necessary

for a visit of this nature, Wright's mind was busy categorizing Wallenger. The profiler saw that here was a dedicated elitist leftist who thought of himself as the champion of the common man, yet had a family background that included privilege and wealth, with access to educational and professional opportunities that were far beyond that of the average American. Some photos of the journalist riding horses were on the desk. Wallenger's personal economic situation certainly allowed him to be part of the "horsey set," but Wright couldn't see him playing polo. He just wasn't the type.

Wallenger had a keen mind, no doubt, yet his perceptions had been clouded by an inability to fully understand the realities of the typical American life—easy to do when one has an abundance of money and no pressing economic problems. The concept of not being able to afford purchasing something was an alien concept to this man, born with that proverbial silver spoon clenched tightly between his teeth. Here, decided Wright, definitely was a well-placed individual who had done nothing to achieve this advantageous position other than being sired by a wealthy pater.

Additionally, Wright saw Wallenger as a pudgy little fellow who had gone through life trying to make up for his lack of physical attractiveness with a sneering display of intellect. No doubt he had known bullying in his boyhood at boarding schools when larger, more aggressive boys harassed him for no other reason that to have some fun at the little fellow's expense. Wright noted another photo on the desk. This one was also of Wallenger in past years, as a cadet at a private military academy. It was quite evident that his father had sent him there for some discipline and toughening up. Any man who would name his son "Dirk" obviously expected him to grow up to be an alpha male. And Wright would have bet his FBI pension that that boy had learned to hate the military with an unending passion. Wright doubted if he had spent more than a year at the institution, probably much less before dismissal as temperamentally unfit.

As Wright analyzed his subject, Bentley spoke in a friendly tone, showing a smile that was almost apologetic. "This is purely an informal call, Mr. Wallenger. I hope you understand that."

"I understand perfectly," Wallenger said coolly. "And please don't think me stupid enough to believe that two FBI agents have called on me to spend an amicable afternoon in pleasant chitchat."

"Well, Mr. Wallenger," Bentley said, "I certainly don't want to give the wrong impression either way. I think you'll agree that these are difficult times we're going through. The whole world is in turmoil because of situations our Western civilization has never faced before. This means that those of us in law enforcement and national defense services must leave the comfort of our offices to go out and speak to people. We are seeking help, and we can only get it by communicating with those we wish to serve."

"How very noble."

As the conversation between the two continued, Wright let his gaze slowly take in the bookcases around the room. Most were political tomes that covered recent history. This could be expected in the library of a contemporary journalist. He also noted that other subjects, such as biographies of Mao Zedong, Che Guevara, and Josef Stalin, were included. A couple of shelves down from that were books on Adolf Hitler, Francisco Franco, and Benito Mussolini. A further search revealed Karl Marx, Heinrich Himmler, Ralph Nader, and William Buckley. Wright smiled slightly to himself; the little guy seemed to be covering all bases in his research. His ultimate decision to lean politically to the left must have been genuine.

In spite of Wallenger's surliness, Liam Bentley remained cheerful and friendly. "I was just wondering something, Mr. Wallenger," he said. "You work for Global News Broadcasting. I'm curious about your employer. That's not a network, is it?"

"No," Wallenger replied. "But we hope to be someday. We're an independent broadcaster and distribute our programs to stations by way of syndication."

"Well, your viewing numbers are very impressive," Bentley said. "You reach one hell of an audience."

Now Wallenger smiled. "Yeah! We're doing quite well, actually. Our president, Don Allen, just announced the addition of stations in Minneapolis, Atlanta, and Phoenix. That's brought us an additional three million viewers."

"Quite an accomplishment," Bentley said.

As their conversation eased over into a discussion of GNB, Wright turned his thoughts to Wallenger's wife, whom the two FBI men had met when they first arrived at the lavish home. Quite a looker. Latest trendy hairstyle, expensive clothing that emphasized a nice body and large breasts, plenty of jewelry to wear that she displayed even there in the house when they were introduced to her. Her name was Linda, and she had given the two FBI men bold looks, not at all intimidated by the fact that they were federal lawmen. Here was a woman who had a lot of experience with men, and that was more than likely done by her in a search for someone to provide her with a luxurious lifestyle. Wright also noted that she was beginning to get a few wrinkles around the eyes, so she was probably in her late thirties or early forties, just a couple of years short of her first plastic surgery. That also meant that she had decided it was time to latch onto a wealthy husband before it was too late. Who better than a short, plump little man who obviously had not had any deep, meaningful relationships with women. He would be easy to manipulate for fun, money, and gifts, and he was gone from home a lot. Wright figured she had a lover by now, and in a decade or so would turn her attention to much younger men who would appreciate the goodies she would lavish on them. All financed by Dirk Wallenger.

When Wright turned his attention back to Bentley and Wallenger, Wright noted that the conversation had segued to a less friendly tone. The journalist's patience was at an end. "This inane conversation is very entertaining, but let's get down to the real reason why you're here, shall we?"

"If you insist, Mr. Wallenger," Bentley said. "We are curious about how you acquired your knowledge of the incident in which a wounded enemy prisoner of war was allegedly executed."

Wallenger crossed his arms across his chest in a defiant manner. "I will not reveal my sources! Period!"

"I'm not asking about your sources," Bentley said. "I would like to know about your personal knowledge of the *facts* of the case."

"I've nothing to say."

"That sounds pretty final," Bentley said. "I don't wish to waste my time or yours. By the way, we already know your source, Mr. Wallenger. He is a cabdriver called 'Ali.'"

"I don't know any cabdrivers by that name," Wallenger said.

"Of course you do," Bentley said. "He's known to be part of a terrorist cell in the D.C. area. He's actually been under surveillance for quite a long time, and you've been seen getting into his cab on numerous occasions."

"Oh, God!" Wallenger exclaimed. "This is so lame! I don't pay any attention to what cab I get into when I want one."

"You pass up others and go directly to his taxi," Bentley said. "And it's always at one of three cab stands. The last time you went for a ride with him, it was from one located where Second Street, Constitution Avenue, and Maryland Avenue all come together."

"This conversation is terminated," Wallenger said. "If you wish to speak to me again, you'll have to give me time to contact my attorney. Now I am asking you to leave."

The two FBI men stood, and Bentley said, "That's your right, Mr. Wallenger. Thank you for your time."

Wallenger led them out of the den and down the hall to the front door. He opened it and stood aside. Bentley and Wright stepped through to the small front porch, then Bentley turned. "By the way, Mr. Wallenger, Ali's real name is Daleel Guellah. I thought you might be interested in knowing that. He's been talking a lot about you lately—to us. Good afternoon."

Wright nodded to their reluctant host. "Have a nice day."

SHELOR FIELD, AFGHANISTAN
4 AUGUST
0845 HOURS

THE nine SEALs—Lieutenant Bill Brannigan, Ensign Orlando Taylor, the two Hit Men and the five Sneaky Petes—had been unexpectedly ordered from their base camp to fly back to Shelor Field the night before. They carried some melancholy cargo with them on the helicopter flight: Two body bags containing Petty Officers Paul Schreiber and Paulo Garcia lay on the deck between the rows of seats.

The most puzzling aspect of the unexpected summons was that they had been instructed to come looking for a fight. Each had his personal weapon and some bandoliers of ammo in addition to Bruno Puglisi packing a SAW and Joe Miskoski an M-203 grenade launcher.

Now the SEALs were back in their old hangar, lounging around the Headquarters cubicle, wondering what the hell was going on. They had enjoyed a good meal at the base mess hall, and were sharing some thermoses of hot coffee the mess sergeant had furnished them after they had finished off a couple of dozen eggs, piles of hash brown potatoes, biscuits, pancakes, sausages, bacon, and a large cheese Danish that Ensign Taylor had gotten for himself. Puglisi belched and stretched. "I wonder what the poor people had for breakfast this morning."

Matty Matsuno grinned. "I don't think there was anything left over for them."

"Man!" Dave Leibowitz said. "When I'm in the field, I think more about food than I do sex."

"Most guys do," Brannigan said, pouring coffee into his plastic cup. "But as soon as that craving for a fully belly is satiated, we turn our wandering thoughts to the delights offered by the opposite sex."

"Oh, yeah!" Connie Concord said. "Females. Say! Is that what them Air Force personnel with soft, round butts are that we keep seeing around here? The ones that seem to need haircuts."

Mike Assad laughed. "Most of 'em. I'm not so sure about a couple I saw."

Further conversation was interrupted by the roar of a motor as Randy Tooley sped into the hangar in his purloined DPV. When Brannigan noticed the man in the passenger seat, he jumped up. "Tinch-*hut*!"

Brigadier General Greg Leroux stepped out of the vehicle, turning to the little Air Force guy. "Thanks for the ride, Randy." He took another look at the conveyance. "Where the hell did you get hold of this DPV, anyhow? I didn't think it was on any Air Force TOA."

"Ask me no questions and I'll tell you no lies," Randy said with a grin as he mashed the gearshift into reverse and gunned the engine for a quick exit.

Leroux laughed aloud. "I never bother a go-getter. The American Armed Forces run on guys like you." He turned to the SEALs. "At ease, men! Sit down and finish your coffee. I need to have a little chat with you."

"Yes, sir," Brannigan said. "Guys, this is General Leroux from the SFOB aboard the *Combs*. He's pretty much running our operation."

"Well, I get some shitty input from Station Bravo from time to time that I have to pass on," Leroux allowed. "But if you're pissed off about anything, I'm pretty much the guy to put the blame on."

"In that case, sir," Brannigan said, "we need some fifties to replace the M-sixties we have in the OA. Those seven-point-six-twos just don't have the punch we need."

"I've already seen to it, Brannigan," Leroux said. "I read the AAR about that little fiasco with them suicidal ragheads. It seemed to me your support folks could have traded a little more fire with the bad guys if they'd been using M-twos." He walked over, grabbed an unused cup, and filled it with coffee. "Okay, let's get down to business. I got to get back to that fucking sardine can of a boat they stuck me on. I called you guys back here for a HALO insertion."

"Christ!" Brannigan said. "Where?"

"Behind that mountain where the bad guys are holing up," Leroux said. "I've already worked out the OPORD so we won't have a briefback on this thing. The gist of the operation is to land on their LZ in the dark, then sneak around and make an attack on their south end and roll up that flank. Shoot the hell out of the place and make great big fucking nuisances out of yourselves."

"That's kind of risky, ain't it, sir?" Puglisi said.

"You'll have the advantage because you'll be firing down their line of defense," Leroux explained. "They'll be caught flat-footed with a very narrow front of resistance to throw up at you. That means the bastards won't be able to mount a counterattack for a while. You're gonna have to judge when they're ready to hit back, then pull out and make a run back to the LZ for exfiltration. You'll be using AFSOC for that. There's nobody better'n the Air Force for that kind of a hairy to-do."

The ever outspoken Bruno Puglisi was still not about to be quiet and withdrawn. "What the hell's this all about, sir?"

"Those Zaheya bastards think they shook you up with that suicide bomber attack," Leroux said. "It seems to me their morale is a bit higher than it should be, since they're feeling smug. Something like this will put the fear of God into 'em."

"The fear of God, hell!" Garth Redhawk said. "It'll be the fear of the United States Navy SEALs."

"I can't argue with you, son," Leroux said. "Now, if one of you would be kind enough to fetch that packet I put in the lower desk drawer there, we'll get into this briefing."

Garth and Matty walked over and secured the documents, handing them to the general. Leroux ripped the sealed envelope open. "We have some detailed maps here made from the latest satellite photos of the OA. These will be real handy as we discuss the ways and means of our operation." He tossed the charts over to Joe Miskoski. "Pass these around, son."

"Aye, sir!"

"God!" Leroux moaned. "I *hate* that Navy talk!"

WHITE HOUSE PRESS ROOM
WASHINGTON, D.C.
5 AUGUST
1400 HOURS

WHEN Owen Peckham stepped into the press room, he exhibited a very obvious bounce in his step. He grinned as he stepped up to the podium and sat his notes down. "Good afternoon, everybody! How are we doing this bright summer day?"

"Well!" Joyce Bennington of the *Boston World Journal* said. "You're in a chipper mood, Owen."

"Why, Joyce, I'm always in a chipper mood," Peckham said. He beamed at his audience. "As usual I will open things up with announcements, or as is the case today, a *single* announcement." He looked around. "Where is Dirk Wallenger? I don't see him here anyplace. Is there anyone else from Global News Broadcasting present? No? Oh, gee, I'll have to go on without them." He paused and cleared his throat. "Ahem! In regard to the information about a wounded enemy prisoner being executed in Afghanistan, we have received an update on that. It seems that the prisoner in question lost his life during an escape attempt."

"Oh, sure!" Brian Mackenzie of the *Ontario People's Advocate* crowed. "Now there's an old story, hey? Shot while attempting to escape. Good God! It's almost a cliché."

"The Pentagon clearly admits the man lost his life during an escape try," Peckham said gleefully. He had received permission to reveal a newer version of the story only an hour before, when the President decided it was best to tell about the snake bite, albeit in a special way. "However, he was not shot." He waited a couple of beats for effect, then announced, "He was bitten by a poisonous snake. A cobra, to be exact. The deadly serpent was in a stand of rocks into which the unfortunate terrorist entered to conceal himself. Cobras are among the deadliest of snakes, and the man died quickly before he could be evacuated to proper medical treatment."

The Canadian Mackenzie wasn't going to give up his argument. "Why didn't the Americans troops treat him for the bite and stabilize him until transportation could arrive?"

"Our troops are not issued any antivenom serum in their medical kits," Peckham explained. "And even if they had any, it would take a doctor to administer it properly. A cobra's bite is fatal in an exceedingly short period of time."

Mackenzie snuffed a bit and scribbled in his notebook.

Peckham gazed fondly at the other journalists. "Well! Let's get down to business. Are there any questions out there?"

A dozen hands were raised.

EXECUTIVE OFFICES, GLOBAL NEWS BROADCASTING
WASHINGTON, D.C.
6 AUGUST
0830 HOURS

DON Allen, the CEO of GNB, sat at the conference table in his office, sharing the large piece of furniture with only one other person: Frank Brice, attorney-at-law, who was on retainer by the broadcasting service. Brice, who styled his hair in a ponytail and sported an earring, was more conventional in the rest of his attire. He wore a skillfully tailored business suit, complete with shirt and tie, and he was shod in an expensive pair of Italian shoes.

When the lawyer spoke, his voice was deep and authoritative. "We do *not* want to go on trial regarding this issue."

Allen wasn't in agreement. "Aren't we dealing with the First Amendment here? If there ever was an incident involving freedom of the press, this is it."

"It's a little more complicated than that, Don," Brice said. "GNB issued a news bulletin stating that American troops had murdered a wounded prisoner during combat action in Afghanistan. That turned out to be false in the *worst* sense, or a mistake in the *best*. And the best here isn't very good."

"Wait!" Allen protested. "It was the fucking Pentagon that said it was false. The sons of bitches are covering their asses with an out-and-out falsehood."

"I don't think they're lying," Brice said. "They've been upfront about atrocities before, so there's no real reason to think they would fudge on this one. So we have to accept what they say as gospel. But we do have some choices here. The best is to blame it on the source."

"That's easy enough."

"But then there would be a demand—not only from the government but also from the public—for you to name that source."

"It's our policy not to reveal sources under any circumstances," Allen said. "We'd rather go to jail."

"Alright," Brice said. "But it's going to make you look like you're dispensing terrorist propaganda. Let's face it, Don. GNB is noted for its leftist leanings. And this isn't like protesting the war. If the public is convinced you're aiding and abetting the terrorists, they'll turn away from you in droves. That also means that the local independent TV stations you depend on will drop GNB like a hot rock. That could be the end of having your voice heard by millions of people." He shook his head. "I hate to say it, but it could be the end of your organization."

Allen was clearly disgusted. "Then what the fuck are we supposed to do?"

"Have Dirk Wallenger issue an apology and announce that he had been victimized by false documentation," Brice said. "He can say he trusted a person or persons who had proven totally reliable in the past. But they let him down on this one occasion."

"Mmm," Allen mused. "Dirk could say he made an honest mistake and is sorry as hell about it. He can also announce he will check his facts with much more care in the future. That will soothe any hard feelings in the White House or the Pentagon."

"Sure," Brice said. "It's just a little incident, anyway." He chuckled. "When you get right down to it, who gives a shit? Right?"

"Yeah," Allen said. "Just a minor happening that means absolutely nothing."

CHAPTER 15

LIEUTENANT Bill Brannigan was stabilized and steady as he streaked earthward at 120 miles per hour. Eight other SEALs similarly occupied in the HALO insert checked the ground thousands of feet below through their NVGs. In spite of the long plunge, they had no sensation of falling. As far as their physical sensations were concerned, they lay motionless on a cushion of air that held them aloft with a bit of buffeting. When the jumpers glanced at each other, they all seemed to be hanging motionless in the night sky; however, the spinning needles on their wrist altimeters gave ample evidence of the controlled plummeting.

As soon as Brannigan noted he was thirty-five hundred feet AGL, he pulled the rip cord. The pilot chute of his rig leaped free, instantly filling with air. The device hauled out the deployment bag and suspensions lines in the blink of an eye, and the canopy cells inflated. This happened at almost the same moment to the other Brigands, and there they were—hanging beneath the deployed parachutes in gentle glides to earth, all relieved that there had been no malfunctions of their equipment.

They didn't want to get too far away from the mountains out in the desert, so they pulled down on the toggles to brake their rate of travel. When they were within a dozen feet of the ground, everyone went into a full brake position until the parachute stalled and their feet gently hit the ground. The one exception was Ensign Lamar Taylor, who wasn't as practiced as the others. This was actually his first HALO jump since finishing the course, and he stalled a bit too soon and tried to recover. This resulted in his striking the ground hard enough to drop him to his knees. He was embarrassed as hell, but he saw the others didn't seem to think he'd done so badly. He quickly got out of his equipment, picking up his M-16 and bandoliers. The used parachute that had brought him safely down from the C-130 would be left abandoned to the elements. This type of mission did not provide enough time for the proper recovery or concealment of jump gear.

Everyone gathered around the Skipper as per the SOP, and it was with mutual relief that nobody seemed to be hurt. Sprains and fractures are only too common during jumps, and in combat situations even a minor twist of ankle or knee can mean disaster for the mission. The only carrying equipment they had was their combat vests, which were attached to pistol belts. This was second-line equipment that provides what's needed to fight effectively and efficiently. These carried a two-quart canteen, battle dressing, and medical kit in the back pouches. Additionally, they individually carried six thirty-round magazines of 5.56-millimeter ammo, with two bandoliers of twelve more slung across their shoulders. Counting the one magazine in their M-16s, this gave each SEAL a grand total of 570 rounds, adding about 36 pounds to their carrying load.

Since Puglisi toted a SAW, he would be lugging four extra bandoliers, providing him with 1,260 rounds. If he fired those as fast as he could, it would take him about a hundred seconds to shoot it all up at the normal rate. Needless to say, the SEAL would be employing short bursts. Brannigan would have liked to have brought along three times that amount for support fire, but Colonel Leroux had limited them to toting only what they could manage as individual jumpers. He also reminded Brannigan that when he returned to his base camp, the newly issued .50 heavy machine guns would be there to provide future support fire. These replacement weapons would soon be under the tender care of CPO Matt Gunnarson and his three crews on the SEAL side of no-man's-land.

On that night's operation Puglisi would be turning loose his full firepower when they made a break for the helicopter during exfiltration. The only other times he was to fire would be during unexpected emergencies. Joe Miskoski with an M-203 on his M-16 was also humping extra poundage because of the grenades. Brannigan teamed him up with Puglisi to give the SAW gunner some added protection so he wouldn't be forced into expending too much ammunition if he ended up in a hairy situation. The Skipper had wanted to leave the SAW behind and have Puglisi lug along a grenade launcher, but Leroux felt the one SAW would be needed.

Out on the DZ, after putting on the LASH headsets and the AN/PRC-126 radios for interteam commo, the small strike force formed up as had been determined back at Shelor Field. Redhawk and Matsuno went on point, followed by Ensign Taylor and Connie Concord. The middle of the formation was made up of the Skipper, Puglisi, and Miskoski. The Odd Couple—Assad and Leibowitz—brought up the rear. When everybody and everything were in readiness at 0335 hours, the Skipper spoke calmly but significantly over his LASH.

"Move out."

0350 HOURS

THE rear of the mountain housing the Zaheya loomed large and menacingly in the darkness. The NVGs gave the point men, Redhawk and Matsuno, a revealing view of the steep terrain's features as they drew closer.

"Objective in sight," Redhawk said. "Two hundred meters ahead."

"Roger," Brannigan said in acknowledgment. "You two move on for a recon. Taylor, you and Concord move forward fifty meters for security, then hold up. Odd Couple, cover the rear."

While the others situated themselves, the two scouts went forward at a slow pace, being careful to stay in the scrub while following dips in the terrain. Although the enemy had no reason to expect an attack from the rear, there was always the chance that some raghead or two with night vision capabilities had been posted at an OP. The SEAL duo walked carefully, avoiding rocks that might be accidentally kicked loose to clatter down into a ravine. As they drew closer to the objective, they slowed even more, this time for studied observations of possible hiding places inhabited by alert sentries. All the Brigands were now very much aware of the professionalism of the enemy they faced, and were aware that any slips in caution could bring fatal results.

The two scions of Native American and samurai warrior traditions barely breathed as they continued their fluid, silent travel upward into the reaches of the mountains. They were fully aware that just on the other side of the valley, the rest of their buddies stood on watch, keeping wary eyes on the Zaheya positions opposite them.

"Wait!" Matsuno hissed into the LASH.

Redhawk immediately dropped to one knee. "What's up?"

"Look just to the right of that cut in the side of the mountain."

Redhawk's eyes went in the direction and found the spot. He pulled out his NVBs and gazed intently. "Yeah! A guard standing by a trail."

"That's where we're supposed to enter their positions," Matsuno said. "They probably stuck the guy there in the off-chance somebody might be going through that area."

"Well now, that was an excellent guess on their part, wasn't it?" Redhawk said. He spoke into the LASH to get the Skipper's attention. "There's a sentry at the entry point. He'll have to be taken out."

"Roger," came back the Skipper's acquiescence. "Do it."

"Here," Redhawk said, handing his M-16 to Matsuno.

Now free of the rifle, he pulled his K-Bar knife from its scabbard. As the senior ranking man between the two of them, this was the Oklahoman's choice. The Japanese-American trailed silently after his buddy as they eased forward toward the Zaheya soldier.

Garth Redhawk unconsciously shed the present and reverted to the past, when his Kiowa and Comanche forebears had existed as warriors, hunters, and plunderers. He truly felt that up in those dense night clouds his male ancestors looked down on him as he moved forward to do what he had to do. It was almost a spiritual experience as he worked himself into position at a point just aft of the guard. He moved silently forward, slapping his left hand around the nose and mouth of the sentry while at that same instant he drove the blade of the K-Bar upward under the man's rib cage. The steel blade slipped in effortlessly and deep, gashing and cutting into vital organs and arteries. Death came fast after only feeble shuddering and gasping, the latter sounds smothered by Redhawk's strong pressure across mouth and nose. He lowered the man to the ground, then stood there looking down at the fresh kill.

"Garth?"

He turned to Matsuno. "Yeah?"

"You're not gonna scalp him, are you?"

Redhawk shook his head. "What makes you think I'd do that?"

"From the way you were looking at him, dude."

"There isn't time anyway," Redhawk said with a slight grin. He turned away, stepping up the trail. "We got to make sure the route is clear all the way to their defenses."

"Lead on," Matsuno said.

0415 HOURS

THE strike force was now gathered at the extreme southern flank of the Zaheya defensive line. The Odd Couple had moved forward to keep watch down the parapets where individual sentries gazed out across no-man's-land to the SEAL positions. Bruno Puglisi with the SAW had set himself up on an elevated position that offered a good view straight over the spot where Assad and Leibowitz now hunkered. Puglisi would be able to provide excellent covering fire for the withdrawal after the raid. He began to carefully lay out his magazines where they would be within easy reach. He kept two of the bandoliers around his shoulders in case they might be needed for a running retreat if the situation went completely to hell.

Now Bill Brannigan brought in the rest of the participants. "Everybody put your selectors on three-round bursts," he said, being careful to whisper as softly as possible. "Firepower is gonna be the name of this game." As soon as everyone had complied, he spoke into the LASH: "Brigand One."

"Roger," said Lieutenant JG Jim Cruiser. He was across the valley on the SEALs' MLR. "Everything is ready on this side, Skipper. And I have a happy surprise: Not only did those fifty-calibers arrive here ahead of time, there was also an extra one."

"Alright!" Brannigan exclaimed.

Cruiser continued, "So Chief Gunnarson has four ready to cover you when you need it. I sent Sturgis and Malachenko over to man the extra weapon."

"Okay, sounds good," Brannigan said. "Here we go."

THE BATTLE

PUGLISI watched as Brannigan led the way down the defensive line. Mike Assad was just behind him with Joe Miskoski and his M-203. Next came Taylor and Leibowitz, with Redhawk, Matsuno, and Concord bringing up the rear. The attack by the SEALs was a classic maneuver called "rolling up the flank." It consisted of hitting a weak extreme side of the enemy line and smashing down its length.

It took but an instant before the nearest Arab sentry glanced their way. When he saw the Americans easing toward him in the trench, he stood open-mouthed in shock at the sight of the unexpected infiltrators. Brannigan pulled the trigger on his M-16, and the resultant burst of three rounds hit the raghead, kicking him back onto a stack of sandbags. The man, already dead, bounced off and crumpled to the ground.

The door to the nearest bunker opened, but before the Arab could step out, Miskoski fired a grenade into the interior. The resultant explosion and screams gave stark evidence of the effectiveness of the projectile. Now, farther down, other fighters emerged from their bunkers, and Brannigan and Assad kicked out several more bursts as Miskoski fired two grenades over their heads that added to the carnage of the fusillades.

SIKES Pasha came wide awake, leaping from his cot in the al-Askerin-Zaubi headquarters bunker. He grabbed his FA-MAS bullpup rifle and rushed outside just in time to see two grenade detonations tear into a trio of his Arab Storm Troopers. He hosed a long automatic burst in the direction of the attackers, then leaped into a parapet where two of his men were trying to find targets to shoot at. The problem was twofold for the defenders. They had no breadth of an MLR to offer resistance to the assault, and the incoming fire was fluctuating rapidly from light to heavy, forcing them to duck for cover. One Arab stood up to deliver a fire burst but caught a chestful of slugs that hurled him against Sikes. Both men went down, but it was the Brit who was able to get back to his feet. He damned the danger and set up rhythmic firing without regard to his own safety.

BRANNIGAN and Assad, with Sikes' bullets splattering around them, moved into an adjacent parapet where a duo of corpses, their upper torsos and heads torn apart by both rifle slugs and grenade shrapnel, were sprawled. Now Taylor and Leibowitz rushed forward, both systematically pulling M-16 triggers to throw out a narrow cone of concentrated fire. With these additional salvos taking some of the pressure off them, the Skipper and Assad joined in with their own bursts.

SIKES felt a heavy blow to his left shoulder that turned him halfway around. His knees buckled and he went down, his numb hands unable to maintain a grasp on his rifle. He immediately felt someone grabbing his collar and dragging him. He looked up to see his faithful warrant officer, Shafaqat Hashiri, pulling him from the parapet and across the walkway toward the entrance to the Headquarters bunker. Hashiri held his own bullpup in the other hand, firing short bursts until he reached the door and pulled his commander inside. Then he quickly slammed the steel portal shut to keep intruders and grenades at bay.

ENSIGN Taylor was now leading the Brigands in their continuing assault, with Leibowitz at his heels. Garth Redhawk and Matty Matsuno were close behind them, with Brannigan and Miskoski following. The latter kept firing the 40-millimeter grenades in short arcs over the heads of the other SEALs to clear the way for them. Detonations, single shots, and automatic bursts of rifles added to the din of shouting, fighting men as the battle continued to evolve.

DOWN on the northern flank, Captain Naser Khadid and his Iranian SF troopers were moving rapidly toward the roar of combat to join in the battle. Suddenly a barrage of heavy machine-gun fire slammed into them. The incoming bullets that missed the men either ricocheted off the metal and concrete of the defenses or plowed into sandbags. Directly above him, Captain Jamshid Komard did his best to set up counterfire against the enfilading volleys, but each time they cut loose with their own machine guns or the automatic grenade launchers, the enemy across the valley would turn their swarms of large .50-caliber slugs on them, forcing the gunners to duck down. Those who didn't find suitable cover died instantly with gaping exit wounds made by the heavy rounds that literally ripped and smashed their bodies, leaving messy piles of meat.

AT that moment Bill Brannigan realized they had penetrated as deeply as feasible and it was time to withdraw. This was not a winnable battle for the Americans, nor was it expected to be. The mission was to get into the enemy's faces, make 'em bleed, then haul ass while the ragheads were still disorganized and demoralized. "Let's get out o' here!" he shouted into his LASH. The loudness of his voice distorted the transmission, but not enough that the SEALs couldn't understand him. They immediately began a withdrawal down the defensive line, leaping over the corpses of dead Zaheya soldiers. Bruno Puglisi went on the alert, ready to support in case of pursuit, but none was mounted against them.

As Brannigan ran with the others, he raised Jim Cruiser over the LASH. "Call in the Air Force, goddamn it!"

"Aye, sir," Cruiser replied. "Gomez is on the horn right now. Get the hell out of there! Chief Gunnarson's four guns have the area saturated with covering fire for you."

When Brannigan and the others reached the original entrance point, they found Puglisi packed up and ready to move out, with all his bandoliers once again slung over his broad shoulders. Assad and Leibowitz led the way back down the trail, with the others following. Heavy fire from the SEAL machine-gun positions across the valley immediately began pounding the small area, the hail of .50-caliber slugs hitting at a combined rate of twenty-four rounds a minute, or forty bullet strikes per second. It was as if each were a blow from a pile driver gone mad. Any Zaheya soldiers desiring to pursue immediately withdrew from the clobbering thunder.

When the SEALs arrived at the flat area behind the mountain, they headed for the rendezvous point where the Air Force Pave Low chopper would pick them up. A scant two minutes passed before the helicopter's engine could be heard approaching the area. Brannigan sent Ensign Taylor to the front of the formation to lead the way to the pickup point. The SEALs had gone no more than fifty meters when they were suddenly in the midst of incoming rifle fire. They looked back and spotted some two dozen enemy soldiers shooting at them.

"Where the fuck did *they* come from?" somebody yelled in loud anger and frustration.

This was not the time when Bruno Puglisi became vocal; this was a call to action as far as he was concerned. He turned the SAW on the closely packed group, hosing them with short bursts. When the first magazine emptied, he quickly replaced it and continued to fire as he withdrew, walking backward. Suddenly he was flanked by Joe Miskoski and Connie Concord. The mixed fire of bullets and grenades forced the attackers to hit the dirt and scramble for cover.

Brannigan's angry voice came over the LASH. "You three get the hell out of there. The chopper isn't gonna wait all day."

The trio turned and rushed toward the waiting aircraft. The firing at them increased until bullets cracked the air around their heads and kicked up spurts of dirt from the ground they ran across. At the same moment that they scurried up the ramp into the interior of the chopper, the pilot worked collective and cyclic to race into a very steep and rapid turn before climbing for altitude.

Good ol' AFSOC!

CHAPTER 16

THE limodriver/bodyguard Lazlo Czernk followed the orders for that evening's ride as he rolled slowly over the Theodore Roosevelt Memorial Bridge toward Virginia. The window between the burly man and his passengers was up, and although he couldn't hear a word that passed between the two men, it was obvious to him that it was not a pleasant conversation.

Dirk Wallenger, with his lower lip protruding, looked like a petulant little boy as he sat pressed up against the side of the car. His eyebrows were knitted into a frown, and he displayed his usual body language expression of anger by crossing his arms across his chest. On the opposite side of the seat, leaning toward him with an intent expression, Don Allen, the CEO of Global News Broadcasting, was speaking seriously in an authoritative tone.

"Dirk, you pay very close attention to what I'm telling you," Allen said. "This is not a situation to take lightly."

"Mmf!" Wallenger said. "You're caving in, Don!"

"Oh, no!" Allen snapped. "Don't take that attitude with me, Dirk. There are certain times when reality must be faced up to firmly and coldly. And I must admit that there have been instances in the past when you went overboard on some of your stories, but I've never reined you in before. However, I'm going to this time. You can be absolutely certain about that."

"Am I supposed to believe you've decided to support that stupid war in the Middle East?"

"I am not supporting the war at all," Allen said. "And what I am telling you to do is not supporting that conflict either. But there is one thing of disagreeing with government policy and another when it comes to turning against the people serving over there."

"These are not draftees, for Chrissake, like in Vietnam!" Wallenger cried. "They are professional killers. They don't deserve any consideration whatsoever."

"Let me remind you of something," Allen said through clenched teeth. "I'll be the first to admit that we at Global News Broadcasting have an agenda. I'm a leftist . . . a socialist . . . a nonconformist . . . a Bolshevik, if you will. And I've grown up with an innate distrust of authority. But the bottom line is that GNB is in business to inform and support the American public. Now, supposedly that's the average guy on the street and his wife and kids. Nowadays, both husband and wife have to work to afford a decent standard of living. Understand? They are not members of our particular social class, Dirk. You and I are both from wealthy families. We had opportunities for education and a lifestyle that the average U.S. citizen can only dream about."

"So what?" Wallenger said. "We didn't choose our families, did we? We were born into advantageous circumstances because of a chance meeting between a certain sperm and a certain egg in our mothers' wombs. I am not going to be apologetic about it. In fact, I am devoting my life to helping that average Joe have a better existence in this unfair world. All I want for him and his family is equality and justice."

"That's fine, Dirk. But you don't help anybody by *attacking* them! You help them by attacking the injustices in the system. And that's the key word—the *system!*"

Wallenger turned his head to glare in righteous indignation at his boss. "I am not attacking the people!"

"When you accuse servicemen and servicewomen of atrocities, you *are* attacking the people," Allen argued. "That's where the soldiers and sailors come from. Our social equals aren't over there in the military. The ones fighting, dying, and getting maimed are the kids of workers—those average Joes we're talking about. I'm sure some of them have committed atrocities, albeit only a minuscule percent. But those who have done so were put in the situations where they lose control by the government you and I hate. When nineteen- or twenty-year-old kids see their buddies killed by a treacherous enemy, some of them are going to eventually lose their heads and strike back most viciously. Instead of condemning those guys, let's take off after the assholes who sent them over there in the first place. Or perhaps I should say the assholes who are making the mistakes that intensify and lengthen this disaster. Does that make sense to you?"

"The guys who killed that wounded prisoner were Army Special Forces," Wallenger said. "They are professional killers. Gangsters! A Mafia in uniform!"

"I've learned they were Navy SEALs," Allen said. "You're not even going after the right guys." He paused. "And that accusation you made is false. The individual who was killed was a prisoner trying to escape who blundered into a deadly cobra snake. He was not wounded and lying helpless on the ground, as you have intimated."

"I was making a point!"

"Oh, my God! That is so fucking lame!"

"The first casualty of war is the truth," Wallenger said. "Both sides of an issue use propaganda. If one doesn't, they will be at a marked disadvantage."

"Now you're being very unprofessional, Dirk," Allen said coldly. "You're lying to back up your own attitudes and opinions. There's no worse sin for a journalist to commit."

"Good can come out of it."

"Do you want to end up like Dan Rather at CBS News?"

Allen asked. "He wanted to nail President Bush so much that he went after him with the wrong data. He should have checked it out, but he let his own agenda trip him up. Once a journalist's credibility is lost, he's no longer useful. Nobody will ever trust his reporting again."

Wallenger sank into deeper pouting. "You've been talking to that son of a bitch lawyer Frank Brice, haven't you?"

"I sure as hell have," Allen said, now at the end of his patience. "And you're going to do just as he says, so listen well, young man. On your next broadcast you will recant your original story. You will say that erroneous information had been given you. You will apologize, saying you should have checked it out more thoroughly. You will make a statement that the Navy SEALs did not shoot the prisoner while he lay wounded on the field of battle. Understand?"

"I'll need time to write it up," Wallenger said sullenly.

"Frank Brice has already composed the delivery," Allen said. "And that's the one you'll use." He leaned forward, picked the intercom handset, and spoke into it. "Lazlo, take us to Mr. Wallenger's home now."

Czernk turned off at the next exit, going under the overpass, then headed back east.

ARMY GENERAL HEADQUARTERS
TEHRAN, IRAN
9 AUGUST
0815 HOURS

MAJOR Arsalaan Sikes, Brigadier Shahruz Khohollah, and Captain Naser Khadid had arrived in Iran's capital city the night before from the OA in Afghanistan. They were given quarters in the transit billets of the local garrison, then picked up by an army sedan and driven to the national army's GHQ that morning. Now they sat in the presence of Major General Nirou Mandji, the Chief of Operations. Sikes had his left arm in a sling from the wound he had taken during the Americans' latest raid.

The general's office was not as luxurious or fancy as would be expected in the bailiwick of a Western officer of his rank. His desk was not made of mahogany or teakwood. In fact, there was no difference between it and that of his sergeant-clerk, stationed outside his door. Two portraits— one of the national President and the other of the Commanding General of the Army—were on the wall. The Iranian flag was mounted on the opposite side of the room. The floor was simple tile and not laid in too expertly, and the windows needed a wash. Sikes almost grinned to himself at the thought of what a British Army sergeant major would do if he charged into the office and saw its deplorable condition.

General Mandji was not a happy man, but it had nothing to do with his work environment. When he spoke, it was with a growl, and he expressed himself in fluent English for Sikes' benefit. "The situation at the Afghanistan border is getting entirely out of control. The Americans have made attacks and gotten away with them. We must bloody their noses when they become aggressive. If they manage to withdraw from the field of battle, it should be disastrous for them no matter the results of the engagement. What I am declaring is that those infidels must return to their positions fewer in numbers and badly shot up." He displayed a furious scowl. "They are *not* afraid of you!"

Khohollah was not intimidated by the officer, who was one rank above him. "Our opponents are from the strongest nation in the world, *Sharlaskar*," he protested, addressing the general by his rank in Farsi. "We are not dealing with Pashtun villagers out there. The enemy can keep whatever level of intensity they desire with the ease of raising or lowering flames under a boiling pot. Their supply lines are unlimited and filled with everything they want or need."

"I am well aware of your opponents in this struggle, *Satrip*," General Mandji said, returning the form of address. "What you must keep foremost in your mind is that the nation cannot afford a defeat in this operation. If we are unable to establish a foothold past the international border, all our plans will fail."

Sikes was not impressed with Mandji. His instinctive feelings of superiority over Arabs and Iranians gave him a defiant attitude. "Let's get a bit logical about this, hey, Gen'ral?

Wot we need is a bigger punch, yeah? More reinforcements straightaway, and that means no less than a hundred or so blokes to beef up our lines."

Mandji looked scornfully at the man he knew had deserted from his own army. "You are forgetting that at this time we must keep as low a profile as possible."

"Then give us seventy-five," Sikes insisted. "But no less than that."

Sikes' attitude emboldened Khadid. The Iranian captain interjected, "And we need mortars, *Sharlaskar*. The grenade launchers we have are little help in counterfire against the heavy machine guns the Americans now have."

"I am not so sure of that," General Mandji said. "The last time the Americans attacked you, they parachuted behind your fortifications. And they were able to penetrate your positions with ease."

"I beg your pardon, sir," Sikes said. "It wasn't *easy* for 'em. Not for one bluddy second it wasn't. We fought back hard." He patted his arm in the sling. "I didn't get this for having tea with 'em, did I?"

"I have no doubt about your collective bravery, Major Sikes," General Mandji said.

"Well, that's good to know," Sikes said. "Anyhow, if we'd had more men, we could've covered our back door, but it just wasn't possible to keep an eye on them bastards over across the valley with so few while trying to repel a surprise attack."

Khohollah decided that he had better take over the conversation, since Sikes could easily upset Mandji. The Brit didn't realize that he could be dragged from the office and taken to a firing squad with just a snap of the general's fingers. The brigadier spoke in a calmer tone. "It is in my opinion that we are reaching the limit of our ability to continue our mission under the present circumstances, *Sharlaskar*. I say this respectfully, and it is my ardent hope that you take my statement seriously. I offer it as both a tactical and a strategic revelation as a professional soldier and a general officer."

Mandji nodded and took a deep breath of frustration. He sank into thought, and the three visitors knew he was considering the big picture of both their mission and how it would affect Iran's imperial ambitions. He finally sighed, raised his eyebrows, and spoke in a much softer voice.

"You have made your point, gentlemen," the general said. "It may surprise you to know that at the meeting of the General Staff two days ago, we discussed the possibility that it was time to change our objectives there on the border. Your candid statements this morning have shown that we must go in a different direction in this initial phase of the invasion of Afghanistan."

Sikes started to speak, but Khohollah put his hand on his arm to stop him. Then the brigadier turned to the major general. "We are anxious to hear what you will expect of us, *Sharlaskar.*"

Mandji leaned forward. "We are going to pull all the stops out now. The velvet gloves are going to be taken off, and we'll hit the Americans so unexpectedly and hard they will be sent reeling. Arrangements have been made for close air support to back you up. Additionally, there will be a heavy armor punch, complete with tanks and self-propelled artillery. All that will be followed by platoons of infantry fighting vehicles filled with brave Iranian soldiers." He now leaned back and smiled. "Within seventy-two hours of that big push, we will be halfway across Afghanistan, and the government there will sue for peace while the Pashtuns flock to our colors."

Khohollah chuckled. "And our terms will include kicking the Americans and other coalition forces out of the country, *na, Sharlaskar?*"

"Exactly," Mandji said. "It will take at least a month for all preparations to be made. In the meantime, you will go completely defensive. Be on your guard for more attacks. We will send you another fifty men and some mortars. But do not make any aggressive moves. Use your additional personnel and weapons to mount a strong, unyielding defense. You must hold that fortress! It will be an anchor around which the invasion will flow." He studied their reaction to the news, liking what he saw. "You are dismissed. Transportation has already been arranged to take you back to the Afghanistan border."

The three officers of the Zaheya snapped-to and saluted.

BONHOMME RICHARD CLUB
ARLINGTON, VIRGINIA
11 AUGUST
2130 HOURS

NOT even the oldest members of the club knew why it had been named after John Paul Jones' famous Revolutionary War ship. Various rumors and conjecturing had gone on for decades until the passing of time made the point moot. For more than two centuries the social group had been a little-known part of life in old Arlington, where it was organized by well-to-do merchants, politicians, and military and naval officers, along with other notables who used the facilities to draw off and be among their peers in society. The club was so exclusive that only members and the staff were allowed into the building. Later, as politics and commerce became more complicated, members were allowed to invite associates for clandestine sessions regarding their various political and commercial concerns. Small rooms were made available for these meetings, where a good number of consequential agreements and deals had been made.

The club had been at its present location near the Potomac River since 1856, and as the world entered the twenty-first century, it remained restricted but without regard to race or religion. The membership, however, was still made up of important, influential men who wielded power and wealth.

DR. Carl Joplin, in the company of Mr. Saviz Kahnani from the Iranian Embassy, walked from the cab up to the steps leading into the club. Jacob the doorman opened the glassed-in portals. The African-American wore a rather unique garb that had been traditional for the greeters at *Bonhomme Richard* since the 1890s. It consisted of a top hat, a bright red, gold-trimmed jacket, and navy blue trousers with a wide red stripe down the outside of each leg. The hot summer weather did not disturb Jacob, since he stayed inside the air-conditioned foyer and peered through the glass door for arriving members. When he spotted the two diplomats, he stepped out to hold the door open for them.

"Good evening, Dr. Joplin."

"Hello, Jacob," Joplin said, gesturing to Kahnani to go in ahead of him. When they entered the lobby, Joplin stopped by the desk to check in. The clerk, a dignified sixty-year-old with thick white hair and a neatly trimmed beard, informed Dr. Joplin that his reserved conference room on the second floor was waiting for him.

Joplin took the lead, and Kahnani followed him up a flight of stairs. From there they went down a long hallway to a spot where a door stood open. When they entered the fourteen-by-fifteen-foot room, they saw a couple of plush leather chairs with a small table between them. The American had already called in to make sure a pot of fresh coffee and a selection of pastries were waiting. Each man served himself in turn, then sat down to sip the coffee and enjoy sweet rolls, making light conversation.

Saviz Kahnani was the Iranian chargé d'affaires, who represented his ambassador on special occasions. He, like Joplin, was one of those silent gentlemen who worked behind the scenes on delicate matters of international diplomacy. This very late get-together was one of those situations.

After a quarter hour of chitchat and munching, the Iranian looked quizzically at his American host, saying, "Well, well. What occasion has brought us together this evening, Carl?"

"A discussion regarding that little situation on the Iran-Afghanistan border seems to be in order," Joplin replied.

Kahnani smiled and nodded. "Why aren't I surprised?"

"Why indeed?" Joplin replied. "The confrontations there, while deadly and explosive, seem to be going nowhere for everyone involved. Don't you think?"

Kahnani only shrugged.

"My government believes it is time to come up with a solution that will save face for everyone concerned," Joplin said.

"Make me trust you, Carl."

"I'll do my best, Saviz. We are at a stalemate. Neither side is going to come out ahead in this thing. Why keep it up?" He was aware that for the Iranian to agree, his government would have to give up their Persian Empire project. The President and the Secretary of State had sent Joplin without really expecting the Iranians to go for a cease-fire, but thought that the meeting would be a good opportunity for them to start giving it serious consideration.

"Perhaps if the Americans and their coalition friends agreed to pull out of Afghanistan, my government would consider what you're proposing," Kahnani said.

"That can't be done," Joplin replied.

"Then we have no reason to consider the proposal," Kahnani responded, telling a lie in the diplomatic sense. "We do not find ourselves in agreement regarding a stalemate."

"Then there's something else to consider," Joplin said. He reached for the coffeepot. "Care for another cup, Saviz?"

"Thank you, Carl," Kahnani said. He watched Joplin refill the cup, then asked, "What is this 'something else' that must be considered?"

"The Israelis might decide to interfere," Joplin said, setting the pot down.

"They would only interfere if they had America's approval," Kahnani said.

"Not necessarily," Carl stated. "They have had their backs up about the Hezbollah for quite some time now. And that includes the support the group receives from Iran."

"Mmm," Kahnani mused. "Well, dear Carl, I have no authority to make a deal with you this evening. However, I shall pass on your suggestions to my ambassador, who will then take them to Tehran."

That was exactly what Joplin expected, but something in Kahnani's tone of voice disturbed the veteran diplomat. It was an implication that a nasty surprise was in store for the Americans. Joplin kept his face inscrutable as he said, "Tell your ambassador not to fail to mention the Israelis."

"As you wish."

CHAPTER 17

DIRK Wallenger sat in his dressing room, the makeup for that evening's show freshly applied by a young intern working at the studio for the summer. The newscaster's tie was correct, and his jacket was over the back of his chair and ready to slip into when he was summoned to the set. Everything was ready for the upcoming broadcast of confessing his error to the public. Some of the crew, in fact, were looking forward to it with a certain amount of unrestrained glee. The newscaster could be an arrogant, demanding ass at times.

Wallenger stared at himself in the mirror as he sank into a mood of self-reflection. Don Allen's censure of the story of the prisoner of war had actually hurt his feelings more than angered him. He had to admit that Don was absolutely correct. He had been so anxious to strike a blow for his own political and philosophical causes that he had broadcast a falsehood fed to him by people wanting to have their sham propaganda over national TV. And to make things worse, he had even put an additional slant on it.

Wallenger now realized that he had gotten a bad perspective on the story because of his passionate hatred of authority in general and politicians in particular. When they conducted war—justified of not—his basic attitudes warped his self-control. Although he abhorred armed conflict, he really wasn't a pacifist and saw no sense in being one. Pacifism would work only if every person on the planet felt that way. But that would never be, since there were always sons of bitches such as the Taliban, Nazis, or Communists who were more than ready and willing to shove their agenda of conquest and domination down the throats of the populations they wished to control. And there were never problems for the despots to get enough followers for them to get the job done.

In truth, Wallenger wasn't surprised about the war against the militant groups of Islam. They were asking for it since 9/11, not to mention the crimes committed in Madrid and London. Those episodes had been as stupid as the Japanese attack on Pearl Harbor. Not only were the Islamic fundamentalists going to be stomped out of existence, but other Muslims who had failed to loudly and publicly condemn the zealots would end up paying a high price as well. Wallenger's problem was that he let his dislike of politicians and financiers such as his father get mixed up in some of the most important areas of his life. He knew he had to stop being a mere commentator on the war and get out there where it was happening to develop a more realistic attitude about the fighting and the people actually doing it. That would be a great way of developing a logical understanding of the process.

He looked at his reflection in the mirror again, noting the fatigue and sadness in his face. He decided what he needed was to go over to Virginia that weekend for some cross-country horse riding. That was one physical activity he was damn good at.

"Mr. Wallenger!"

The voice startled him, and Wallenger spun around. He

saw Fred, the floor director, standing in the dressing room door with clipboard in hand. "Mr. Wallenger, it's time for you to come out to the set."

"Thanks, Fred."

Wallenger slipped into his jacket and grabbed his script, walking out of the room and down the hall. When he stepped onto the set, he saw Don Allen standing by the cameras. Allen came over to him. "How are you feeling, Dirk?"

"Okay," Wallenger said. "Don't worry. I'll do exactly as Brice said. But at the end of crying mea culpa, I have an announcement to make. I want you to pay close attention to it and acquiesce to what I plan to do."

"Now just a minute!" Allen said, walking toward the news desk at the journalist's side. "What is on your mind?"

Wallenger sat down. "You just listen."

"I'm warning you, Dirk. Any smart-ass action on your part could mean the absolute end of your career as a newsman."

"Quiet!" Fred hollered loudly. He looked at Wallenger. "Five, four, three, two, one, go!"

"Good evening, ladies and gentlemen," Wallenger said the as the red light lit up on the center camera. "This is Dirk Wallenger with the news." He paused for a quick moment, then turned his eyes directly into the lens. "One of the most nutritious meals—spiritually nutritious, that is—is humble pie. And I am about to consume a great, big heaping dish of that bittersweet food."

Don Allen felt a little better, but he was still worried about what would be said at the end of the spiel.

"I made a mistake," Wallenger said. "A big mistake by journalistic standards. I inadvertently was given some erroneous information by a previously unimpeachable source and broadcast it to you without properly determining its veracity. The story to which I am referring is the one regarding a wounded Arab prisoner of war who was shot to death by his American captors. I informed you that they did this because they did not wish to be burdened with carrying him to a place where he could receive medical treatment for his injuries.

"The story is not true.

"The prisoner in question was indeed killed. But he was not wounded. In fact, he was in perfect health and attempting to escape. He was running away and refused to respond to orders to halt and ran into a rocky area, where he was bitten by a poisonous cobra snake. Unfortunately, the U.S. Navy SEALs who had captured him were unable to save his life because of a lack of proper medical supplies. He died from the reptile's bite rather than being summarily executed. Thus there was no violation of the Geneva Convention. No war crime was committed in this instance. It was a terribly unfortunate misadventure brought on the prisoner by his own actions.

"I apologize to you for my error and I promise you most sincerely and solemnly that I will never—*never*—repeat such misconduct. I consider it a sacred trust to get you the truth, the whole truth, and nothing but the truth in my broadcasts. I shall be most diligent in following this self-appointed requisite in the future. I can only humbly beg you to keep your faith in me. I was wrong. And I am sorry for it.

"However, let me emphasize that my deep disapproval of the conduct of this war and the individuals in our national government who are mismanaging it continues unabated and stronger than ever. It is because of their incompetent arrogance and self-absorption that situations such as the faulty passing of information occur. They have, in fact, set up an environment of half-truths, outright lies, and other deceptions to cover up their errors in management and judgment in their so-called leadership in this tragedy in the Middle East."

Don Allen now breathed easier, but he felt a twinge of nervousness when Wallenger looked straight at him.

"Therefore," Wallenger continued, "rather than gather my news here in Washington, I intend to travel to the war zone, to be embedded with one of our fighting units. I will never again rely on what others tell me. I will report back to you from the battlefields and the field hospitals to give you the unvarnished truth of what is going on in that hellhole our government has created."

Fred the floor manager announced, "Fade to commercial! Three minutes!"

Allen walked over to the news desk. "Well done, Dirk. Are you serious about wanting to go to Iraq and/or Afghanistan?"

"That is my request, Don."

"Granted."

BALTSCHUG-KEMPINSKI HOTEL
MOSCOW, RUSSIA
25 AUGUST
2300 HOURS

THE hotel's luxury suites at its front corner looked out over the Moscow River, giving a magnificent view of the Kremlin. The red star mounted above the structure glowed a bright scarlet over the walls as Dr. Carl Joplin sipped coffee and gazed at the sight. It made him think of Josef Stalin and his cruel domination over the large populace of the now-defunct U.S.S.R. He thought of purges, arrests in the middle of the night, the Gulag with its myriad of death camps, and other horrible features of the despot's reign of terror. Somehow that historical knowledge gave not only the Kremlin but also the nearby St. Basil's Cathedral an aura of evil and hopelessness.

THIS long trip across the Atlantic and the Scandinavian nations into Russia had been unexpected and quite inconvenient. He had been hoping for a call from Saviz Kahnani, the Iranian chargé d'affaires, in regard to the standoff along the border separating Iran and Afghanistan. There was always the possibility of some sort of breakthrough when least expected, but Secretary of State Benjamin Bellingham had summoned him to his office with orders to go directly to Moscow. It was one of those "get over there yesterday" decrees that reminded him that he worked in an atmosphere in which his superiors exercised so much authority over his professional and personal life. To make matters worse, Bellingham had absolutely no idea what was going on.

"All I can say, Carl," the Secretary of State said irritably, "is that you are to meet your Russian counterpart in Moscow. I believe his name is Crash-Sinko or something."

"Krashchenko," Joplin said. "His name is Yuri Krashchenko."

"Oh, yeah, that's the guy," Bellingham said. "He wants you to be available at the usual spot sometime in the evening of the twenty-fifth. So you better hurry."

NOW Joplin was in the "usual spot," and he had been there since ten o'clock that morning. A bit more than thirteen hours had gone by since his arrival, and he was a trifle irritated with the delay. What if Kahnani was at this very moment trying to summon him? It was four o'clock in the afternoon back in Washington. The Iranian might want another one of those sessions at the *Bonhomme Richard* Club.

A knock at the door broke into the peevishness that Joplin was beginning to actively nurture. He walked from the living room to the hall, past the bathroom to the suite entrance. A glance through the peephole revealed a husky, athletic young man standing on the other side. That most certainly was not Yuri Krashchenko. Joplin opened the door.

"Dobriy vyechyir," Joplin said.

The young man ignored the greeting. *"Tih Doktor Joplin?"*

"Da," Joplin answered. Then he saw the short, stout figure of Krashchenko standing by the elevator. Joplin grinned and switched to English. "Come on in, Yuri. There are no secret agents here. I'm sure you can cross the hall in safety."

Krashchenko made no reply as he walked over with a briefcase shoved under his arm. He entered the suite, and since the brawny greeter showed no inclination to follow, Joplin closed the door. He took Krashchenko to the living room.

"Nice view, huh?" Joplin asked, gesturing toward the window.

"You have vodka?"

"Sure," Joplin replied. "Right over there, at the bar. All sorts of liquor came with the suite. Help yourself."

Krashchenko walked across the room and pulled a tumbler

from the shelf. He filled it from a bottle of Dolgoruki brand vodka, put it to his lips, and downed the whole thing in three gulps. After refilling the glass, he walked to the sofa and sat down.

Joplin joined him, settling into an easy chair on the other side of the coffee table. "What can I do for you, Yuri?"

"We are aware of situation on Afghanistan border with Iran," the Russian said. "We do not want to get involved."

"I think our President already knows that."

"But we can help in this particular instance," Krashchenko said. "Most surreptitious. That I emphasize. You understand?"

"I understand perfectly."

Krashchenko placed the briefcase on the coffee table, opened it, and pulled out a packet of blueprints. "Here. For you. It must not be known you have received this in Moscow."

Joplin opened the package and looked inside. "Mmm. I see. It seems to be a mine or something. And it's all in Russian."

"Is that problem?"

"Not really," Joplin said. "And what are we to do with these?"

"Here for you are complete plans of fortified mountain where Iranian and Arabs are being where you fight them on the Afghanistan and Iran frontier," Krashchenko said. "All bunkers, trenches, entrances, and exits are clearly shown."

"Good God!" Joplin exclaimed. "Yeah! That place was constructed by Russian military engineers, wasn't it?"

"We are hoping these will be help for you."

"They certainly will! Thank you very much."

Krashchenko downed the second glass of vodka and stood up. "Now I am going. Good-bye, Carl."

"Good-bye, Yuri."

Joplin accompanied him to the door, opening it. "Thank you again for the blueprints."

"What blueprints?" Krashchenko said, shrugging. *"Da svidaniya."*

**SEAL BASE CAMP
HEADQUARTERS BUNKER
28 AUGUST
1000 HOURS**

BRANNIGAN had called an officers and chiefs conference, and Lieutenant Jim Cruiser, Ensign Orlando Taylor, SCPO Buford Dawkins, and CPO Matt Gunnarson were all seated on rough-hewn stools waiting for the Skipper to begin the proceedings.

"I'm getting a lot of pressure from Carey about that goddamn DPV I gave to Randy Tooley," Brannigan said. "And Carey in turn is getting leaned on real heavy from Station Bravo supply. The damn thing is on their property books, and they want an accounting—in writing—*now*! I need some serious intelligent input and advice on this situation."

The senior chief spoke up first. "Lie about it, sir."

"It's going to have to be a pretty clever lie," Brannigan said.

"Not necessarily," Cruiser said. "You can claim it was lost in the normal course of things."

"I'd have to pay for it."

"Tell 'em the enemy stole it," Chief Gunnarson suggested. "Or destroyed it with hostile fire."

"How can I do that?" Brannigan said. "We won all the battles."

"Bad luck," Cruiser said, and then quickly added, "Well, you know what I mean."

Ensign Taylor spoke up. "I have a suggestion, sir."

Cruiser chuckled. "All due respect, Ensign, but I don't think you've been in the Navy long enough to get down and dirty about a situation like this. Figuring out a way to get away with it will take a lot of savvy and experience."

Taylor shrugged. "I suppose you're right, sir."

"C'mon!" Brannigan said. "Let's give the young man a chance. Out of the mouths of babes, right?"

"Well, sir, I've noticed that Petty Officer Murchison has a way with words," Taylor said. "Sometimes it's very difficult to understand him. Perhaps if he wrote up an explanation in an ambiguous way that really didn't say anything but looked impressive, the people at Station Bravo could write off the vehicle easily and quickly. They could attach it as an endorsement to their own report of the affair."

"Great idea!" Brannigan exclaimed. "They really don't want the damn thing back, but they have to cover their asses. That supply officer doesn't want to pay for the vehicle any more than I do."

"Murchison is in my section," Dawkins said. "I'll brief him on the problem."

Monty Sturgis, the petty officer of the watch, stepped into the bunker. "Chopper's coming," he announced. "Two visitors. Can't see who they are from here."

"Right," Brannigan said. "I can't wait to see who they might be." Then he added under his breath, *"Not!"*

Ten minutes later, Lieutenant Commander Ernest Berringer entered with PO Doug MacTavish. The SEAL who had been wounded was in good spirits as he reported in. His face, which had taken a combined load of shrapnel, rocks, and dirt in the explosion that injured him, still showed the effects of the incident. But it was obvious he was healing nicely. There was none of the tattooing that Doc Bradley had feared.

Ensign Taylor was happy to see his SAW gunner back in action. "It's great to have you home again, MacTavish. We've had need of your expertise. You play pretty tunes on that squad automatic weapon."

"Glad to be here, sir," MacTavish said.

Berringer spoke in his usual somber manner. "He's not going to be here long. And neither are the rest of you. A detachment of Army Rangers is coming in to relieve you. You're to be back at Shelor Field by tomorrow at the latest."

"What's with this shit, sir?"

"All I know is that orders came down to move you guys back to Shelor Field," Berringer explained. "And I don't think it's for R and R."

Brannigan pointed over to the informal supply dump just outside Doc Bradley's clinic. "It's gonna take us a hell of a long time to pack all this stuff up."

"Leave it for the Army," Berringer said. "All you lug out

of here is your personal weapons and equipment. Leave the fifty-caliber machine guns too."

"Aren't I charged with all that?" Brannigan asked in way of a protest.

"Your name is removed from all supply and ordnance considerations here," Berringer assured him.

"Does that include the DPV?" Brannigan asked.

"There's never been a desert patrol vehicle up here on Operation Battleline," Berringer said. "And you're still going to have to answer for the one that was misplaced during Operation Rolling Thunder."

"Not to worry," Brannigan said. "The paperwork is in the mill." He turned to his section leaders. "You heard the commander. Go round up your guys. It's moving day."

"The chopper will be here at fourteen hundred hours," Berringer said.

The officers and chiefs left the bunker to muster their sections and teams.

SEAL HANGAR
SHELOR FIELD
30 AUGUST
1300 HOURS

BRUNO Puglisi sat next to his buddy Joe Miskoski among the other SEALs scattered around on folding chairs. The last two days had dragged by very slowly. Puglisi whispered, "They might as well leave this meeting stuff set up permanent."

"Yeah," Miskoski agreed. "I'm beginning to feel like I've spent half my Navy career getting briefed in this freakin' hangar."

Mike Assad, in the row just behind them, leaned forward. "Yeah. But this time we're gonna really be able to go at the bad guys down and fucking dirty, man!"

"Sail on!" Puglisi agreed with a wicked grin.

Brannigan, Jim Cruiser, and Orlando Taylor were in the cubbyhole of an office with Commander Tom Carey and Lieutenant Commander Ernest Berringer. When the latter

two officers had shown up at Shelor Field after the Brigands'
impromptu transfer from the OA, they had kicked up everyone's adrenaline with the revelation of the blueprints of the
Zaheya mountain fortress. A well-hidden and skillfully camouflaged rear entrance was plainly shown on the plans. Now
they knew how the ragheads had managed to get out and
catch up with them during the exfiltration after the HALO
attack.

The officers came out to join the rest of the detachment.
The Skipper, Cruiser, and Taylor went behind the chairs and
stayed on their feet for the briefing that was about to be delivered. Carey and Berringer tacked a blown-up reproduction of
the fortress layout on the wall. Then Berringer stepped aside
while Carey took the floor.

"I can see the eagerness in your eyes," Carey said. "It's
show time! You're going into that goddamn place via that
hidden entrance. We're going to issue a vocal OPORD to you
this afternoon, and when that's done, you'll draw some concussion grenades to take the place of the M-two-oh-threes.
There won't be any machine-gun support per se, but the fire
support section will all carry individual SAWs. That procedure will be explained later."

"When do the festivities start?" Pech Pecheur asked.

"HALO insertion will be in the early morning of one
September," Carey said. "You will launch your attack immediately after landing. You're not going to have a lot of room
inside that damn fortress, so you can forget the fire-and-
maneuver drill. I'm not going to try to fool you guys. This is
gonna be tough and deadly. Figure some hand-to-hand in the
deal. And also keep in mind how confined it's gonna be in
those tunnels and bunkers." He turned and indicated the layout on the wall. "The one thing you won't have to worry
about is having the bastards come at you from all directions.
When the Russians built that place, they kept it simple and
orderly. For all intents and purposes there is only one passageway, but it leads to each separate bunker."

"Man!" Pete Dawson exclaimed. "The few guys in front
are going to catch all the hell."

Brannigan interjected himself into the proceedings.
"We've taken that into consideration. Fire teams will be

rotated as we progress through the place. That will be the section commanders' responsibility. And as soon as the last team of a section has put in its time, the next section will immediately take over."

SCPO Dawkins turned in his seat and looked at the Skipper. "Sir, what about a rear guard? Those Zaheya guys can send some of their own riflemen around the back and come in behind us."

"That's going to be Chief Gunnarson's responsibility," Brannigan responded. "His fire support section with those SAWs is going to set up a perimeter around the area of that rear entrance. There'll be half a dozen of 'em with beaucoup ammo."

Gunnarson now spoke up. "I've been wondering about that, sir. We could end up getting hard-pressed out there in the back. SAWs are great, but I'm sure gonna miss those beautiful fifties we left them Army guys."

"That's been taken into consideration, Chief," Brannigan said. "Gomez is going to be with you. He'll bring along his faithful Shadowfire radio for long-distance transmissions. He'll also have his AN/PRC-twenty-six to keep in touch with me. So if things get real hairy back there, he can call in CAS from Shelor Field. There'll be half a dozen F/A-eighteens from the local CVBG standing by if needed. They're due to arrive here early this evening."

"What about medevac, sir?" Doc Bradley asked.

"That won't happen until the show comes to an end," the Skipper said. "You'll set up an aid station at that rear entrance close to Gomez and the SAW gunners. We'll bring any wounded down to you during the fighting. You'll have to do your best with 'em there until the situation is under control."

Carey said, "I might add that those carrier guys will also be able to plaster the front of the fortress, if it becomes necessary. However, don't forget the Army Rangers in your old trenches. They'll be keeping an eye on the enemy's front lines, so if you need their help, let 'em know. Any questions or comments about the air or fire support? Okay, then. I'm going to jump to the exfiltration phase, since Lieutenant Brannigan will be covering the procedure you're going to use inside the fortress." He checked his notes. "When it is decided it is time for you to withdraw and you've pretty well shot the place up, you'll make a careful exit and head out the same way you entered. The AFSOC choppers will be in to pick you up. If things didn't go real well and you're under pressure, you'll have to fight a delaying action while you pull back. Once you're out in the open, those F/A-eighteens will be there to turn the back part of the mountain into molten lava. And, of course, the Air Force will make their usual timely appearance. So! I'll let your esteemed commanding officer take over now."

Brannigan walked to the front of the room and gave his men a solemnly proud look. "Guys, this is gonna be a fucking load. So be mentally prepared for it." He walked to the wall, turning his laser pointer on the blueprint. "Now you can tell there are eight—I say again, eight—bunkers inside this place. Each has two entrances, or exits, depending on which way you're going. One leads to the trenches and fighting positions outside and the other to that connecting tunnel within the mountain. It's those interiors we'll be wading through first. That means when you charge into one of those rat holes you'll be exposed to fire coming from outside. The advantage at that point is they'll be firing through a narrow opening."

Matty Matsuno raised his hand. "How's us headquarters weenies gonna be organized, sir?"

"Puglisi and Miskoski are gonna be my goons," Brannigan replied. He looked at the two SEALs. "That means you stick close to me. I'll be directing things and I'll need you two to cover my ass while my attention is directed elsewhere."

"Aye, sir!" the pair responded.

Brannigan swung his eyes to Connie Concord. "The Sneaky Petes are gonna be under your direct command. You'll be the last in the assault column. We'll let Assad be your grenade toter. I'll get to that part of the operation in a minute."

"Understood, sir," Connie acknowledged.

"Now, our basic procedure is going to be simple and calls for everyone to think fast and clearly," Brannigan said.

"We'll all have to be adaptable because each time we hit a bunker the situation is gonna be different. Basically, here's how we'll do it. The team grenadier may not have his M-two-oh-three, but he'll be carrying four concussion grenades. These are something we normally don't deal with, since our application of handthrown explosive devices is to tear up living meat. However, Station Bravo sent some down from their prison."

"What do they do, sir?" Puglisi asked, disappointed that they wouldn't necessarily "whack" anybody.

"They have a stunning capability," Brannigan said. "The reason we chose them was to keep from having our own shrapnel whip back on us. I'd rather we got headaches then a bellyful of pellets or fragments. So each time the lead team comes to a bunker entrance, the grenadier tosses one in, and as soon as it goes off, the entire team charges into the interior. The backup team will then move to the entrance for support, being ready to rush in and lend a hand if necessary."

Jim Cruiser was thoughtful. "If each team has four concussion grenades, then we'll be carrying in a total of twenty-eight. That's more than enough. Hell, with eight bunkers that means we'll have more than three for each one."

"Not if we have to take and retake some of those bunkers four or five times," Brannigan said.

"Oh, shit!" Cruiser remarked.

"Yeah," Brannigan said. "Oh, shit."

Ensign Orlando Taylor was leaning forward in his chair, his concentration and attitude showing he was looking forward to the coming action. "You said we were going to do some battle drill, sir. What was that all about?"

"The Air Force has some unused storage sheds east of the landing strip," Brannigan said. "We'll use them as simulated bunkers and work out the best way to get the job done." He looked at his watch. "Well, we'll start right away. There's only about forty hours before we jump into the OA. Tomorrow we draw ammo, supplies, parachutes, and other goodies." He nodded to Dawkins. "Senior Chief, get the detachment outside."

"Aye, sir!" Dawkins said. "Off and on! Move it!"

Carey and Berringer watched the men get to their feet

and move toward the exit. Berringer was more morose than normal, and he turned to his fellow staff officer, speaking in a low tone. "I wonder how many of 'em are coming back, sir."

"I don't even want to think about it."

CHAPTER 18

ENSIGN Orlando Taylor worked the toggles on his parachute by the book, and he stalled enough to land as gently as if he were stepping off a curb. He grinned happily and looked around to see if any of the others had seen this Class A act. The smile faded as he realized his triumph was not witnessed by any of the other SEALs, who had been occupied with their own PLFs.

A few more light skidding and thumping noises of others landing sounded before everyone was down. The jumpers quickly shucked their chutes and organized M-16s, bandoliers, and grenade pouches as they readied for the bloody job ahead. Within three minutes the detachment was formed up. CPO Matt Gunnarson and his SAW gunners, along with Doc Bradley and Frank Gomez, brought up the rear. Gomez had the combined twenty pounds of the Shadowfire radio and battery to lug, while Doc was burdened with extra medical gear he deemed would be necessary for the mission. He anticipated the worst-case scenario, with several badly wounded men to care for.

Up at the front, Garth Redhawk and Matty Matsuno acted as point, with Mike Assad and Dave Leibowitz backing them up. The middle of the column was formed by Lieutenant Jim Cruiser's First Section, Ensign Orlando Taylor's Second, and SCPO Buford Dawkins' Third. Lieutenant Bill Brannigan and Connie Concord had buddied up as Tail-End Charlies until they could rejoin the Sneaky Petes for the assault on the mountain fortress.

0105 HOURS

REDHAWK and Matsuno had the same deadly task as in the first HALO assault, but this time it would be in a different place. The original attack outflanked the southern enemy positions and worked its way down the Zaheya MLR. This time the two point guys would be taking out a guard or guards at the camouflaged entrance to the fortress interior. In fact, the Brigands would literally be going in through the back door.

It took twenty minutes of careful maneuvering to get into position to sight the ingress within the heavy thorn vegetation and boulders. The two SEALs' NVGs showed only one guard on duty, and he didn't seem to be too attentive to or concerned about the assignment. The ragheads obviously considered the place secure, and had posted a sentry simply because it was SOP to have someone at each entrance and exit. Redhawk and Matsuno had agreed that it was the Japanese-American's turn to tend to this latest unpleasant silent killing, and he pulled his K-Bar knife from its scabbard.

Matsuno moved softly through the darkness, working around a stand of tangled brush, then easing between a camouflage net and the mountainside. The dozing guard squatted at the entrance, facing forward with his back against a rocky outcrop. Matsuno moved in, bent down, and drove the sharp blade into the guy's throat, then pushed the blade sideways, slicing around to the jugular vein. The gurgling and gagging were muffled by the SEAL's hand and did not last long.

Matsuno spoke into his LASH. "The entrance is cleared."

Brannigan replied, "We're moving up. Go ahead, First Section."

Jim Cruiser and his men appeared at the entrance a couple of minutes later. Rick Morales, the grenadier of Alpha Fire Team, led the way in, a concussion grenade in his hand. Gutsy Olson and Pete Dawson were on his heels, with Cruiser behind them. The Bravo Fire Team followed the section commander.

The Sneaky Petes left the entrance area and made their way back down the column until joining with Brannigan and Connie Concord. Then they assumed a fire team formation and trailed closely behind the senior chief's section. The column had now penetrated 100 percent into the interior of the fortress.

When the last man entered, Chief Matt Gunnarson kept his men outside, arranging them in a defensive perimeter, with the SAWs around the ingress site. At the same time, Doc Bradley and Frank Gomez found a good place within a stand of rocks to set up their combination commo and medical center. The dead guard still lay slumped over, the last of his life's blood now pumped out of him through the large, jagged wound inflicted by Matty Matsuno.

0115 HOURS

THE going was slow, since sound discipline was vital at this stage of the assault. There were a couple of places where the tunnel either narrowed perceptibly or made sharp turns. The tight spots required extra care to avoid bumping weapons or equipment against the stone sides. Any noise created in such incidents would be intensified in the tubular environment. The tunnel was also leading upward at a ten-degree angle, meaning that it required extra sound discipline because of the tougher walking conditions.

A light glowed dimly ahead, getting steadily brighter as they moved toward it. Suddenly Morales sighted the entrance to a bunker. "We're ready to make the big move."

"Do it," Brannigan said.

THE BATTLE

MORALES looked into the bunker, noting that the men inside were sleeping. A glance to the right showed the egress to the trench in front. He looked back to get the combined attention of Gutsy Olson and Pete Dawson, then pointed to it. They nodded to indicate they were ready.

Morales pulled the pin on the concussion grenade and tossed it into the interior. The explosive device clattered across the rock floor, then detonated. Morales leaped in, his M-16 spurting three-round automatic bursts into the sleeping men. Gutsy Olson and Pete Dawson covered the exit to the trenches, and a moment later a Zaheya man stepped inside, totally bewildered by what had just happened. His arms flew up and he staggered back into the trench, to collapse under the impact of the combined volley cut loose by the two SEALs. Olson led the way outside to the trench, with Dawson half a step behind. They rushed across the narrow, open area to a sandbagged parapet, then turned their weapons down the Zaheya defensive line, squeezing out more bursts at ragheads rushing their way. The impromptu enemy attack broke off as they took casualties. The survivors sought shelter in bunkers and ramparts.

Now Monty Sturgis and Andy Malachenko of Bravo Fire Team joined Morales as he pulled another concussion grenade from his pouch. He went to the entrance of the next bunker and tossed the explosive inside. As soon as it exploded he jumped in, but before he could fire, he caught a four-round volley straight in his chest. He died immediately, and both Sturgis and Malachenko leaped over him, chopping down his killers. They cleared the place with a few more fusillades, then turned their fire on the two enemy soldiers in the trench outside. At the same time, Olson and Dawson advanced up the line to the next redoubt in the defensive line. Lieutenant Jim Cruiser led Malachenko and Sturgis outside to join them. Now the Brigands' attack was a double-pronged operation, moving through the fortress, through the bunkers, and down the trench.

This was when Ensign Orlando Taylor brought his Second

Assault Section up to take over the advance position of the attack.

BRIGADIER Shahruz Khohollah was having a hell of a time figuring out what was going on. All discipline among the Zaheya units had fallen apart, and the babbling over the LASH commo sets had merged into a steady, unintelligible noise of combined Arabic and Farsi.

Sikes Pasha had hurriedly dressed and grabbed four bandoliers of ammo for his FA-MAS rifle. His first reaction was that the Americans were storming the trenches, but he quickly determined that if they were, it was a pretty weak assault. He made some quick inquiries of nearby Zaheya soldiers, learning that a couple of the fighting sites had fallen, but that was all. A full five minutes went by before he was able to figure out that the attack was actually inside *and* outside the fortress. He rushed toward the fighting through the complex until brought to a stop when he encountered Warrant Officer Shafaqat Hashiri desperately directing the defense inside a bunker now under fire. Hashiri was glad to see his commanding officer.

"Sikes Pasha! Two of our bunkers have fallen, and they are pressing the attack against this one," Hashiri reported breathlessly. "The enemy is outside in the trenches, and we cannot engage them without sustaining many casualties. I fear they have complete control of the battle."

"Right then," Sikes said, quickly realizing what had to be done. "Pull out o' this one, hey? And we'll set up in the next one back. There's some cover in there you can use. *Kawam!* Hurry it up!"

Hashiri issued the orders, and the bunker was quickly abandoned, leaving three dead Arabs sprawled on the floor.

UZI Melech, the grenadier for Charlie Fire Team, quickly surmised that the bunker ahead of them had been abandoned. But instead of rushing in, he wisely threw his concussion grenade across it and into the next one. Then he and

Pech Pecheur charged in firing, with Ensign Taylor behind them.

The trio ran through the empty bunker to the next entrance, with Delta Fire Team deployed as backup. Suddenly a lone Arab leaped into view and cut loose with his bullpup rifle. Melech caught it in the belly, and he crumpled just as Pecheur blew the Arab away. But other Zaheya soldiers inside had taken cover behind a stack of surplus sandbags that had been filled as replacements for any damaged in future battles. The Arabs popped up and quickly shot off an uncoordinated but effective fusillade that cut down Tony Valenzuela and George Fotopoulos.

"This is Brigand Two," Taylor said. "I've got three casualties in the third bunker. We've taken fire from the fourth. The guys in there have cover. It's either a pile of sandbags or an interior defensive position. I surmise it is the former rather than the latter."

"Keep the door under fire and hunker down!" Brannigan ordered. "Brigand One, are you still outside?"

"Roger," came back Cruiser. "I have four guys with me. I've lost Morales, but I can throw fire down on that fourth bunker."

"You're gonna have trouble hitting anybody in there," Brannigan said. "Concentrate on keeping the enemy from coming down the trench and reaching us here."

"Aye, sir!"

The Skipper started to order the senior chief to move his section forward but was interrupted over the LASH by Frank Gomez. The RTO spoke quietly and efficiently. "I've received a relay over the Shadowfire, sir. The Army Rangers on the other side of the valley want to know if we need fire support."

"Negative! Negative! Negative!" Brannigan yelled. "We can't tell them where to put it because we don't know where we'll be from minute to minute. Cruiser and his guys would be hit. Tell the Army to hold their fire!"

"Aye, sir," Gomez said.

"Everybody on the net listen up," the Skipper said. "Assault sections, press forward and trade shot for shot. Better yet, two shots for every one of theirs. Sneaky Petes along with Puglisi and Miskoski, move forward!"

The fighting in the tunnel and bunkers grew more desperate for both sides. Sikes Pasha left his Arabs in charge of Warrant Officer Hashiri and hurried to answer a summons to the brigadier's Headquarters bunker. When he got there, he found that Captain Naser Khadid and Captain Jamshid Komard had already arrived.

"What's with this meeting?" he asked angrily. "Me blokes are down there up to their ears in Yanks!"

"We realize the situation is grave," Brigadier Shahruz Khohollah said. "It is obvious the Americans have learned about the hidden entrance to the mountain. Once again we have been betrayed."

Khadid was mortified. "I cannot believe that anyone on the General Staff would be sending information to our enemies. The traitor must be getting millions of dollars from Washington for his disloyalty. And, of course, the rewards would include political asylum and a new identity for living in America."

Komard was coldly furious. "He will not live long enough to enjoy that arrangement."

"There could be another source of treachery," Khohollah suggested. "I am thinking it is perhaps the Russians."

"Right now we ain't got the bluddy luxury of thinking about that, do we?" Sikes snapped. "The bastards are in here and we got to throw 'em out, yeah?"

"Of course," the Brigadier said. He turned to Khadid. "Captain, I want you to take ten of your men and go around the northern flank and down the mountain. You are to go directly to the camouflaged entrance. If you meet resistance there, destroy it, then move into the fortress and attack the Americans from the rear."

"I can leave immediately, Excellency!" Khadid said.

Now Khohollah addressed Captain Komard. "Send two of your grenade launcher teams with him for support."

"Yes, Excellency!"

"I shall collect them on my way out," Khadid said, rushing to obey the order.

The Brigadier looked over at Sikes, who had taken the arm of his wounded shoulder and pulled it from the sling. "How are you doing, Major Sikes? You seem to be able to function."

"I'll do me bit, don't worry none about that, sir," Sikes said.

"Excellent," the Brigadier said. He turned his eyes on Captain Komard. "While Captain Khadid is making his attack, you and Major Sikes must combine your forces and pin down the Americans. When we catch them between your group and the detachment of Captain Khadid, we will have the battle won."

The two officers rendered quick salutes, then left the bunker to tend to their duties.

ONCE again the fighting in Operation Battleline had evolved into one of attrition. The four survivors of Ensign Taylor's assault section had now been joined by the seven men of SCPO Dawkins' outfit. Dawkins led his men forward, working to spots within the Second Section's firing line. A moment later the seven Headquarters weenies joined the crowd, adding their firepower to the mix.

Meanwhile, out in the trench, Lieutenant Jim Cruiser was in excellent cover with five SEALs. They were keeping busy preventing Zaheya troops from entering the third bunker from the trench to attack the Brigands in the interior. Several dead ragheads who had been caught in defensive fusillades were sprawled at the entrance, piled one on top of the other. All this happened in the roaring pandemonium of the battle. Any additional Zaheya fighters would have to use interior ingresses to join the fighting, and that put them under the direct fire of the Second and Third Sections.

OUT in the natural cover and concealment around the rear entrance, Chief Matt Gunnarson had arranged his men in a semicircle, with each one able to combine his zone of fire with the guys on both sides of his position. Their SAWs were locked and loaded, and they had plenty of ammo at hand.

Greg Beaver was on the extreme right flank of the Chief's defensive line, which covered the fortress's hidden ingress. Beaver perceived a line of skirmishers that suddenly appeared to his right front. They were moving rapidly toward the SEALs.

"Enemy sighted off my flank," Beaver reported.

An instant later, four incoming grenades from one of the rapid-fire LAG launchers splattered around the SEAL, blowing his life away. The other five SAWs immediately responded by hosing out long fire bursts into the scampering riflemen moving toward them. The attackers responded with two more grenade barrages among the SEALs. The resultant detonations claimed the lives of Arlo Bartholomew and Terry O'Rourke.

Matt Gunnarson sighted one of the enemy grenadiers and fired a quick burst from his M-16, cutting the guy down. "Brigand Boss, this is Big Gun," the Chief said into his LASH. "We're under heavy attack out here from rifles and grenade launchers. I've taken three casualties in the past couple of minutes."

Brannigan's voice came back, calm in spite of the bad news. "Have Gomez call in air support, Chief. Those F/A-eighteens are out there someplace."

"No can do, sir! The enemy is in too close and moving closer. We'd be in as much danger as the bad guys."

"Do your best then, Chief," Brannigan said. "I'll send Puglisi and Miskoski out to you. As of the moment they're the only ones I can spare."

"Send 'em ASAP, sir!"

SIKES had managed to get the jabbering over the LASH quieted down and was able to issue orders to his men in the fourth bunker. He had given up on sending an attack down the trench line to rush into the third bunker, but left a couple of rifleman to keep the Americans outside occupied.

The rest of the Arabs were well protected behind the stack of sandbags. The incoming fire from the third bunker ricocheted off the walls, but all ended up slamming harmlessly into the burlap containers. Now Sikes Pasha's Storm

Troopers didn't bother to aim as they sent blasts of automatic fire into the other bunker, knowing that the slugs
bouncing around in the interior would eventually find live
flesh to plow into.

BRANNIGAN realized the only way they were going
to take that fourth bunker would be to storm through the narrow entrance into the interior. He had fifteen guys with him,
more than enough to get the job done. The only problem was
that the first three or four were sure to be mowed down like
wheat stalks in a Kansas harvest. He couldn't order his men
into a situation of certain death unless he led the way. He
looked over at the SEALs nearest him. His old stalwarts
Mike Assad and Dave Leibowitz were at his side. The Skipper took a deep breath, knowing it was close to being his last.

"We're gonna storm through that door en masse. We'll
have to go in shooting. Leibowitz and Assad, get behind me.
As soon as the three of us get through there, the rest of you
come in on our heels. And pump out those three-round auto
bursts. If you aim just over the sandbags into the wall, your
rounds should ricochet down into the ragheads."

The SEALs were astounded and stopped firing for an instant, then renewed their salvos. Everyone—including Mike
and Dave—knew that they and Lieutenant Bill Brannigan
had as much chance as that proverbial snowball in hell once
they entered the other bunker.

"Everyone put in a fresh magazine," Brannigan ordered.
"Get ready! On my—"

Frank Gomez's voice crackled over the LASH headsets.
"Skipper, word just came over the Shadowfire. Cease fire!
Cease fire and pull out!"

"Say again!" Brannigan angrily demanded.

"We have received orders to cease fire and withdraw."

"Goddamn it, Gomez!" Brannigan said. "Did you authen-
ticate that transmission?"

"Yes, sir."

Brannigan swallowed hard, almost stunned by the as-
tounding news as he managed to utter, "Cease fire."

Now it was CPO Matt Gunnarson over the net. "Brigand

Boss, this is Big Gun. The enemy attack has broken off. They've pulled back."

"Same out here," Jim Cruiser reported. "The enemy is no longer firing. There are no ragheads in the trench."

The quiet that had suddenly descended over the scene of the battle left their punished ears buzzing. Everyone looked at each other in puzzled confusion. Now they heard scuffling in the fourth bunker, and the sounds suddenly faded away. Ensign Orlando Taylor took a cautious look into the interior.

"Skipper, they've withdrawn," he reported. "The place is empty."

"What about that shit," Mike Assad commented. "The war's been called off."

For a long moment, Brannigan said nothing. Then he turned and gestured toward the exit. "Alright! Get the hell out of here."

The SEALs grabbed their dead and abandoned the position, the bodies slung over sturdy shoulders.

OVAL OFFICE
WHITE HOUSE
3 SEPTEMBER (LABOR DAY)
0715 HOURS

THE President showed an apologetic half smile. "Hell of a thing to ask you to work on a holiday, gang."

Arlene Entienne, Carl Joplin, Colonel John Turnbull of the SOLS, and Secretary of State Benjamin Bellingham shrugged it off.

"Well!" the President continued. "The Iranians accepted a cease-fire on the Afghanistan border. The deal was negotiated by Carl with their chargé des affaires here in Washington. Or should I say in Arlington, since it was hashed out at the *Bonhomme Richard* Club."

"Well done, Carl!" Arlene exclaimed. "How in the world did this come about?"

"Saviz Kahnani contacted me about wanting to make a deal," Joplin explained. "He had left a message that I received upon my return from Moscow. Tehran wanted to wrap up this whole brouhaha. I can only assume they sensed they were headed for a disaster and decided to negotiate an end to the affair."

"At any rate," the President said, "the deal was so secret that the Iranian Ambassador didn't know a damn thing about it."

Bellingham was slightly miffed. "And neither did the American Secretary of State. That is who I am, just in case anybody forgot."

"Now, Ben," the President said with a wink, "you and I are only temporarily in Washington until the next administration. Our dear Dr. Joplin is a permanent resident and a career diplomat."

"Our timing was pretty bad, though," Joplin said. "But it couldn't be helped. When the message was sent out, the SEAL team was already heavily engaged in the interior of the enemy mountain fortress."

"The order to cease fire must have surprised them," Arlene commented.

Colonel Turnbull nodded to Joplin. "What's the procedure from this point on, Carl?"

"The idea of the cease-fire was for Iran to make a withdrawal from the border under certain conditions," Joplin replied.

"What about us?"

"Our situation goes on as before," Joplin explained. "We and our partners in the coalition are deeply involved in complicated military operations in Afghanistan. Therefore we gave no quarter."

"Way to go, guy!" Turnbull exclaimed.

"And best yet," Joplin said, "the Iranians have also agreed to negotiate an end to the Persian Empire scheme as well as to begin discussions regarding their nuclear program. It appears they've realized they're going nowhere."

"The UN sanctions didn't hurt," Arlene added. "But what about their dealings on Hezbollah?"

"They're not bringing that to the table," Joplin said.

"Ha!" Turnbull remarked. "That's gonna really piss off the Israelis."

"Yes, it will," Joplin said. "My friend Kahnani gave some

strong hints that Tehran may wish to discuss the Israeli situation with us."

"And there we are," the President said, pleased. He glanced at Benjamin Bellingham. "Well, Mr. Secretary of State, are you ready for a trip to Geneva for a tête-à-tête with your Iranian counterpart?"

"I'm happy to go," Bellingham said.

"There is one very sad aspect of this great accomplishment," the President observed. He had obviously quickly sunk into a somber mood. "Late last night I received a call from the Pentagon. They informed me that the SEAL detachment that took such an active part in this operation suffered almost twenty-five percent casualties."

Colonel Turnbull nodded. "It's called soldiering, Mr. President."

"It is also called a tragedy," the President quietly commented.

CHAPTER 19

BRANNIGAN'S Brigands were back aboard the *Daly*, battered but proud. The detachment was battered by the intense combat and casualties they had endured in Operation Battleline, but proud they could honestly proclaim those words most respected in the world of military professionalism: *Mission accomplished*.

When they evacuated the Zaheya fortress after the astonishing order to cease fire and withdraw, they made their way to the LZ for the rendezvous with the USAFSOC helicopters. They even had time to secure the parachutes off the DZ, and this included a few from the first jump. True to SEAL tradition, the Brigands left no one behind. Their seven dead came out, borne among the twenty-seven living, and were respectfully and lovingly placed aboard the choppers to begin their somber journey back to hometowns and families, to be honored and mourned.

They weren't at Shelor Field long before another aircraft came in, to retrieve them for a surprise flight back to the

Daly that same day. Twenty-four hours later, the detachment was assembled in their usual briefing room aboard the ship, where they learned from Commander Tom Carey that the reason for the cessation of hostilities in the OA was that the government of Iran had capitulated, willing to give up their goal of a Persian Empire as well as enter into serious negotiations with the West in regard to their nuclear ambitions. The mountain fortress in which the fiery battle had been fought in its interior was to be abandoned, and all Iranian troops and their Arab volunteers had been withdrawn from the Afghanistan border. The Zaheya fighters were back in garrison in northwestern Iran, their unit now deactivated.

There was no cheering among Brannigan's Brigands, only a quiet acceptance of the outcome of Operation Battleline. Now they needed some time and space to catch their breath, and work themselves back to their premission way of life. The grinding of a few administrative wheels brought about some transfers of the newer men, since there was no longer a lot for them to do aboard the *Daly*. James Duncan, Lamar Smith, Tom Greene, J. T. Snooker, Chuck Betnarik, Tiny Burke, and Hump Dobbs said their good-byes and were carried away via a U.S. Navy Seahawk chopper to the nearby CVBG for further transportation to other duty stations. That left twenty-four total members of the detachment; five more than they had before the onset of Operation Battleline. Some of the other new men—Ensign Taylor, Matsuno, Benson, Sturgis, and MacTavish—were now permanently assigned to the detachment.

These unexpected reinforcements made the Brigands slightly suspicious. Perhaps the powers-that-be had some future heavy-duty plans for them. Anything could happen in that part of the world.

8 SEPTEMBER
1400 HOURS

ONE sign that the SEALs were ready to get on with things as before was that the BVBL—Brigand Volleyball League—was back in business, reorganized and ready to play its particular brand of the sport. That meant outrageous bad-mouthing, charging under the net and tackling opposition players, refusal to give up the ball when a side's service was ended, and other irregularities that added so much charm to the contests. The two permanently organized teams had no names other than those given them by their opponents, such as the Dickheads, Candy Asses, Ass Faces, and a colorful one from the mind of Chad Murchison who christened the other team as the Ignoble Flâneurs. Bruno Puglisi like the sound of the name until he learned it meant Despicable Loafers. Even then he wasn't quite sure if it was really an insult.

Now, in the second game of the new season, a particularly competitive contest was under way, with a nothing-to-nothing tie score that had held for quite a while. This impasse had occurred because of things such as taped rolls of gasket material being thrown at the servers while they tried to hit the balls over the net. The gaskets were stolen from the engine and maintenance compartments on the vehicle decks forward of the launching dock, and rolled into projectiles that weren't heavy, but stung sharply when they struck anybody. With a little creative effort, the duct tape used in the construction could be fashioned into sharp edges.

Ensign Orlando Taylor thoroughly enjoyed the rough-and-tumble version of volleyball. He found this disregard of any sort of rules or discipline refreshing and stimulating after the strict upbringing in his father's house, where obedience to decorum was paramount. This included forbidding participation in sports because Mr. Taylor considered them detrimental to getting a good education.

The scoreless game that day followed the usual procedures, but things went even more awry when Bruno Puglisi punched Monty Sturgis through the net after he spiked the ball. Sturgis went ape, charging through the stringed barrier so hard that he ripped it in two. He and Puglisi went at it, swinging hard punches and counterpunches viciously as the melee developed. They eventually began kicking at each other amid bellows of encouragement from the other players. The two-man riot could have gone on for a lot longer until a bawling voice drowned out the noise of the ruckus.

"What the fuck is going on?"

The sound of the Skipper's bellowing brought instant peace over the scene. Everyone turned his way, seeing that SCPO Buford Dawkins was with him. The senior chief walked up to the damaged net. "You heard the commanding officer. Answer the question."

Taylor felt it was his responsibility, since he was the senior ranking man present. He stepped forward with a salute, saying, "Sir! We are playing volleyball."

"Ah, yes," Brannigan said. "The BVBL, hey? And there seems to be a league violation of some sort here. At least a somewhat serious disagreement as to whether an infraction has occurred."

"Yes, sir!" piped up a few voices.

"Well, well," Brannigan mused. "Something must be done about this, as in any other sport." He was thoughtful for a few moments, then made an announcement. "As of this moment I am appointing Senior Chief Petty Officer Buford Dawkins as the Commissioner of the Brigand Volleyball League." He turned to Dawkins. "I expect you to hold a hearing on this incident, Commissioner, and see that proper justice is dispensed to all concerned. And remember that good sportsmanship must be encouraged. As the old saying goes, 'It isn't whether you win or lose, but how you play the game.'"

"Aye, sir!" Dawkins said. He glared at the players. "Alright! Assemble in the shade at the aft side of the island. Do it *now!*"

Brannigan walked off as the players headed for the meeting place, with the senior chief following. When they arrived at the spot, each team split off to keep separate from their opponents, and Dawkins gave them yet another scowling glare.

"As officially appointed Commissioner of the Brigand Volleyball League I do hereby call this hearing to order, and that means ever'body shut the fuck up." He paused to make sure his authority was recognized. "Alright! This team on my left. You, Miskoski. What started this ruckus?"

"Well, Senior Chief, my good buddy Petty Officer Second Class Bruno Puglisi of the United States Navy was playing volleyball," Joe announced.

"Was he playing in an officially sanctioned game of the Brigand Volleyball League?" the Senior Chief asked.

"Yes, Senior Chief, and Petty Officer Puglisi was playing a straight-up game when all of a sudden one of them hooligans by the name of Sturgis hauled off and pasted him in his snot locker. For no reason! Then, o' course, Petty Officer Puglisi had to perfect hisself to keep from getting the shit beat out of him."

"Okay," the Senior Chief said. "That's enough. Now I need a spokesguy from the other team. Murchison, you"—he stopped speaking—"on the other hand, nobody can understand what you say. So Assad, you testify."

"Right, Senior Chief. And I'd like to say straight off that Miskoski is a goddamn rotten liar and I wouldn't trust him any further than that snake that bit the raghead. And I mean that in all respect."

"So noted," the Senior Chief said. "Proceed with your testimony."

"Well, my teammate and gentleman Petty Officer *First* Class Montgomery Sturgis, who I would like to remind you outranks his assassin, was attacked and nearly killed during the game by Petty Officer *Second* Class Bruno 'the Brute' Puglisi right after making a legal, authorized spike of the ball. And I ain't sure, but I thought Puglisi pulled a knife on Monty. Anyhow, he attacked poor Monty out of pure meanness."

"Okay, that's enough," the Senior Chief said. He appeared to lapse into deep thought for a few moments, then said, "I've reached a verdict. Both Puglisi and Sturgis are guilty of poor sportsmanship, cheating, and assault and battery, along with conduct unbecoming a human being. I therefore fine them four cases of beer each. They are to have said brew purchased no later than two bells in the evening watch, and see that it is placed iced-down and cold in the ready room. At that time the beer will be consumed by all members of the SEAL detachment commanded by Lieutenant Wild Bill Brannigan. I have rendered my decision in this matter, and it is final! Dismissed!"

Everyone, with the exception of Puglisi and Sturgis, cheered the outcome of the hearing. The sharing of this costly punishment wiped away the animosity between them.

Things were back to normal.

IRANIAN SF CAMP
NORTHWESTERN IRAN

THE camp actually had no name, and was referred to as *ordu makhus*—the special camp—by both the Iranian government and the Army.

One of the small garrison's denizens, Major Archibald Sikes—aka Sikes Pasha—had recovered completely from his shoulder wound suffered during the fighting on the Afghanistan border. It was still a bit stiff and if he turned over on it in his sleep, it smarted enough to wake him. However, he had full use of the arm, and there didn't appear to be any permanent disability involved. But he wasn't worried about the injury anyway. He had only half a dozen survivors of his Arabs, including Warrant Officer Shafaqat Hashiri, and he was fretful as hell about his situation.

The whole Iranian thing he'd been sucked into was falling apart. In fact, the Iranians were now showing more concern about themselves than any grandiose plans of conquest that encompassed the entire Middle East. There was no more talk about their Persian Empire or the program to develop Shiite insurgencies as part of their armed forces. If Sikes were thrown out on his ass, he would be what is known as persona non grata—unwanted, useless, shunned, and shit-out-of-luck no matter where he went in the world. As a man with no country or passport, he would be vulnerable to arrest by British authorities. And that would mean long years in a military prison.

He needed a drink bad, but here he was, deep in the Islamic world, where consumption of alcohol was considered a sin.

1900 HOURS

THE officers in the camp were quartered in tents like everyone else, except they had wooden slat floors so they didn't have to walk on the dirt inside their domiciles, like the lower-ranking men. Their furnishings were slightly better as well, with a cot, chair, small table with a drawer, and a simple frame wardrobe. There was also a net to keep insects out, stretched across the front of the canvas structure. The exception among the officers was Brigadier Shahruz Khohollah, who had a comfortably furnished bunker complete with a carpet.

Sikes shared the accommodations with his former mentor, Khalil Farouk, but the old friendship had faded quite a bit. The Brit no longer trusted his Arab companion, and kept his personal feelings about the current situation to himself.

Sikes sat in his chair, his feet upon the table, smoking a Turkish cigarette from a carton given him by the brigadier, when he noticed some commotion toward the main gate to the garrison. He walked to the tent opening and stepped outside. He could see a car drive up from the camp interior to meet another, larger sedan, which had just arrived. Soldiers scurried around to get out some luggage, while a man wearing safari-type garb made up of a khaki shirt, trousers, and desert boots stepped out of the vehicle. A gray felt Australian hat with the brim turned up on one side topped off his attire.

Sikes grinned to himself at the familiar individual he could recognize even at a distance. It was the arms dealer Harry Turpin, who had a contract with the Iranians to provide them with the latest in modern military weaponry, vehicles, and equipment.

"I wonder what that bluddy old bastard is up to," Sikes mused.

2100 HOURS

SIKES wasn't sleepy, and he lay on top of the covers listening to the deep breathing of his companion, Farouk, across the tent. Boredom pressed down so heavily on Sikes that he didn't care if a vehicle drove up and a couple of Iranian secret police goons got out and dragged him off to be summarily shot. In fact, he would welcome it.

Then a car did come to a stop outside the tent.

Sikes sat straight up, then relaxed at the sight of the man getting out. "Hello, Harry," he said. "I saw your arrival a coupla hours ago." He got to his feet and opened the net to let the Cockney enter the tent.

"'Ow are you, Archie, me lad?" Turpin said in his East End London accent. He nodded to Farouk, who had awakened. "And 'ow are you, Farouk, you ol' rascal?"

"I am very well, thank you," Farouk said. "It is so nice to be seeing you again."

"Oh, I'm good news for the two o' you," Turpin said. "You can bet your last shilling on that. Or pence or Euro or whatever the bluddy 'ell they're using in Blighty nowadays."

"Sit down, Harry," Sikes said. "Sorry, but we got no proper drinks to offer you."

"Sobriety is the scourge of Islam," Turpin said. He winked at Farouk. "No wonder you blokes are always looking for a fight."

"I admit I have enjoyed a whiskey now and then," Farouk confessed. "But here we have no choice. But we do have some canned fruit juice."

"I've got me own refreshments back in the bluddy tent, thank you," Turpin said, settling on the camp chair while Sikes and Farouk went back to sit down on their respective bunks.

Sikes leaned forward. "Wot d'you mean, you got good news for us, Harry?"

"Wot do I mean?" Turpin said with a wide grin. "I'll tell you, alright. I'm a vanguard, that's wot I am, see? I'm an 'arbinger of good news. I 'ave just made arrangements to bring in surplus East German tanks from Belarus, 'ey? Right straight to this camp. Also plenty o' small-arms ammo, shells for artill'ry and mortars and the like. And this deal also includes self-propelled cannons."

"And you're having 'em delivered here?" Sikes asked.

"Right 'ere where we are this very minute," Turpin said.

"You lads are gonna take part in a big push. A bluddy invasion, that's wot it's gonna be."

Sikes and Farouk looked at each other, then back to Turpin. Farouk shook his head. "I am not understanding what you say to us, Harry. We have just pulled back from the Afghanistan border. Where on Allah's earth will we be going?"

Turpin laughed loudly. "Right back to where you come from, mate. You and this lot are gonna be storming across the international line straight into Afghanistan. Not only are more Iranians coming 'ere, but Shiites too."

Sikes was so astounded that he stood up. "But Iran has just made an agreement with the Yanks to stay away from Afghanistan."

"Well, Archie me lad, then it looks like the Yanks are in for a great big fucking surprise, ain't they?

MANCHESTER, ENGLAND
9 SEPTEMBER
1930 HOURS

CHARLIE and Nancy Sikes sat in their small parlor, watching TV. Neither one was paying much attention to the program, which was a sitcom involving a dysfunctional family feuding with their neighbors, who were another dysfunctional clan unable to cope with life's little problems.

Charlie and Nancy had real-life worries and saw no humor in the comic performances of the actors in the program. Their son Archibald, a soldier in the British Army, had deserted his unit in Iraq and had not been heard from for many long months. They didn't know if he was dead or alive.

The doorbell rang, and Mrs. Sikes walked out to the hall and down to the entrance to the house. She opened door and saw two bobbies in full uniform and helmets at the simple portal. "Good evening, madam," one of the policemen said. "Is Mr. Charles Sikes at home?"

Mrs. Sikes didn't answer. She turned and hollered. "Charlie! There's a couple o' coppers asking after you."

Mr. Sikes appeared in the hall from the parlor with a puzzled expression on his face. "Wot can I do for you?"

"We'd like you to come down to the station, if you please, Mr. Sikes," the spokesman said.

"Wot for?"

"A routine inquiry, sir. We must ask you to come straight-away, please."

"I'll get me coat." He reached over to the hooks on the wall and pulled off his jacket and an American baseball-style cap, then stepped past his wife. "I'll be back soon. Maybe we'll learn something about Archie."

"Alright, Charlie."

The two policemen took him down to their car and opened the back door. Mr. Sikes settled in for the ride, with heavy sus-picions that this unexpected happening would indeed have something to do with Archie. This wasn't the first time some official had come around to make inquiries. But it was the first time he had ever been taken anywhere.

When they reached the station, they went around to the back and parked. Once more Mr. Sikes was under close es-cort as they took him inside, going straight to a room with a small table that had one chair on one side and two on the other. The policemen took him to the single seat.

"Sit down, Mr. Sikes. Someone will be with you quite soon."

"Right. Thanks."

Five minutes later, two men entered. Mr. Sikes knew one of them. He had been out to the house on at least three occa-sions. The man's name was Falkes, and Sikes figured him for a military policeman. In actuality, he was MI-5, and the man with him was from a special unit of Scotland Yard that worked the terrorist detail.

Falkes nodded a greeting as he and the other man sat down. "How are you, Mr. Sikes?"

"Fine, thanks," he said, glancing at the other man. "Who's he then?"

"This is Inspector Jenkins from Scotland Yard."

"Are we gonna be talking about me son Archie?"

"In a roundabout way," Jenkins interjected. He reached in his suit pocket and pulled out a pair of four-by-five photo-graphs. "Do you know these two men?"

Sikes studied the portraits. "Yeah. This one here is Hasim

and the other is Afsar. I don't know their last names. That is, I don't remember 'em. Them kind o' names are hard to re-collect."

"Where do you know them from?"

"They work at the same warehouse where I do," Sikes replied. "They're stock boys."

Falkes asked, "Do you see them at places other than work?"

Sikes shook his head.

"What about the pub? Have you ever gone out and had a pint or two with them?"

"They ain't the type I'd choose for friends," Sikes said. "I don't like Pakos or Arabs or none o' them Wog blokes. And I don't think their religion lets 'em drink beer or whiskey anyway. I wish to hell they'd all go back where they come from, that's wot I bluddy wish. Let England be England, by Gawd!"

"They're from Iraq," Jenkins said. "The same country where your son deserted from the Army."

"All that trouble started when them swells in that Dragoon regiment wouldn't give Archie a commission," Sikes said defiantly. "He was good enough to be a sergeant, by God, and he was good enough to attend officers' training school and go to another regiment, but they said he wasn't acceptable in their precious mess, hey? Archie ain't the type to take being snubbed quiet. One thing led to another and it ended up with him taking French leave."

"He did more than that," Falkes said. "He didn't just go off without permission, he left without the intention of re-turning."

"Wot's that got to do with the price o' tea in China?"

Falks leaned toward him, resenting the flippant remark. "I'll tell you what it's got to do with, Sikes. It's got to do with you and your son. We now know an Iraqi was instrumental in getting your son away from the military. And Archibald Sikes has been actively working with the terror-ists in Afghanistan."

"Now, I don't believe that for an instant," Sikes said.

"And those two Iraqi lads are now in custody for taking part in a bombing in Leeds," Jenkins said. "And we know they have a contact here in the United Kingdom. And we know he's an Englishman."

"Well, I ain't working with no bombers!"

"We got a few questions to put to you, Sikes," Falkes said coldly. "And we advise you to cooperate. It'll be for your own good."

"Bluddy shit!" Sikes exclaimed. "I want me solicitor!"

"You've been brought in under the Antiterrorist Act, Sikes," Jenkins said. "And if you want some advice, here's some. You better cough up the truth when it comes to answering our questions. One slip! One rotten lie, and you're for it. Understand?"

"Oh, bluddy shit!"

"Get ready, Sikes," Falkes said. "It's going to be a long night."

10 SEPTEMBER
1000 HOURS

MRS. Nancy Sikes didn't know whether to worry or not. Her husband, Charlie, had gone off the night before with two policemen and still wasn't home. Surely there hadn't been an accident or anything. She would have been informed. Maybe they had some news about Archie. She left the kitchen and went to the front window for the tenth time that morning. On this occasion she was rewarded with the sight of a police car pulling up to the curb. Charlie got out of the back and walked toward the house. It was easy to see he was dead tired.

She ran to the door and jerked it open. "Charlie! Wot's been going on then?"

He came in and hung up his cap and jacket. When he turned toward her, she could see his bloodshot eyes and the paleness of his face. He shook his head slowly. "Oh, Nancy! Them coppers been giving me bluddy hell all night. Two of them Wog lads at the warehouse was arrested for a bomb plot. They figured I was in on it because o' Archie. I had a god-awful time convincing 'em I didn't know nothing about it."

"Oh, poor Charlie," Nancy said. "Come out to the kitchen, love. I'll make you a nice cup o' tea."

He followed her, saying, "I thought they might have some news about the lad, but all they told me was that he was a terrorist or something."

Mrs. Sikes went to the stove to put on a pot as Mr. Sikes sat down. He sighed audibly. "I better call work and tell 'em why I ain't in yet."

"Well, you tell 'em why," Mrs. Sikes said. "It wasn't your fault, Charlie."

"They know about Archie deserting, Nancy, and some o' the blokes has been making remarks about it. This is probably the excuse they've been looking for to give me the bluddy sack."

"The union won't let 'em do that, Charlie."

"The union ain't exactly sympathetic toward me," Mr. Sikes said. He suddenly slammed his hand down hard on the table. "Goddamn it! That boy of ours has got us into some deep shit!"

Mrs. Sikes stifled a sob, then recovered and wiped her eyes. "The tea will be ready in a minute, love."

CHAPTER 20

CUSTIS FARM, VIRGINIA

THE facility, made up of three hundred acres of U.S. government property, was not a working agricultural site, although the people who used it referred to it as "the Farm." It was far off the beaten track, surrounded by deep sections of forest and bog, and kept under rigid security. A narrow dirt lane that wound ten miles off the main county road was the only way to reach it overland. The likelihood of some wandering stranger blundering onto the property was not probable but possible. Therefore, to discourage any exploration by the curious, the two creeks on the acreage were not bridged. Although the water was no more than a couple of feet deep, it was enough to keep anyone from wanting to venture farther in their automobile or truck. And just in case some weekend adventurer with his off-road vehicle showed up, roving teams of guards who appeared to be rather tough-looking farmers provided further dissuasion. These individuals were part of a large staff that performed security and service functions for the Farm. They were rotated every two weeks from the isolated assignment.

Persons who used it for official functions preferred to come by air, utilizing either the helicopter pad or a short airstrip in the center of the bucolic estate. The Farm's main building was a one-story, split-level rambling ranch house that seemed completely out of place. It appeared as if belonged more in a California suburb than the environment of rural Virginia.

Undersecretary of State Carl Joplin, PhD, was the only government official who maintained a permanent office in the place. His boss, Secretary of State Benjamin Bellingham, had not been assigned any space within the large house, nor had he ever been to the Farm, though he was aware of its existence. Like all other people who held his office, Bellingham's tenure in the nation's capital was not a permanent arrangement. He worked for a specific president and would be around only as long as his sponsor was in office. Joplin, on the other hand, had nothing to do with political appointments, and he had visited Custis Farm dozens of times during his career. He used it for meetings and discussions with unique persons who, for the most part, enjoyed extremely friendly and intimate working relationships with the U.S. government. A good number of defectors had enjoyed sanctuary on the Farm as they were debriefed and interviewed. When those processes were taken care of, the majority were given new identities and provided with official federal law enforcement protection.

On the other hand, there had also been a few special antagonists whose conduct or activities made it necessary that they be dealt in the most clandestine ways. Several of the latter ilk had never been seen again. They were the ones who were taken care of by those "farmhands" who had a sinister, sleepy-eyed look about them.

10 SEPTEMBER

CARL Joplin and his guest, Avigdor Peled, from the Israeli Embassy, had arrived at Custis Farm in an unmarked government helicopter. Circumstances made it impossible for them to use the *Bonhomme Richard* Club. The business to be conducted by the two men was much too complicated for a quick meeting.

Their flight to the Farm had begun in the late evening, at a small airport in the vicinity of Coleburg, Maryland. After landing and quickly settling in, the two went to the dining facility to enjoy a quiet pancake supper. After the meal, they retired to the main salon for coffee. Peled could not discuss any business with Joplin until he received confirmation by phone from his ambassador that he was cleared to do so.

When the call came, Peled was given the phone by one of the staff, who plugged it into the wall next to his chair. After identifying himself, the Israeli listened to a fifteen-second message. Then he hung up, looking over at Joplin.

"I am not cleared to speak with you until zero-six-forty-five tomorrow."

11 SEPTEMBER
0630 HOURS

JOPLIN and Peled, enjoying the relative coolness of the early morning, strolled through the woods a few dozen yards away from the house. Both men were dressed for the occasion, wearing light jackets, blue jeans, and sneakers. They had consumed continental breakfasts with plenty of coffee, and both were buoyed by heavy doses of caffeine.

Joplin knew that the reason his Israeli counterpart had requested the meeting at the Farm had to be of great import. But the man's attitude indicated there were no critical elements of urgency or time constraints involved. Or it could be that perhaps his people didn't want to give the Americans the opportunity to respond too quickly to whatever information he had to pass on. The Israelis were independent thinkers and doers, and did not appreciate nor seek any critiques of their various projects.

Peled had picked up a thin branch on the ground and walked with it, idly swinging it back and forth. Another five minutes of the stroll continued; then he checked his watch. Now was the time to get down to business.

"I am sure you are familiar with a certain Iranian Special Forces camp, Carl. In fact, we are informed that you have scored a victory of sorts on the border between Iran and Afghanistan."

Joplin smiled. "Tell me, Avigdor: Is there any place at all in this world where the Mossad does not have agents?"

Peled chuckled. "I know of none."

"Then you are aware that our aims there were fully met," Joplin said. "And, although it is not yet announced publicly, I am sure I would not surprise you if I said the Iranians are now ready to negotiate everything we've demanded of them."

"Yes," the Israeli said. "We are aware of those conditions. However—"

Joplin interrupted. "Uh-oh! Whenever you say 'however' I know you're going to lower the boom."

"We have irrefutable intelligence that Tehran has no serious intentions of negotiating anything with you," Peled said. "In fact, they are about to show their worst side to America, the world, and to us."

"What are our Persian antagonists going to do now?"

"They are going to invade Afghanistan," Peled said. "They backed off from that series of battles they had engaged in with your SEALs because they finally realized they would gain no advantages from the situation. Even now they have gathered leftover East German armor, artillery, and munitions to make a big strike that will carry them deep into that poor, backward country."

"How soon is this supposed to happen?" Joplin asked.

"We estimate that around the last of September or the first of October," Peled replied.

"Your revelation will be much appreciated," Joplin said. "If we move fast enough we'll be able to meet them head on."

"That won't be necessary," Peled said. He stopped walking and turned to face his friend. "We are going to bomb that camp. We'll be concentrating our strikes on the recently arrived military hardware assembled for the invasion."

"Oh, God!"

"The Iranians have gotten quite sassy since our confrontation with their Hezbollah stepchildren. The sons of bitches seem to think they won a great victory in Lebanon."

Joplin knew this would both please and displease the American government. He nervously cleared his throat. "Ahem. Please go on, Avigdor."

"We are going to fly into Iran's sovereign territory and plaster the treacherous bastards billeted at that camp," Peled remarked matter-of-factly. "We are going to pound them into smoking charcoal. And that information, dear Carl, is why I came to the Farm. Now you know. Please do us the favor of informing the President of the United States."

"I do believe he will be interested," Carl said, recovering slightly from the shock. "May I tell him the exact date and time that you plan this air strike?"

"That information we will keep to ourselves," Peled said. "Now! The matter is closed and is not open for negotiations or discussion." He gestured forward with the branch. "Shall we continue our stroll?"

"I really must get back to Washington, Avigdor."

The Israeli laughed. "I am not surprised."

OVAL OFFICE
WHITE HOUSE
1500 HOURS

THE Aladdin Committee had been dissolved. The mysterious informer had made no transmissions for several weeks, and since the Iranians had now shown a much better attitude, the group was dismissed as per an executive order. The big item for that afternoon's impromptu session was to discuss the intelligence passed on to Carl Joplin by the Israelis earlier that morning.

The President of the United States was not happy. He looked at Joplin with near pleading in his eyes. "Isn't there a damn thing we can do about this aerial attack, Carl?"

"I'm afraid not, Mr. President," the career diplomat answered. "That East German weaponry has convinced them that the fall of Afghanistan would be the first step in a long war that would eventually reach the borders of Israel."

The four others in the office—Arlene Entienne; Edgar Watson of the CIA; Liam Bentley, the FBI Liaison Officer; and Secretary of State Benjamin Bellingham—shared the chief executive's concern.

"It would be better if we could contact the Iranians and warn them," the President said. "If they found out we had diverted a bombing of their sovereign territory it would be a great incentive for them to be more cooperative."

"Yes!" Bellingham agreed. "It would convince them of the benefits of friendlier relations with the United States."

Joplin shook his head. "I don't think that will happen."

"I still don't like this bombardment," the President insisted. "You've proven in the past that you have contacts galore. Surely there is *some*one *some*where who can *some*how call this Israeli air raid off."

"I'm sorry, sir," Joplin said. "The Israelis timed the revelation so that we would not have any feasible opportunities to circumvent their plans. They are bound and determined to get that particular thorn out of their sides. They think this is necessary to stifle any misleading feelings of triumph the Iranians may have because of their positive relationship with Hezbollah. The Israeli population is unhappy with the way their government dealt with the terrorist group in the past, and the leaders don't want additional disapproval that would result from an Iranian invasion of Afghanistan."

"Oh, God," Bellingham moaned. "The reaction from the Islamic world is going to be violent and long. And what about the UN? They're going to assume that we encouraged Israel in this act."

"As will the rest of the world," Arlene said.

"I'll tell you one thing for sure," Joplin said. "It certainly won't upset the American public."

The President's concern seemed to be growing with each passing moment. Now he turned his attention to Edgar Watson. "What does the CIA have to say about the happenings in Iran?"

"The only such weapons shipments we are aware of were

shipped to Belarus," Watson answered. "It is not known what happened to them after their arrival in that country."

"But would it be possible for that warmaking matériel to be sent farther south, into Iran?" Bellingham asked.

"It would have to go through several countries," Watson replied. "The Ukraine and Georgia first, then Armenia and Azerbaijan before crossing the border into Iran."

"The logistics of such a thing are staggering," Arlene remarked.

"Not only the logistics," Watson said, "but also the number of palms to be greased would be plentiful and greedy. However, with enough money . . ." He shrugged.

"But how did the Israelis learn about it?" the President asked.

"The Mossad has its eyes and ears in a lot of hidden corners throughout the world," Joplin said. "And if Israel says there is a big arms buildup in Iran for the invasion of Afghanistan, you can rely on it completely and irrevocably. And they are going to destroy it with an aerial attack."

"Oh, Christ!" the President said. "And not a thing we can do about it."

"Sir," Watson said, "the CIA has a suggestion. It is official and I've been authorized to pass it on in this meeting."

Bentley, the White House Liaison Officer from the FBI, finally spoke up. "The Bureau is aware of this suggestion and concurs, Mr. President."

"Don't keep us waiting, damn it, Edgar, I am not a patient man this afternoon!"

"Alright, Mr. President," the CIA man said. "We recommend that the Brits join us in aiding the air raid. We have our AWACS aircraft, and the Royal Air Force has aerial refueling capabilities in the area."

"I second the motion," Joplin said. "It's going to happen anyway, so let's join in and make it easier for our Jewish friends."

The President sighed. "Alright. Do it."

Joplin wasn't finished. "Sir, there is one way we can take advantage of the situation. After the Israelis bomb the hell out of the place and level it, I advise you to send in some of

our SPECOPS people to mop up and try to capture some
EPWs."

"Yes, Watson agreed. "If these captives were shipped off
to Barri Prison in Bahrain they will prove most invaluable.
We have an interrogator there who could ring them dry in
record time."

"That seems a good idea," the President allowed. "Is it
feasible to expect a group of our guys to be able to get in and
out of there fast and accomplish that mission?"

"Of course, sir," Arlene said. "That's why they're called
Special Forces."

"It would require the best of the best then," the President
said. He leaned back in his chair and became thoughtful for
a moment. "Who should we deploy?"

"Only one outfit I know of, Mr. President," Joplin said.
"Brannigan's Brigands."

USS *DAN DALY*
12 SEPTEMBER
0900 HOURS

THE letter from S-4 of Station Bravo in Bahrain came
through the official mail, and after being offloaded with the
regular shipment from the Seahawk, it was inserted into the
ship's administrative distribution system. An hour later, a mail
clerk made his deliveries to the various command and staff
sections of the vessel and dropped it off in the SEAL in-box at
the small office maintained by SCPO Buford Dawkins. He
pulled it from the container and ripped the envelope open. After reading the missive, he broke into a wide grin.

Ensign Orlando Taylor's suggestion to have PO Chad
Murchison write a letter filled with ambiguity, confusion,
and logical illogic had paid off. Station Bravo's supply officer sent a statement taking away all responsibility for the
missing desert patrol vehicle that had disappeared during
Operation Rolling Thunder. The DPV was now written off,
putting it into that great logistical obscurity in the sky. Randy
Tooley at Shelor Field would never have to give up that gift

from Lieutenant Bill Brannigan as a token of appreciation for a job well done.

1130 HOURS

WEAPONS maintenance had been the main activity that morning. All the M-16 rifles, M-203 grenade launchers, M-249 squad automatic weapons, and even the AS-50 sniper rifles had to be detail-stripped and given thorough cleanings. This included submersion in boiling water to make sure the grit and grease that had worked into the smallest of the moving parts was dissolved. Afterward, after a complete wipe-down as the residual water evaporated, light coats of oil were applied.

It was not really a messy job, but hands got oily and dirty and were wiped as much on BDU trousers as on the rags furnished by the ordnance division that serviced the ship's weaponry. Ensign Taylor had been in charge of the activity, and he gave the men some extra time to wash up for chow. When they returned from the head to form up for the trip to the mess deck, they stepped into the compartment and halted.

Commander Tom Carey and Lieutenant Commander Ernest Berringer stood with the Skipper, Lieutenant Jim Cruiser, and SCPO Dawkins. They were obviously waiting for them.

"Uh-oh!" said Mike Assad.

"Oh, shit!" uttered Bruno Puglisi.

"This portends lugubrious developments," Chad Murchison stated.

It was the senior chief who made the announcement. "You won't be going to chow. Box lunches will be sent up to the ready room. So go there immediately if not sooner. There's business to attend to."

ONCE again Brannigan's Brigands were scattered among the seats in the ready room, as they had been several times in the past. The officers and senior chief situated themselves off to one side, while Carey and Berringer stood at the front of the room.

Carey didn't waste any time with salutations or an introductory statement. He cut to the chase. "Mission statement," he announced. "You will do a mop-up operation on an Iranian Special Forces camp after it has been bombed and strafed by the Israeli Air Force."

The awe and shock at the announcement was shown on every face.

Carey continued, "I want to emphasize from the very get-go that this is a highly—I say again—a *highly* classified mission. It is illegal, immoral, and reprehensible." He paused and grinned. "In other words, right up your alley."

"Ha!" Puglisi said with a laugh. "What brought this shit down?"

"I'm just about to tell you, Petty Officer Puglisi," Carey said. "The Iranians have secretly—they think—reneged on engaging in negotiations regarding their Afghanistan and nuclear ambitions. They are planning a full-scale invasion of Afghanistan, complete with tanks, armored infantry units, self-propelled artillery, and close air support. They fully expect they can be hundreds of kilometers into the country before the coalition forces will be able to react."

Monty Sturgis, like the others, could hardly believe what he was hearing. "Where do the Israelis come in on this? Are we coordinating our efforts with them?"

"I'm sure they'll be provided with some sort of clandestine aid, but that's just my opinion," Carey answered. "But all that is separated completely from what you're going to do. They will inform us at the last minute of the exact time of their attack, and at that point you will board USAFSOC choppers for a quick trip into Iran to the site of the action."

Ensign Taylor was also not quite catching on. "Just exactly what is this 'mop-up' aspect of our mission?"

"Exactly that," Carey said. "You will unass the choppers, form up as skirmishers, and move through the mess the Israelis made. Your mission is to police up any EPWs among the survivors or anything that may be of interest to our intelligence people."

"How long are we expected to be on the ground?" CPO Matt Gunnarson asked.

"No more than twenty minutes," Carey replied. "The Air Force helicopters will be waiting for you with rotors turning. The Iranian Air Force will undoubtedly send some recon flights over to see what happened. So as soon as you've made your walk through the debris, return immediately to the aircraft for evacuation back to Afghanistan."

"What part of Afghanistan?" Dave Leibowitz wanted to know.

"The same place where you'll take off from," Carey said. "That will be the LZ behind your former positions where you faced the Zaheya forces. The Air Force is going to pick you up here on the *Daly*'s flight deck."

"What're we gonna be toting in with us?" the SAW gunner Tex Benson asked. "Is any special equipment called for?"

"Everyone will carry one M-sixteen rifle, two bandoliers of ammo, and a canteen," Carey responded. "You'll leave the SAWs behind, along with the grenade launchers." He glanced over to where Puglisi and Miskoski sat. "No calls for snipers on this trip."

"Now, sir," Garth Redhawk said, "I know we're supposed to going in light, but I'm not the optimistic type. I'd like to bring along my personal medical kit, a two-quart canteen, a couple of MREs, and my compass."

Brannigan interjected, "That's a good idea. And any other small items you want. And I emphasize that means no real additional bulk or weight." He glanced at Carey. "How's that, sir?"

"Approved," Carey answered. "And as far as commo goes, you'll use the AN/PRC radios with LASH headsets. Forget any night vision stuff. This is strictly daylight. Any questions so far? Alright! Commander Berringer has some intel notes to run by you."

Berringer now took the floor. "You were told to look for items that would interest the intelligence community. I want you to consider the big picture, and by that I mean keep in mind the CIA and others. Look for documents, videotapes, CDs, books, letters, and those sorts of things that might be scattered around the area. If it's feasible and you run across dead officers, search their pockets. Tear insignia off uniforms so we can use them to figure out orders of battle and ID certain units. And above all, do your very best to get EPWs. And that includes wounded personnel who would survive being carried back to the choppers. And I have these." He held up a handful of pamphlets. "These are charts showing the Iranian Army's insignia of ranks that I'm going to pass out to you. If you see anybody wearing shoulder straps, check carefully to see if they can be evacuated. And if they're sporting stars and wings on the epaulets, bring 'em back, dead or alive. Those would be generals, and I suppose there's a chance there might be one or two out there. It's plain and simple, and you guys have been around enough to recognize what is needed."

Carey took over again. "That's it. There's nothing left to do until we get the word when to move out. The Israelis are playing their cards close to their chests, so we won't know when they'll launch the air strike until the last minute. Commander Berringer and I will stay aboard the *Daly,* and if we get additional information, we'll pass it on to you ASAP." He nodded to the Skipper. "Lieutenant Brannigan wants a word with you now."

"Right," Brannigan said. "We're down to twenty-four guys now, so we have to reorganize. I'm going to wait until we're on standby over at our former base camp to shuffle you guys around. It's going to take a bit of doing, but be ready for changes. And remember! These assignments are not negotiable."

"Okay," Carey said. "I'll leave you guys to it. We'll be in constant touch with you."

He and Berringer left the compartment, and all eyes were turned to Brannigan. The Skipper gestured to Buford Dawkins. "Under the new setup you're the detachment chief. Get the ball rolling."

"Aye, sir!" Dawkins responded. He turned to the others. "Alright! Let's go, people!"

"Hey!" Bruno Puglisi yelled. "Where the hell are them box lunches?"

CHAPTER 21

IRANIAN SF CAMP

THE principal officers who had been commanders in the now defunct Zaheya Force were ecstatic. After the long weeks of being nothing but glorified squad leaders in a clandestine struggle that was going nowhere, they had finally been assigned to meaningful command positions in an important upcoming combat operation in which they would spearhead nothing less than a full-blown invasion. And to make things even sweeter for Captains Naser Khadid and Jamshid Komard, they had been promoted to the rank of major. Komard was not assigned a larger unit to lead, but he was advanced from being Brigadier Shahruz Khohollah's adjutant to the post of chief of staff. This was a prestigious assignment in which he would wear a bright yellow aiguillette attached to his left epaulet as indication of his important new position.

Major Arsalaan Sikes, while not promoted, was given the command of no less than forty tracked infantry fighting vehicles, which meant he would lead a total of ten platoons consisting of more than 520 men. His vehicles were MT-LBs, which had formerly been in the Soviet Army's inventory but had been mothballed for a decade after loan to East Germany. Each had a driver and gunner and could transport eleven infantry soldiers. Sikes Pasha truly felt he was back on the career track to the glory he had dreamed about since his desertion from the British Army.

Newly promoted Major Khadid now had fifty vehicles under his command. These were self-propelled 2S3 Akatsiyas howitzers, which sported both a 152-millimeter main gun and a 7.62-millimeter antiaircraft machine gun. The TO of this newly activated unit gave Khadid a bit more than 400 men, including both the weapons crews and a small command and service unit to aid in the logistics and administration of the equipment-heavy outfit. This command would take him out of Special Forces and into the conventional segment of the Iranian Army, but he could rightly expect to make quick rank either during or immediately after the invasion of Afghanistan. That, of course, would also mean an even more prestigious place in the national army's chain of command.

But the happiest of those old sweats from Zaheya was Brigadier Shahruz Khohollah. Along with the outfits of Sikes and Khadid, his expanded command responsibilities now included an entire battalion of T-72 tanks. Like Sikes' IFVs and Khadid's SPAs, these armored vehicles had begun their service life as part of the Soviet Union's army before transfer to East Germany's armed forces. This new development meant Khohollah would be leading a grand total of sixty-four of the armored monsters, along with a Headquarters and service battalion, making his spearhead invasion force number 2,500 men, along with all those vehicles. This was not a large command when compared with other great land battles, but was enough to punch deep into Afghanistan. And a strong combined arms corps–size force would be coming right behind them to mop up and consolidate the gains. After that the operation would turn south, into Pakistan. And that would mean a division or corps would be placed at the brigadier's disposal.

The great invasion was set for 20 September.

HARRY TURPIN'S QUARTERS
13 SEPTEMBER

HARRY Turpin was seventy years old, and he looked every day of it plus a hell of a lot more. The old Cockney was tired. Decades of bartering international arms deals with the risks, stresses, and uncertainties were finally taking their toll. No less than a dozen contracts had been taken out on his life by rivals, and that didn't include government agents from nations that had grown disenchanted with some of the deals he had made with their enemies. These unpleasant individuals had been charged with assassinating him, and had come close to succeeding half a dozen times.

In fact, the whole arms dealing business had become more complicated in the past decade, what with computers keeping track of transactions and having permanent, accurate entries in their databases. This electronically stored information had caused a couple of his less than honest arrangements to collapse when certain facts surfaced at very inopportune moments.

Of course, there had been good times too. Harry owned villas in Switzerland and Italy, not to mention luxurious hideaways in Singapore and Monaco. The arms broker had never been lacking for the companionship of beautiful women. He had even had spasms of romantic affections in which he kept some particularly charming and beautiful females with exotic sexual talents stowed away in deluxe apartments in several European capital cities. One of these affairs lasted almost a year, but eventually ended, like all the others, when he paid for a final six months of residence, a rather generous farewell bonus, and some lavish presents. Harry wasn't required to be so generous, but he had a soft side to him when it came to his sexual playmates, even if he wasn't really in love with any of them.

But as the years passed, he began to have spells of erectile dysfunction. Of course, the several drugs available to jump-start his lovemaking abilities took care of that small problem. Lately, however, he had begun not to care when those old desires couldn't be satisfied, and this was mainly because he wasn't having too many of those erotic cravings. The passing of several decades had brought about a "been there, done that" attitude on his part when it came to sexual liaisons with women.

This last deal for the Iranians, with all the preparation, bribery, cajoling, threats, and logistical nightmares of gathering up infantry fighting vehicles, self-propelled artillery, and those goddamned tanks, had really drained the old boy. The officers of the Ukrainian and Russian armies were a rotten bunch and very difficult to set decent prices with. He had to admit this Iranian caper was the crowning achievement of his entire arms-dealing career, but it left him spiritually exhausted. The millions of Euros he made on the transactions soothed his anguish to a great degree, but he finally reached a conclusion: Things were getting too big and too complicated for even the great Harry Turpin to handle alone.

2300 HOURS

HARRY had a special guest that evening. Archibald Sikes—he would never be Arsalaan or Sikes Pasha to his compatriot—had been invited over to take pleasure in something he hadn't enjoyed in a long, long time.

English beer!

Harry had several cases of Tetley's with him that were neatly stacked in the rear of his tent. The crates that held them were labeled with the Farsi words *"mive ab,"* so that any casual glance by an Iranian Muslim would make him think the Englishman had brought in some fruit juice. Even though the arms dealer had done a lot of business with the Iranians in the past, he still had to be careful about bringing alcohol into one of their military garrisons. Imbibing was seriously frowned on in the Islamic religion, and even enjoying a few brews by himself was considered taboo.

It was because of this that he had invited Sikes over at such a late hour. They could safely enjoy a few pints if they kept the lantern turned low, the tent flaps shut, and their conversation quiet. Sikes seated himself in a camp chair.

Englishmen prefer to drink their beer warm, so there was

no need to ice down the goodies. Sikes seemed almost orgasmic as he took the first few tentative sips. After smacking his lips, he quickly consumed three deep gulps.

Harry grinned at him. "So 'ow's that then, Archie lad?"

"Have I died and gone to heaven?" Sikes replied with a wide grin.

"Well, I thought you needed a taste o' Blighty after all the time over 'ere," Harry said.

"I must admit I've missed those good times in the pub," Sikes said. He took a deep breath, then drained the mug. "Gawd! I ain't never gonna see England again, am I, Harry?"

"It's 'ard to tell, lad."

"But things'll look up for me after this invasion," Sikes said. "I'll have a large command and a promotion along with a couple of medals, I should think."

"D'you miss 'ome much?" Harry asked.

"O' course."

"I don't want to make you no worry, lad," Harry said. "But yer mum and dad 'as been 'aving a terrible time of it."

"Oh, Gawd!" Sikes exclaimed. "I was afraid o' that. I ain't heard nothing from the old folks, o' course, but I had a notion that the Army would be going after 'em because o' me."

"It's more'n the Army, Archie," Harry said. "The antiterrorist coppers have been coming 'round too. They took your dad in one time and kept him under interrogation for a whole bluddy night. It liked to 'ave drove him to an 'eart attack."

"How'd you know about all that then?"

"I got me eyes and ears in Blighty, lad," Harry said, "along with a lot o' other places. Yer folks is worried Mr. Sikes might get the sack at his job."

Sikes grinned and shook his head. "That's not gonna happen, mate. The union looks after their own in a case like that. There'd be plenty o' trouble. I know, 'cause I worked there meself for a year or so. I wasn't worth much, let me tell you, but the foreman didn't dare do nothing about it." Archie laughed. "Management was real happy when they learnt I was leaving to join the Army."

"Everybody's down on your dad," Harry said. "The union

too. Since them Wogs blew up the Underground, the whole bluddy population has got a new attitude toward things. It seems there's a couple o' Arab blokes down at that warehouse that's come under suspicion. It was thought your dad might be involved with 'em."

Sikes reached over and picked up another bottle of beer from the bunch on the floor. After opening it, he settled back in the camp chair, glancing at his older friend. "I know things might look bad, Harry. I went from good to bad soldier after that commissioning thing, y'know?"

Harry shook his head. "I never understood that, Archie. Don't get upset with me, but it seems you 'ad a good chance for a commission, but in a different regiment. You shoulda took it, lad."

"There's such a thing as pride, Harry," Sikes said testily. "The fact they said I wasn't good enough for 'em just set me off, hey? Maybe it wasn't logical, but that's the way I felt, and I ain't sorry about it. I ain't sorry about nothing."

Harry eyed him carefully. "Ain't you even sorry about deserting from the Army?"

"Hell, no!" Archie exclaimed loudly, then quickly quieted. "They was gonna kick me out when we got back to Blighty anyhow. They ruined me life, Harry. There I was doing fine in the Army, a sergeant and all, and then they turn around and treat me like shit. It wasn't my fault!"

"I can see yer point, lad," Harry said. "I ain't putting no blame on you."

"It's gonna turn out alright, don't you worry none about that," Sikes assured him. "I got a good command for this invasion, and when we finish up in Afghanistan and take over Pakistan, I'll be sitting pretty in the Iranian Army. I'm a major now and expect to be at least a brigadier when we start our operations over on the other side o' the Persian Gulf. I got real glory ahead o' me, Harry. I'll be able to make up for all that trouble and bother I caused me mum and dad."

Harry smiled. "O' course you will. No problem with that, 'ey?"

"I'll have a lot o' money," Sikes said. "I can send 'em enough to buy a nice house, and my dad won't have to worry

about his job. If I'm a gen'ral, the British government and
Army have got to forgive me past sins, hey? Maybe I'll even
be able to go home for a visit. I mean, they got to show respect to a bluddy gen'ral, ain't they?"

"I would think so," Harry said. He lowered his voice and
leaned closer to the younger man. "'Ere, Archie. I notice
there ain't no birds around 'ere. When's the last time you got
yourself a bit o' tail, 'ey?"

Sikes grinned and shrugged. "I had one of them temporary marriages when I was with the Pashtuns. A thirteen-
year-old. But she was mature for her age, Harry. It ain't like
I was having it on with a little kid."

"Sure," Harry said. "Them Pashtun girls grow up fast."
He winked at Sikes. "I know a place up near Tehran called
Khoshi. It's a special place for foreigners. Lots o' liquor and
women. We could go up there, you and me, and 'ave us a bit
o' fun. Know what I mean?"

"Oh, yeah!" Sikes said. "I feel bluddy deprived, I do. But
ain't that risky what with Islamic law and all that?"

Harry shook his head. "The government knows about the
place. Them Muslims ain't all stupid. They know they need
a place where special guests from the West can get away and
ease up a bit."

"I bet a lot them Iranians go there too, hey?"

"They'd be in deep shit," Harry said seriously. "There's
times when them mad followers of Islam are 'arder on their
own kind than on us infidels."

"I switched to Islam," Sikes reminded him.

"Nobody over there is gonna know about it," Harry said.
"You'll just be another soul damned by Allah as far as they'll
know."

"The invasion is set for the twentieth," Sikes said.

"That's a week away," Harry said. "We could go up there
tomorrow morning and be back in a couple o' days. There's
plenty o' time."

"Yeah!" Sikes said. "I'll turn the comp'ny over to Hashiri."
He raised the beer bottle. "Let's do it, Harry!"

"Alright, lad," Harry Turpin said. "I'll take care o' everything."

SIKES' QUARTERS
14 SEPTEMBER
0200 HOURS

UNDER normal circumstances, Sikes would have been fast asleep after an evening in which he had consumed a dozen bottles of beer. But he was so excited about getting away to that fleshpot for sex, serious drinking, and celebrating, that the effects of the brew had evaporated.

He was also sobered by thoughts about his parents. He hadn't realized the amount of trouble he had caused them. When he deserted, he figured they would be embarrassed, but that that would blow over after a while. The idea of his father enduring a night of police interrogation pained him deeply. His mother's anguish also bit deep into his spirits of well-being. She was fully devoted to his father, and any suffering he went through would be felt doubly by her.

He lay on his bunk, looking up at the darkness of the canvas above him, turning his thoughts to what he could do to help his parents. He smiled as his mind ran through a scenario in which a telegram arrives at his old home. It comes in the early evening, and his mother answers the door. She takes it into his father, who is watching the telly from his usual easy chair. He opens the telegram, then leaps to his feet. He shouts, "It's a wire for fifty thousand pounds . . . it's from Archie . . . there's more money to come . . . lots more . . . and Archie is a general in the Iranian Army!"

Sikes smiled sleepily to himself, then eased into a deep slumber.

CHAPTER 22

IT had been one hell of a day for Archie Sikes, the wandering lad from Manchester, England.

He and his mate, Harry Turpin, had arrived at the airstrip outside the small but modern and chic town of Khoshi at 0830 hours after a short hop from the city of Sabzevar aboard a Cessna Citation S-11. Harry, always insisting on traveling in style, had chartered the aircraft from a private company in Tehran. The trip from the Special Forces camp to the airport hadn't been particularly luxurious, however. They had to hitch a ride in an army supply transport truck, sitting in the front with the driver while their luggage bounced around in the back.

But the dusty ride was forgotten when the Citation landed at Khoshi and the two revelers disembarked from the aircraft. The pilot would be waiting for them for some twenty-four hours, and the international arms dealer had gotten him a room in the same hotel where he and Sikes would be settling in.

Almost immediately after checking in at the Ritz-Kraus, a German-run hostelry, the two Brits left the place to begin exploring the delights offered in the desert sin city. In comparison to Las Vegas, U.S.A., it was a minor-league resort, but to Sikes, who had spent long months in the hinterlands of the Iran-Afghanistan border as well as an isolated military camp, it was like arriving on the French Riviera. Paved streets! Sidewalks! Restaurants! Theaters! Bars! And, best of all, women!

Harry knew the place well and served as an expert and considerate guide. The first place they went was to Khoshi's finest bordello, called Le Baron. Although it was early in the morning, the place was in full operation. When they walked in, Sikes noted that the "parlor" was actually a bar furnished like a living room, with sofas, love seats, and easy chairs. It was plush and heavily decorated with heavy drapes, a deep Persian rug, and scantily clad females. The clientele, all foreigners stationed in Iran, were having the times of their lives, and a couple of them appeared as if they might have been in the brothel two or three days. These were all Europeans and were doing their best to have some fun during a short respite from their places of employment in the midst of Islamic law.

Harry was well known in the place, and a huge African bouncer greeted him like an old friend. The proprietress, a middle-aged, fleshy Algerian woman named Lola, rushed to the Brit, giving him a tight hug around the middle while planting a wet kiss on his cheek. Lola had once worked in a regimental brothel of the French Foreign Legion, and although Harry hadn't known her during his own legion days, he had visited his own unit's mobile military whorehouse countless times between operations against the Algerian rebels.

After enduring the emotional salutation from Lola, Harry laid his hand on Sikes' shoulder. "'Ere now, Lola, this is a mate o' mine from England. 'Is name is Archie."

Lola gave Sikes a big grin, speaking in a French accent. "Welcome to Le Baron, Archie!" She gestured at the scantily clad females sitting on sofas along the wall. "Our ladies are waiting to pleasure you. We can promise delights of which you have never dreamed. *C'est la vérité!*"

Archie eyed the prostitutes with the longing of a starving man gazing at a T-bone steak. Harry laughed and pointed. "Well, now, Archie. Wot in 'ell are you waiting for, then? Take care o' that itch. Then we can start a day of doing nothing but enjoying ourselves."

Thus began an entire day of sex and alcohol for Archie, with Harry as his host and mentor. When the younger man showed a bit too much inebriation, the older steered him to a restaurant for a good feed and thick, hot Iranian *ghahve-ba-khame*, a sweet coffee drink with enough of a caffeine kick to cancel out the effects of Scotch whisky. When Archie was back in reasonably good condition, they would head back for Le Baron to allow him to renew his sexual assaults.

The temporary Islamic marriage that Archie had enjoyed with the Pashtun girl Banafsha had taught him the pleasures of having a single female playmate who would learn what he wanted and liked during sex, then see that he got it. By mid-afternoon he had settled on a dark beauty by the name of Javahere, and Harry forked over enough Euros to Lola in exchange for a guarantee that Javahere would be available for Archie any time he wanted her.

While Archie went slightly mad in his controlled orgy, the old man Harry Turpin slowly imbibed gin tonics while visiting with Lola in her office. In bygone days he would have run through the roster of whores like a lion through a herd of gazelles, but his libido just wasn't up to the task anymore. Lola, a good friend, understood, and made him welcome as they talked about what the Foreign Legion had been like in the days of the Algerian War.

2130 HOURS

TO say Archie Sikes was satiated would have been a total understatement. In reality, he was slaked, quenched, and fulfilled to the ultimate. To also state that he was drained to the physical weakness of a baby would have been another minimized depiction. The young Englishman's energy level had sunk close to collapse. However, because of Harry's regulation of his drinking, at least he was not sick or hungover.

Now they sat on the balcony of their hotel room, both consuming some light snacks and beer as the twinkling glare of Khoshi's lights cut upward into the night sky. Harry gazed with amusement at his companion. "Well, Archie, me lad, it appears you've 'ad quite a day, 'ey?"

Sikes chuckled. "You're right about that. And after all them weeks in the desert and mountains, believe me, I deserved it."

"That you do," Harry said. "Are you ready to settle down to a bit o' seriousness, then?"

Sikes was slightly surprised by this somber turn in events, but gave an affirmative nod.

"Them Iranian mates o' yours are a bunch o' sods," Harry said, unsmiling. "And 'ere's something else for nothing, my lad. They're right on the bluddy edge o' disaster."

"Wot the hell are you talking about, Harry?"

"They've been too cheeky for their own good," Harry said. "That's wot I'm talking about. And they're for it. The Iranian people, particularly the young ones, are restless and angry, and the next revolution is gonna send them mullahs packing. And that goes for any poor sod that supported them. And you can believe there's plenty o' outside interests who want to see that 'appen."

"I suppose you're talking about the Americans," Sikes commented.

"I'm talking about nearly the whole of the United Nations," Harry said. "All this nuclear shit and supporting the 'Ezbollah is coming back to 'aunt 'em. So 'ere's a warning for you to heed. Get the 'ell out o' Iran as fast as you can."

"I think I got a future with 'em, Harry," Sikes said. "I ain't got much choice but to stick with 'em."

"If you go back, you're gonna get killed," Harry said.

"Oh, yeah? And by who, may I ask?"

"The Israelis."

Sikes was surprised by that. "Now, how're they gonna do that?"

Harry instinctively lowered his voice. "By bombing the 'ell out o' that camp you just came from." He looked around at the nearby balconies to make sure there was nobody lounging on them before he spoke again. "They know about the Iranians buying all them tanks and armored vehicles from me. They know about the planned invasion of Afghanistan, and they damn well know the Iranians are going to continue their operation of taking over the whole o' the bluddy Middle East and build up WMDs to boot."

"Ha!" Sikes laughed. "Now, how do they know all that?"

"Because I told 'em."

If Sikes still had any lingering effects from the day's drinking left, it quickly faded away in the shock of this revelation. "Wot this all about then?"

"I always know which side me bread is buttered on," Harry said. "In me business you can't choose causes, right? You got to look after yourself and do what's best for you personally. After I made the deal with the Iranians, I got 'old of the Mossad, and told 'em every bluddy thing I know." He cleared his throat and grabbed his bottle of beer. "Ahem. I'm on their payroll."

"Well, this puts me in bluddy deep shit, Harry!" Sikes said angrily. "Thank you very much."

"You can come out of it smelling like a rose, me lad," Harry said. "I need a younger man for an 'elpmate, 'ey? Someone with youthful energy, know what I mean? A smart, energetic partner. That's you, mate."

Sikes was silent for a moment. "Are you offering me a job, Harry?"

"That's it, Archie," Harry replied. "You'll get rich, lad. I got no son o' me own to leave nothing to, and you'll do fine. You got guts and you're smart."

"Wot'll I do for you, Harry?"

"You'll be me legman," Harry answered. "I'll still set up the deals and you can give me an 'and whilst you're learning the business. And when there's trips to be made and deliveries to check on, I'll send you out."

"I ain't got a passport, Harry. And I'm a deserter from the British Army, or have you forgot that?"

"I ain't forgot," Harry said. "And I can get you a passport from *any* country with *any* name we prefer. Think about this—a starting salary of two hundred and fifty thousand Euros a year plus bonuses when deliveries are made." He leaned toward him. "And imagine just 'ow much 'elp you can give your mum and dad when you're rich, 'ey?"

"There's something else," Sikes said. "Me warrant officer, Hashiri, has been a great help to me. He even saved me life the day I was wounded. How about taking him out with me?"

"Can't be done," Harry said. "The first reason is that we ain't going back to that camp, so we can't fetch 'im. And the second is that 'e's a bluddy Wog, so 'e won't be the first 'eathen to die for an English master."

"That's the way it is, hey?" Sikes asked.

"That's it. Now, wot d'you say, lad?"

Sikes grinned. "When do we leave, Harry?"

"Later tonight. That plane I chartered is set up to fly us to my bungalow in Singapore instead of returning us to Sabzevar."

FORMER SEAL BASE CAMP
IRAN-AFGHANISTAN BORDER

THE Army Rangers had offered to share their bunkers with Brannigan's Brigands, but because of the short time involved in the upcoming mission, the soldiers' proposal was refused with thanks. Lieutenant Brannigan thought it best that they stay out on the LZ and stay in close proximity of the USAF Pave Low chopper and its crew.

Security was no longer an issue in the vicinity, and several campfires made from dried branches of thorn bushes had been lit to heat water for coffee. It was late for a detachment meeting, but there had been a lot to do that day. The checking and rechecking in with Commanders Carey and Berringer at Shelor Field took up a lot of time, as did the breakdown of ammunition, rations, and some other supplies. Only when SCPO Buford Dawkins informed the Skipper that "every swinging dick" was squared away, shipshape, and ready to go was Brannigan able to take the time to organize for the mop-up of the Iranian Special Forces camp.

2200 HOURS

LIGHTS from dying campfires flickered off the side of the helicopter. The crew was inside sleeping as the SEALs settled in a semicircle around the Skipper, who stood in front of the aircraft's open ramp.

"There's quite a few less of us than when we started out on Operation Battleline," Brannigan said. "So I've worked out the new TO." He pulled a sheet of paper out of a side pocket of his BDU and unfolded it. "Now hear this."

Everyone sat up a bit straighter, anxious to find out the new configuration.

Brannigan looked at the document for a moment before speaking. "Alright! Headquarters and the Sneaky Petes will stay the same. Under these circumstances we can be considered a reinforced fire team." He glanced over at Bruno Puglisi and Joe Miskoski. "Puglisi, you'll go to Alpha Fire Team, and Miskoski to Bravo. That takes care of the First Assault Section."

Ensign Orlando Taylor stood up to receive the word on the changes in his command.

"Okay," Brannigan said. "Here's the Second Assault Section, under Ensign Taylor. Chief Matt Gunnarson takes over Charlie Fire Team. Devereaux goes to that team as a rifleman. Senior Chief Dawkins takes over Delta Fire Team, and Murchison goes with him as a rifleman. Anybody whose name I didn't call will stay in the same place you started out in. Got it?"

"Yes, sir!" answered a chorus of voices.

"Now here's our formation for moving through the enemy camp for mop-up and other assignments," Brannigan continued. "The left flank will be First Section; the center will be Headquarters and the Sneaky Petes; and Second Section will be on the right flank." He took another look at the diagram he'd drawn. "That's it. We won't be moving out of here until we get the word. There's no telling when that'll be, but when the word comes, we're gonna have to move fast. Any questions or comments? Good. We've got an important job to do, so let's make sure we stay on the ball all through the mission. Dismissed!"

The Brigands got to their feet and ambled back to their campfires.

ARABIAN SEA
VICINITY OF 64° EAST, 20° NORTH
15 SEPTEMBER
0205 HOURS

THE twelve-plane squadron had flown close to a thousand miles, violating the airspace of one country for some minutes, then streaking across the entire width of another while being monitored by a foreign but friendly military force stationed there. This small aerial armada was made up of Kfir C.2 fighter-attack aircraft of the Israeli Air Force. And they were loaded for bear. Each carried 12,700 pounds of ordnance that included Vulcan 20-millimeter guns, one heavy general-purpose bomb, and six air-to-ground high-explosive missiles.

With another 700 miles to go, the squadron leader suddenly gave the word to form into a tight orbit. He had reacted to a transmission from a U.S. Air Force E-3 Sentry AWACS aircraft with a very busy seventeen-man crew.

A short distance away, two other large aircraft, these a pair of KC-135 refueling tankers bearing the roundels of Great Britain's Royal Air Force, were being vectored to the orbiting Israelis. Their mission was a simple but vital one, in that they were tasked with topping off the fighter-attack squadron's fuel tanks so they could continue their journey to the objective. Both the E-3 and the KC-135s would be waiting at the same spot to service those same fliers on their return flight.

IRANIAN AIR FORCE RADAR STATION
SOUTH OF BANDAR-E-BUSHER

THE radar operator yawned and stretched, keeping his eyes on the cathode ray tube to his direct front. The images he studied were confusing and busy, with hundreds of blips indicating ships and planes. All this among the usual activities of a large concentration of naval forces.

The sergeant in charge sat across the room, listlessly reading a week-old sports magazine giving international soccer scores. He glanced up and could see over the operator's shoulder at the radar set. He got to his feet and strolled to where the soldier still watched the blips.

The sergeant laughed. "Ha! It appears that the *Amrikayaan* are having night training, *na*?"

"Well, they have no one to bomb at the present," the operator said. He smiled. "Too bad they have to go without sleep."

"They will be allowed to stay in bed late this morning," the sergeant said. "The American Navy sees that their pilots are pampered and well treated."

"Not like us," the operator said. He looked at the screen again. "This is boring."

"But better than being in the infantry," the sergeant commented. He went back to his desk.

The operator dully noted some circling blips, then got to his feet. He walked over to where the sergeant sat and leafed through newspapers and magazines to find something to read. He was happy to discover a photojournal. He picked it up and took an empty chair beside the desk, quickly lost in scanning the photographs and captions.

Across the room, the radar tube continued to display what its antenna picked up out on the Arabian Sea.

0235 HOURS

THE last Israeli fighter-attack aircraft had been refueled, and the squadron turned northeast toward its destination.

The two men in the radar station were engrossed in their reading, while the blips of the departing squadron flitted across the screen, unseen and unheeded by either one.

CHAPTER 23

THE little Austrian Haflinger utility vehicle rolled away from the guard tent, with a sergeant at the wheel and a lieutenant as a passenger. They were part of an artillery battalion that had been assigned to serve aboard the self-propelled howitzers lately delivered to the invasion force. The unit was made up of professional soldiers, competent and disciplined, and between stints of learning the proper operation of the big tracked guns, they did housekeeping chores around the camp, such as trash collecting, cleanup, and—like the two men in the Haflinger were presently doing—guard duty.

The lieutenant was a keen young officer only recently commissioned, and the sergeant was an old soldier, grumpy as hell about being rousted off the cot in the guard tent. He would have preferred getting some much-needed sleep rather than making rounds with a puppy out to enjoy his new rank. When they reached Post One, the sentry properly challenged them, then recognized and allowed them to approach. He promptly and correctly responded to the lieutenant's questions regarding the special orders for his post, but was dressed down for having a button undone on his jacket.

With that done, and satisfied that he had given the soldier a proper reprimand about the pocket, the lieutenant jumped back into the vehicle, to be driven to Post Two. The lieutenant was in a grimly determined mood to build a reputation as a disciplinarian. "We'll catch one of these fellows sleeping yet."

The sergeant said nothing, knowing that the headlights and the motor noise were enough to wake even a dozing sentry, warning him of approaching inspectors. As could be expected, when they reached Post Two, they were once again properly challenged. This time the sergeant also got out of the vehicle, wanting to stretch his legs. As the officer questioned the sentry about his duties, a growl could be heard in the distant sky. The three men looked at each other in puzzlement.

Then the slight growl evolved into a dull roar, and suddenly burst forth into a full-blown thundering of jet engines that could be felt as well as heard. Several aircraft burst into the moonlight from the clouds, heading straight for the camp. They swept over in four "Vs" of three as a large cylindrical object dropped from each. Immediately a series of explosions worked their way across the camp in evenly spaced rows; then the planes swept back up into the clouds, breaking off into separate groups.

This attack scored hits on the vehicle park, pulverizing tanks, IFVs, and the self-propelled howitzers as brilliant flashes of explosives and ignited fuel lit the night. The sentry was rattled by the destruction and yelled out as he had been instructed to do in emergencies.

"Sergeant of the Guard, Post Two!"

"*Ahmagh*—idiot!" the sergeant bellowed. "I *am* the Sergeant of the Guard!"

The lieutenant was speechless and seemed unable to move. He stared upward into the moonlit sky at the irregular cover of scattered clouds. He had received no instruction at the military academy regarding airplanes suddenly appearing and dropping bombs in the middle of the night.

Now one of the groups of aircraft came in from the north, sweeping down and firing off a total of eighteen air-to-ground missiles that exploded in a pattern that spread southward. Immediately a second group came in from the west, also cutting loose with the same ordnance. The explosions continued the destruction begun by the heavy bombs as third and fourth attacks were launched from the east and the south. Once again the target was the vehicle park, and a total of seventy-two rockets punched through armor, ripping the vehicles apart until the entire motor pool was burning as if molten lava had flowed across its expanse.

Figures of men could be seen emerging from their tents. Most only stepped outside and stood in stupefied wonder at the hell raining down in their midst. The thought of seeking cover did not occur to them. Then the ammunition dump at the far end of the camp exploded with one roaring boom that was quickly followed by two more as the initial blasts triggered additional detonations.

The aircraft made another run in the same order, but this time they fired heavy 20-millimeter Vulcan ammo at a rate of more than 600 rounds per minute. Their targets were now the rest of the camp, and the heavy shells struck rapidly and hard into the unprotected men and tents. The canvas structures were instantly shredded, and pieces of poles somersaulted through the air. A group of soldiers standing together at the end of a camp street was chopped to pieces in an instant as hunks of their corpses spun off and bounced along the ground.

Panic set in when the living saw the dead. It was pitiful as they ran aimlessly and uselessly in all directions while the heavy slugs swept over them like steel curtains being drawn across the camp. The lieutenant, sergeant, and guard were horrified when they spotted three aircraft flying in a direct line toward them. The officer and soldier stood stupefied as the sergeant dived under the vehicle. The two in the open died immediately as they were rendered into slices of meat, and the sergeant's life was abruptly ended a moment later when the gas tank in the guard car exploded, wrapping him in flames.

And then the detonations ended, and the twelve aircraft once again climbed above the clouds, turning westward, leaving the area quiet except for the crackling of flames, an occasional late explosion, and the screams of the maimed and burned.

0445 HOURS

THE instant the two Pave Low choppers set down, the Brigands inside unassed the aircraft and formed up by sections to get ready for a quick sweep through the burning camp.

Brannigan was the last out, and when he stepped to the ground and looked around, he didn't say anything for a moment. The rest of the detachment also stood silently, gazing at the carnage spread before their eyes.

The camp was flattened, with numerous small fires burning throughout the site. Craters from bomb and missile hits dotted the area, giving it the look of a moonscape that had lately been pounded by an immense storm of fiery meteorites. Here and there were recognizable human corpses, but there also were hunks of smoking meat of those dead who had caught the full brunt of a weapon detonation. A smoky, acrid stench hung over the scene, which displayed a nightmarish surrealism in the predawn gloom.

Brannigan turned to the detachment. "Alright! Let's form up for a sweep through the . . . the . . . well, the mess out there. Remember that time is of the essence, so we have to be back here at the chopper in less than half an hour. A reminder for you! We want items of intelligence value and EPWs most of all."

Bruno Puglisi shook his head. "I don't think there's anything living out there, sir."

"You could be right," Brannigan said. He waited until the Brigands were formed in a skirmish line. "Move out!"

The sights of horror in the camp grew more frequent with each step the SEALs took. Things that looked like shapeless lumps evolved into skulls with patches of flesh and hair; arms and legs were scattered helter-skelter among torsos that had been ripped open, displaying scorched entrails. Chad Murchison walked across the remnants of a tent floor, noting some papers in the mess. He picked them up and noted that the scribbling on them was in handwritten Arabic. He surmised them to be no more than letters from home to some Arab volunteer, but he stuck them in his pocket just in case they revealed some gleam of information that would make the intelligence boys dance with joy.

Joe Miskoski grimaced at what he saw as he stepped through the rubble. When he looked over at Doc Bradley, he called out to him. "Hey, Doc, do you have any training in psychology?"

"Nope," Doc replied. "If you need a shrink after this, you'll have to wait until we get back to the *Daly*. I'll write out a sick slip for you and they'll take you over to the CVBG. They have a small psychology clinic aboard the carrier."

Dave Leibowitz chuckled without humor. "Fix up one for me too, Doc."

Garth Redhawk was walking with Matty Matsuno when he spotted an arm still in a sleeve. He knelt down when he noticed an insignia on the hunk of cloth. He pulled it off the limb, and stood up, glancing at Matty. "My ancestors mutilated their enemy dead in the belief that they would go to the spirit world maimed and crippled."

"If that's true, then there had better be a lot of parking spaces for the disabled up there in the Kiowa afterlife after what the Israelis did to these poor bastards," Matty remarked.

Monty Sturgis and Andy Malachenko stepped down into a dip in the ground where they discovered a flattened pile of corpses. It was impossible to tell how many there were, since they had been torn up and burned to the point where they appeared to have melted together.

"I wonder what happened here," Andy wondered aloud.

Monty studied the macabre scene for a few seconds. "I figger them guys dived into this depression looking for cover. They prob'ly caught a combination of concussion and fire from a nearby hit."

"Ruined their whole day," Andy commented drily.

Over on the right flank, Ensign Orlando Taylor walked a few paces ahead of his section. He pointed out the few spots of interest for investigation he was able to spot. All that his men found were more dismembered dead and the normal items of trash common in any military installation. Then Arnie Bernardi yelled out and pointed off to the west.

A lone figure stood up some fifty meters away. He had risen from a pile of rubbish to his immediate front. Everyone swung their M-16s his way. The man yelled out something unintelligible.

"Stay where you are!" Taylor hollered back. "And raise your hands!"

The man, confused and dazed, hesitated for a moment, than complied with the demand. He stood looking at the SEALs in perplexed puzzlement as they slowly approached him. His face and uniform were stained with smoke and dirt to the extent that the insignia on his epaulets were obscured and impossible to decipher.

"Search him," Taylor said to Arnie Bernardi. As the SEAL patted the EPW down, the group was joined by Lieutenant Brannigan. The young ensign proudly announced, "We have a prisoner, sir."

"So you have," Brannigan said. "Well, done, Mister." He checked his watch. "We're running out of time. Let's hustle this guy over to the choppers and haul ass."

The prisoner seemed to recover from his bewilderment. "Are you Americans?"

Brannigan glared at him. "We'll ask the questions. First of all, I'm curious as to how you survived this slaughter."

"I was in a bunker," the man responded. "Not a tent."

"Lucky you," the Skipper commented. "And secondly, who are you?"

The man straightened and spoke with an authoritative tone in his voice. "I am Brigadier Shahruz Khohollah of the Iranian Army!"

OVAL OFFICE
WHITE HOUSE
16 SEPTEMBER
0915 HOURS

THE President of the United States had only one item on his agenda for that morning's meeting—the incident at the Iranian Special Forces camp.

Those in mandatory attendance were Dr. Carl Joplin, Undersecretary of State; Arlene Entienne, White House Chief of Staff; Colonel John Turnbull of SOLS; and Liam Bentley, the official liaison between the White House and the Federal Bureau of Investigation. If Edgar Watson from the CIA's Iranian desk had not been in the Middle East, he would have been present too.

"Well," the President began, "it seems our Israeli friends did exactly what they told Carl they would do. I received an official report via Colonel Turnbull's SOLS office on the result of that aerial attack." He paused, then muttered, "Devastation. Pure devastation!"

"Iran is already raising hell," Arlene said. "There's going to be a special session of the UN later this afternoon."

"I imagine they'll suspect we're involved right off the bat," Joplin remarked.

"Yes," the President said. "Even when the Israelis eventually claim responsibility, the rest of the world is going to figure we were behind it."

"As long as nobody is aware of the guidance and protection provided by our Air Force AWACS aircraft, we should stay in the clear," Arlene said.

"Britain's contribution of inflight refueling must remain unknown as well," the President reminded her. He glanced over at Turnbull. "What about those SEALs? How did their part in the operation go?"

"Faultless, sir," Turnbull replied. "In and out nice and quick. I suppose you heard they got an EPW, right?"

"I'm surprised they were able to find one from the way that place was flattened," the President said. "Do you think the fellow will be of any value?"

"He's their equivalent of a brigadier general," Turnbull

answered. "We're not sure of his exact position right now, but I would venture the opinion that he was probably the camp commander. And I wouldn't be surprised to learn that he was going to spearhead the invasion of Afghanistan."

"Is he being held at Barri Prison in Bahrain?" Joplin asked.

"Negative," Turnbull said with a shake of his head. "He's been ensconced deep in the bowels of the USS *Combs*. General Leroux and the intelligence boys are having at him even as we speak." He chuckled. "I almost feel sorry for the poor bastard."

"I suppose I do too," the President said. "It must be a frightening experience to be in the complete control of your enemies and isolated from your own people."

"He's worse off than that, Mr. President," Turnbull said. "General Leroux has been in a bad mood ever since he was assigned to that floating SFOB. He'll take out all his anger and frustration during interrogation on the guy. I'm afraid our prisoner could get a healthy slapping around."

"What?" Joplin said. "No instant rapport between two brigadier generals?"

"Not in this case," Turnbull said.

The FBI man Bentley said, "I've been instructed to look deep into this situation. We'd like to have a go at the guy too. We're very interested in building up a good file on any Iranian terrorist cells in this country."

"Don't worry, Liam," the President responded. "The Bureau will get their turn along with everybody else."

A knock on the door startled everyone. No interruption of presidential conferences was allowed unless something of the greatest and/or gravest of importance occurred. When the door opened, it was a communications clerk. He walked wordlessly to the Chief Executive and dropped a message form on his desk, then just as quickly departed the office.

The President unfolded the paper and read it. "Well, I'll be damned!"

"What's going on, sir?" Arlene asked.

"We have Aladdin!"

CHAPTER 24

"SO you're Aladdin, are you?" Carl Joplin asked the man sitting across from him in the dining room during the luncheon meal.

Brigadier Shahruz Khohollah nodded as he spooned some of the vegetable soup into his mouth. "I, of course, was not aware I had been assigned a code name. I made my transmissions from my own headquarters when the opportunity presented itself. Naturally, there were long periods of time when I could do nothing because of my communications center being occupied. I was obliged to wait until none of the radio operators was present. This occurred irregularly."

Edgar Watson of the CIA had arrived with Khohollah from the Middle East the day before. He occupied a seat at the head of the table. "Every single bit of intelligence you sent us was timely and accurate. Without it we could well have failed to stop Iran from moving forward in attaining its goals."

"Actually I was never aware of whether you received my transmissions or not," Khohollah said. "However, when I perceived actions that could have resulted from the information I passed over to you, I would be encouraged to continue."

"May I inquire as to your motivation?" Joplin asked.

"It was patriotism for my native country that drove me to betray the government," Khohollah said. "You may note that I said I betrayed the *government*, not Iran, the *nation* of my birth."

"We understand perfectly, General Khohollah," Joplin assured him. "Now that your request for political asylum in America has been approved, you'll be staying here on the Farm for a while."

"And for that I am most grateful," the Iranian said.

"I trust you will be patient with us," Joplin said. "Certain very secret and sensitive arrangements must be seen to."

"I have no trouble with that, sir."

"Does that mean you have no intention of ever returning to Iran?" Watson asked.

"My fondest dream is to return to my homeland," Khohollah said. "But only if it is free and democratic. The young people there today yearn for that. I plan to use my contacts and influence to nurture that desire, and when appropriate to direct a popular uprising. I must tell you that Islamic insurrections, suicide bombings, and all that will go on until they are brought to a halt by more enlightened mullahs. But these gentlemen can do nothing until the right circumstances are arranged for them."

"It sounds as if you wish to set up a government-in-exile," Watson said.

"That is exactly what I plan to do," Khohollah said. "That, of course, will include a military branch. And I humbly recognize that this cannot be done with the moral and financial help of the United States government."

"We at the CIA are working with Iranian dissidents on a regular basis," Watson said. "It is hoped to bring all of you together under our sponsorship. As of now we will see that you are made head of the movement."

"I am honored by your faith in me," Khohollah said. "I

promise to do my best to build a solid organization with the funding and facilities furnished for us."

"But aren't you afraid of what might become of your family back in Iran?" Watson wanted to know.

"I have no family there," the Iranian replied. "I am an old widower without even close friends to worry about."

"I am curious about a few things," Joplin said. "Do you have any bad feelings about some of the things that happened through your transmissions? I'm thinking of that ambush in which reinforcements were wiped out."

"They were young Arab extremists and terrorists."

"And the secret entrance to the mountain fortress," Joplin said. "Why did you not tell us of that?"

"I was wrestling with that dilemma," Khohollah confessed. "It would have led to a slaughter on both sides. And it did, as you are aware. If that cease-fire had not been offered, probably everybody fighting within the complex would have been killed." He took a sip of coffee. "I still do not know how you learned about it. But I have my suspicions."

"I'm afraid that is something that cannot be revealed to you under the circumstances," Joplin said.

"I understand."

Further conversation was interrupted when the main course of the lunch was brought in on a serving cart. The three men sat in silence as the waiter put the plates of lamb chops, stewed tomatoes, and green beans in front of them.

The rest of the meal was continued in silence.

GREEN EMERALD RESORT AND SPA
SINGAPORE
21 SEPTEMBER

HARRY Turpin had settled his protégé, Archie Sikes, into his beach bungalow to prepare him for entry into the complicated environment of high-class international dealings in arms. But before the actual lessons were begun, the two took a quick flight to Harry's tailor in Hong Kong to obtain a new wardrobe for the younger man. Business suits, casual attire, shoes, socks, ties, jackets, overcoats, raincoats—the whole nine yards in haberdashery—were prepared for the new assistant. Like any other sales agent, the future dealer in death had to make a good impression on the clientele.

With the attire taken care of, it was time for grooming. Archie had kept his hair clipped short to the scalp during his soldiering in Iran and Afghanistan, and his beard had simply grown any way it wanted to. A tonsorial treatment was in order, and the lad from Manchester was turned into a regular Beau Brummel with styled hair, a neatly clipped goatee, and manicured fingernails. With that taken care of, Harry turned to the commercial side of their partnership.

This was nothing less than a combination apprenticeship and business course. Archie had the proper background in military hardware, but he had to learn the current prices, sources, and outlets for everything from platoon-size orders of T-72 tanks to the going rate for a single rocket-propelled grenade. All these transactions were extremely complicated. Most of the time the acquisition of the merchandise involved desperately crooked military officers from the old Soviet bloc. They were underpaid and resentful, driven to perform paperwork miracles in which they hid away whole inventories of the most destructive weaponry in the world. They drove hard bargains, and it took just the right combination of toughness and diplomacy to make a profit in these cloak-and-dagger dealings.

Archie Sikes turned out to be an enthusiastic student, and within a short time he was well into his studies, learning fast, and anxious to get out and make some money. The international arms industry now had another member in their ranks, more than willing to turn a profit off the blood and cruelty of others.

**USS *DALY*
PERSIAN GULF
21 SEPTEMBER**

THE Brigands were back into their shipboard routine with one exception. The ship's skipper, Captain Jackson

Fletcher, issued specific orders that the BVBL—Brigand Volleyball League—was to be dissolved and that under no circumstances would the SEALs participate in that or any other type of athletic competition aboard the vessel. This message was delivered rather forcefully to Lieutenant William Brannigan, with a stern warning that disobedience would lead to his OER looking like a criminal rap sheet in the civilian world.

Thus the Brigands returned to a more conventional training schedule, which included a vigorous PT program featuring innumerable laps around the deck; classroom—"skull sessions" in which Ensign Orlando Taylor taught and reviewed small-unit tactics; weapons and equipment maintenance under the stern supervision of Lieutenant JG Jim Cruiser; and other housekeeping details necessary to keep them in a state of readiness for the next operation.

It wasn't long before SCPO Buford Dawkins was worried about his guys. The predictable routine was beginning to sap their morale and enthusiasm, and he realized that if something invigorating wasn't done, they'd begin to lose that fighting edge that had to be kept honed at all times. Then he had a great idea. The ACV *Battlecraft*, which they had used in their seaborne operations against the al-Mimkhalif terrorist group, was berthed in the docking well of the *Daly*. He made some inquiries within the naval administration aboard, and the captain made the craft available for their use in training. Better to have them whipping around on the ocean than trying to kill each other in the vicinity of a volleyball net.

The next day the detachment took the *Battlecraft* out to sharpen their boat-handling skills and also to employ it as a platform for SCUBA diving. From that point on, many hot afternoons were spent deploying and recovering CRRCs under the blazing Arabian sun, as old skills were brought back up to a high degree of professionalism.

Jim Cruiser wrote to his wife, Veronica, back in San Diego about once again being aboard the *Battlecraft*. She had served in the Navy as an electronic weapons officer, and designed the armament system for the ACV. Veronica had even gone on combat operations with the detachment and was an honorary member of Brannigan's Brigands. It was during this time that the romance between her and Cruiser blossomed, ending in marriage before she left the Navy to work in a local electronics manufacturing firm.

Even though the SEALs enjoyed the recreative aspects of these latest activities, a collective restlessness began to emerge among the group. No matter what was going on, there would always be anxious glances toward the horizon in the direction of the USS *Combs*. That was where Commander Tom Carey and Lieutenant Ernest Berringer would appear from someday, sitting in a Seahawk chopper with another WARNO in their briefcases.

Then it would be isolation, briefback, and an insertion back into hell.

MANCHESTER, ENGLAND
22 SEPTEMBER
1430 HOURS

CHARLIE Sikes had gotten the sack.

This was the reason he sat in front of his telly, dully watching a BBC sports broadcast in the middle of the afternoon. Because of his son's desertion from the Army in Iraq, the union representing the workers at the warehouse where he had been employed was disinclined to contest his firing. Now he was watched by the police, unemployed, and unlikely to find another job. There was every possibility that he would be on the dole for the rest of his life.

His wife, Nancy, sat across the room on the sofa, also gazing at the screen without really noting what was on. Both parents were bitterly disappointed in Archie's conduct and what it had brought on the household.

"He bluddy thinks only of himself, and he's always been that way," Charlie suddenly said aloud.

"You're right, love," Nancy said. "He's all but destroyed us. It was horrible what he done, and I'm his mum and I'll say that to anybody."

"If I had anything worth anything, I'd damn well disown the rotter," Charlie said bitterly. "He's chucked out o' me life, Nancy. There's no room in me heart for him no more. He's come to being no more than a criminal and a disgrace."

"I feel the same," Nancy said. "Who woulda thought—"

The sound of the doorbell broke over the scene.

"Oh, bluddy shit!" Charlie said. "It's the coppers again."

"I'll tell 'em you ain't home, love," Nancy said, getting up.

"It won't do no good," Charlie said as she walked from the room.

When the woman answered the door, it wasn't a policeman. Instead it was a messenger boy from the telegraph office. "Wire for Mr. and or Mrs. Charles Sikes," he announced. He thrust a pad at her. "Sign for it here, if you please, madam."

Nancy signed and took the envelope back to the living room, handing the envelope to Charlie. He opened it with a great deal of hesitation and slowly pulled the message out of the envelope. After a disheartened sigh, he began to read. Five seconds later, he was on his feet, shouting, "Blimey! Blimey! Blimey!"

"Oh, Gawd!" Nancy wailed. "Wot is it, Charlie?"

"It's a bluddy money wire, that's what it is!" Charlie exclaimed. "For fifteen thousand bleeding quid!"

"Who's it from then?"

"It's from Archie, and he says there's more on the way!" Charlie yelled. He sat down and handed the wire over to Nancy. "It's from Hong Kong."

She trembled as she looked at it, then smiled sweetly. "Oh, that Archie!"

"Y'know, something?" Charlie said, smiling and reaching for his pipe. "I always knew that lad would amount to something big."

EPILOGUE

TWELVE-YEAR-OLD Reshteen stood on the rooftop with his wool serapelike *pukhoor* hanging loosely over his shoulders. It was still a couple of months before the onset of winter, yet a rare preliminary coolness was in the air. After the heat of summer, it was a refreshing change. The steppes were much warmer and fifteen hundred meters lower than the Kangal Mountains, to the east across the Tajikistan border. Up in that frigid high country, hundreds of glaciers had been carving through the depthless rockbeds for aeons. These deep slabs of ice, some more than five kilometers wide, eased across the mountaintops in a steady progression that was so slow the human eye could not perceive the movement.

Reshteen, like all boys his age, took his turn on lookout duty, and that's what he was doing on top of old Mohambar's house, which was the tallest in the village. This was a vital necessity in the living routine of those particular Pashtuns. Fierce bandits roved unchecked through the area, and raids happened once or twice a year. Mostly, however, the attacks by the murdering robbers occurred when people, alone or in small groups, were traveling across the steppes to other settlements.

The boy guards such as Reshteen kept part of their attention focused on the distant horizons to the south and west. When they turned to the north and east, they took extra time to study the view. That was where the rugged, boulder-strewn foothills of the Kangals joined the flat country, and it was much more difficult to discern anyone approaching from that direction.

Reshteen took off his rolltop cap and scratched his head as he gazed out across the steppes in boredom. There was nothing there but the dancing blur on the horizon that distorted distant view. Sometimes, when he tried very hard, his mind could conjure phantom donkeys or goats in the haze. This time his eyes could make up nothing to amuse him, and he swung his attention toward the mountains.

"Awrede!" he hollered, loudly enough for the whole village to hear. "Two horsemen to the east!"

VALENTIN Surov and Yakob Putnovski reined in as the village came into view. Both horsemen were in the same attire in that it was a mixture of native costume and Russian Army uniforms. Their boots were definitely military-issue, and the open-collar camouflage jackets were the type used by the KGB border guards. The rest of their clothing was the traditional type found in Afghanistan and Tajikistan. The cartridge pouches across their shoulders were the leather type available in the bazaars of the larger towns. These were handmade, and exhibited the craftsmanship of the saddlers who designed, cut, and stitched them together.

Putnovski took his binoculars and studied the small community. "Is this the place we're looking for?"

"Just a minute," Surov said. He reached into his jacket and pulled out a map, unfolding it carefully.

Putnovski glared at him. "Fucking officer!"

Surov sneered. Both of them were veterans of the Russian Army, and the practice of not instructing enlisted men in map reading was a Soviet tradition. The reason behind the practice was to keep any discontented soldier with itchy feet from finding someplace to flee from the Peasants' and Workers' Paradise. Surov studied the terrain around them, then traced his finger along an elevation line. "*Da!* This is it. Come on!"

THE fact that Rasheen had sighted only two riders did not alarm the villagers, but they fetched their weapons just the same. The pair could be scouting for a larger bandit gang lurking somewhere else nearby. Most of the men stayed inside their huts, ready for trouble. The women and children went about their normal activities, whether it was indoors or out, while half a dozen men with their AK-47s concealed under their *pukhoors* lounged on benches in the village square.

The two Russians rode slowly and warily into the village, their AKS-74 assault rifles slung across their backs to make it obvious they were no threat. Each was aware the locals were armed to the teeth and that disturbed Pashtuns had a disagreeable habit of shooting first and asking questions later—provided there was a survivor or two to converse with. The Russians brought their horses to a halt at the well, nodding to one of the men standing there.

"*Staray me she!*" Surov said in his working knowledge of Pashto. "Are any of your *spinzhire* around?" He used the Pashtun word for "graybeards," which was the way they referred to their elders.

The Pashtun man called out, and an old fellow named Mohambar appeared in the doorway of the nearest hut. He said nothing, but looked up at the Russian on the horse.

"I have been sent by Luka Yarkov to give you a message," Surov said. "He has been informed that this village made much money selling opium poppies to a fellow called Awalmir Yousafzai."

Old Mohambar nodded.

"Awalmir did not give Yarkov's share to him," Surov said.

"It is a *malya*—a tax. It must be paid. Since you were paid money by Awalmir, you must pay a share to Luka Yarkov because he has enough fighting men to control everything that happens on the Steppes. Do you understand?"

Mohambar stared at him without expression or emotion.

"If you do not pay Luka Yarkov what is due him, he will be angry."

There was still no reaction from the elderly Pashtun.

With anyone but Pashtuns, this would have been the beginning of some sort of negotiations, protests, or a discussion. But Surov did not expect any verbal response to his announcement. It was enough that he had made it, and that these villagers would pass the word on to their brethren across the steppes.

The Russian turned his eyes from the old man and glanced around at the other villagers, who also did no more than gaze at him. He nodded, saying, "*Khuday peaman—*good-bye."

The two foreigners rode slowly from the village, their weapons still slung across their backs. The Pashtuns looked at each other, knowing this was the start of big troubles on the Pranistay Steppes.

APPENDIX

The letter composed by PO3C Chadwick Murchison to explain the loss of the desert patrol vehicle on Operation Rolling Thunder:

SEAL Detachment
USS *Dan Daley*
Persian Gulf

10 September

SUBJECT: Missing Desert Patrol Vehicle

TO: Commanding Officer
ATTN: S-4
Station Bravo, Bahrain

The vehicle in question was lost in combat during Operation Rolling Thunder last May. This compunctious misadventure occurred as a result of an exigent oblation that occurred during a traumatic period of active campaigning against a miscreantful enemy force.

By the profligation of the DPV, I was able to gain salient amelioration both on the field of battle and in the logistical relucts of conducting a combat operation.

The DPV may be gone, but its loss was outweighed by the outcome of the operation. I am sure I need not remind you that Operation Rolling Thunder was a mission accomplished.

I therefore resepectfully request that the vehicle be classified as lost in the line of duty as a result of enemy action.

WILLIAM BRANNIGAN
Lieutenant, U.S. Navy
Commanding

GLOSSARY

2IC: Second-in-Command
2-Shop: Intelligence Section of the staff
3-Shop: Operations and Training Section of the staff
4-Shop: Logistics Section of the staff
AA: Anti-aircraft
AAR: After-Action Report
ACV: Air Cushion Vehicle (hovercraft)
Afghan: Currency of Afghanistan: 43.83=$1.00
AFSOC: Air Force Special Operations Command
AGL: Above Ground Level
AKA: Also Known As
Angel: A thousand feet above ground level; e.g., Angels Two is two thousand feet
AP: Armor-Piercing or Air Police
APC: Armored Personnel Carrier
ARG: Amphibious Ready Group
AS-50: .50-caliber semiautomatic sniper rifle with scope
ASAP: As Soon As Possible
ASL: Above Sea Level
Asset: An individual who has certain knowledge or experiences

that make him helpful to an individual or units about to be deployed into operational areas

AT: Antitank

AT-4: Antiarmor rocket launchers

Attack Board (also Compass Board): A board with a compass, watch, and depth gauge used by subsurface swimmers

ATV: All-Terrain Vehicle

AWACS: Airborne Warning and Control System

AWOL: Away Without Official Leave—i.e., absent from one's unit without permission; AKA French leave

Bastion: Part of a fortification or fortified position that juts outwardly

BBC: British Broadcasting Corporation

BDU: Battle dress uniform

Blighty: British slang for their home nation

Boot: A rookie or recruit

Boot Camp: Navy or Marine Corps basic training

BOQ: Bachelor Officers' Quarters

Briefback: A briefing given to staff by a SEAL platoon regarding their assigned mission; this must be approved before it is implemented

BUD/S: Basic Underwater Demolition SEAL training course

Bushido: The philosophy and code of conduct of Japanese samurai warriors.

BX: Base Exchange, a military store with good prices for service people; in the Army, AKA PX for Post Exchange

C4: Plastic explosive

CAR-15: Compact model of the M-16 rifle

CAS: Close Air Support

CATF: Commander, Amphibious Task Force

CDC: Combat Direction Center aboard a ship

CG: Commanding General

Chickenshit: An adjective that describes a person or a situation as being particularly draconian, overly strict, unfair, or malicious

CHP: California Highway Patrol

CLU: Command Launch Unit for the Javelin AT missile

CNO: Chief of Naval Operations

CO: Commanding Officer

Cover: Hat, headgear
CP: Command Post
CPU: Computer Processing Unit
CPX: Command Post Exercise
CRRC: Combat Rubber Raiding Craft
CRT: Cathode-Ray Tube
CS: Tear gas
CSAR: Combat Search and Rescue
CVBG: Carrier Battle Group
Dashika: Slang name for the Soviet DShK 12.7-millimeter heavy machine gun
DDG: Guided-Missile Destroyer
DEA: Drug Enforcement Agency
Det Cord: Detonating cord
DJMS: Defense Joint Military Pay System
DPV: Desert Patrol Vehicle
Draeger Mk V: Underwater air supply equipment
DZ: Drop Zone
E&E: Escape and Evasion
Enfilade Fire: Gunfire that sweeps along an enemy formation
EPW: Enemy Prisoner of War
ER: Emergency Room (hospital)
ERP: En route Rally Point; a rally point that a patrol leader chooses while moving to or from an objective
ESP: Extrasensory Perception
ETS: End of Term of Service
FLIR: Forward-Looking Infrared Radar
Four-Shop: Logistics Section of the staff
French Leave: See AWOL
FRH: Flameless Ration Heater
Front-Leaning Rest: The position assumed to begin push-ups; it is customary to place malfeasants or clumsy personnel in the front-leaning rest for punishment, since it is anything but a "rest"
FTX: Field Training Exercise
G-3: The training and operations staff section of a unit commanded by a general officer
GHQ: General Headquarters
GI: Government Issue

GPS: Global Positioning System

Gunny: Marine Corps for the rank of Gunnery Sergeant E-7

HAHO: High-Altitude High-Opening parachute jump

HALO: High-Altitude Low-Opening parachute jump

Hamas: Palestinian terrorist organization that has been voted into office in Palestine; their charter calls for the destruction of Israel.

HE: High Explosive

Head: Navy and Marine Corps term for toilet; called a latrine in the Army

HEAT: High-Explosive Anti-Tank

Heel-and-toe: See watch-and-watch

Hell Week: The fifth week of BUD/S that is more than five days of continuous activity and training with little or no sleep

Hezbollah: A militant Islamic terrorist organization located in Lebanon; it was organized in response to the Israeli occupation and is still active

H&K MP-5: Heckler & Koch MP-5 submachine gun

Hors de combat: Out of the battle (expression in French)

HSB: High-Speed Boat

IFV: Infantry Fighting Vehicle

Immediate Action: A quick, sometimes temporary fix to a mechanical problem

IR: Infrared

IRP: Initial Rally Point; a place within friendly lines where a patrol assembles prior to moving out on the mission

Island: The superstructure of an aircraft carrier or assault ship

JCOS: Joint Chiefs of Staff

JSOC: Joint Special Operation Command

K-Bar: A brand of knives manufactured for military and camping purposes

KD Range: Known-Distance Firing Range

Keffiyeh: Arab headdress (what Yasser Arafat wore)

KGB: Russian organization of security, espionage, and intelligence left over from the old Soviet Union

KIA: Killed In Action

KISS: Keep It Simple, Stupid—or more politely, Keep It Simple, Sweetheart

LBE: Load-Bearing Equipment
Light Sticks: Flexible plastic tubes that illuminate
Limpet Mine: An explosive mine attached to the hulls of vessels
Locked Heels: When a serviceman is getting a severe vocal reprimand, it is said he is having his "heels locked"—i.e., standing at attention while someone is bellowing in his face.
LSO: Landing Signal Officer
LSSC: Light SEAL Support Craft
LZ: Landing Zone
M-18 Claymore Mine: A mine fired electrically with a blasting cap
M-60 E3: A compact model of the M-60 machine gun
M-67: An antipersonnel grenade
M-203: A single-shot 40-millimeter grenade launcher
MATC: A fast river support craft
MC: Medical Corps
MCPO: Master Chief Petty Officer
Medevac: Medical Evacuation
MI-5: United Kingdom Intelligence and Security Agency
Mk 138 Satchel Charge: Canvas container filled with explosive
MLR: Main line of Resistance
Mossad: Israeli Intelligence Agency (ha-Mossad le-Modiin ule-Tafkidim Meyuhadim—Institute for Intelligence and Special Tasks)
MRE: Meal, Ready to Eat
MSSC: Medium SEAL Support Craft
Murphy's Law: An assumption that if something can go wrong, it most certainly will
N2: Intelligence Staff
N3: Operations Staff
NAS: Naval Air Station
NAVSPECWAR: Naval Special Warfare
NCO: Noncommissioned Officers—i.e., corporals and sergeants
NCP: Navy College Program
NFL: National Football League
NROTC: Naval Reserve Officer Training Corps

NVB: Night-Vision Binoculars
NVG: Night-Vision Goggles
NVS: Night-Vision Sight
OA: Operational Area
OCONUS: Outside the Continental United States
OCS: Officer Candidate School
OER: Officer's Efficiency Report
OP: Observation Post
OPLAN: Operations Plan; this is the preliminary form of an OPORD
OPORD: Operations Order; this is the directive derived from the OPLAN of how an operation is to be carried out; it's pretty much etched in stone
ORP: Objective Rally Point—a location chosen before or after reaching the objective; here a patrol can send out recon on the objective, make final preparations, reestablish the chain of command, and perform other activities necessary either before or right after action
PBL: Patrol Boat, Light
PC: Patrol Coastal vessel
PDQ: Pretty Damn Quick
PIA: Pakistan International Airlines
PLF: Parachute Landing Fall
PM: Preventive Maintenance
PMC: Private Military Company; these are businesses that supply bodyguards, security personnel, and mercenary civilian fighting men to persons or organizations wanting to hire them
PO: Petty Officer (e.g., PO1C is Petty Officer First Class)
POV: Privately Owned Vehicle
PPPP: Piss-Poor Prior Planning
PT: Physical Training
Puhtee: An Afghan rolled stocking cap that can be worn in many ways
RHIP: Rank Has Its Privileges
RIB: Rigid Inflatable Boat
RIO: Radar Intercept Officer
RON: Remain OverNight; generally refers to patrols
RPG: Rocket-Propelled Grenade
RPM: Revolutions Per Minute

R and R: Rest and Relaxation, Rest and Recuperation, and a few other things used by the troops to describe short liberties or furloughs to kick back and enjoy themselves

RRP: Reentry Rally Point; a site outside the range of friendly lines, to pause and prepare for reentry

RTO: Radio Telephone Operator

Run-flat tires: Solid-rubber inserts that allow a vehicle to run even when its tires have been punctured

SAS: Special Air Services—an extremely deadly and super-efficient special operations unit of the British Army

SAW: Squad Automatic Weapon—M249 5.56-millimeter magazine- or clip-fed machine gun

SCPO: Senior Chief Petty Officer

SCUBA: Self-Contained Underwater Breathing Apparatus

SDV: SEAL Delivery Vehicle

SERE: Survival, Escape, Resistance, and Evasion

SF: Special Forces

SFOB: Special Forces Operational Base

Shahid: Arabic word for martyr (plural is *shahiden*)

Shiites: A branch of Islam; in serious conflict with the Sunnis

SITREP: Situation Report

SNAFU: Situation Normal, All Fucked Up

Snap-to: The act of quickly and sharply assuming the position of attention with chin up, shoulders back, thumbs along the seams of the trousers, and heels locked, with toes at a forty-five-degree angle

SOCOM: Special Operations Command

SOF: Special Operations Force

SOI: Signal Operating Instructions

SOLS: Special Operations Liaison Staff

Somoni: Currency of Tajikistan: 2.79=$1.00

SOP: Standard Operating Procedures

SPA: Self-Propelled Artillery

Special Boat Squadrons: Units that participate in SEAL missions

SPECOPS: Special Operations

SPECWARCOM: Special Warfare Command

Stand-to: Being on watch or at a fighting position

Sunnis: A branch of Islam; in serious conflict with the Shiites

Superstructure: The part of a ship above the main deck

T-10 parachute: Basic static-line-activated personnel parachute of the U.S. Armed Forces; primarily designed for mass tactical parachute jumps

Tail-End Charlie: Brigand terminology for the last man in an operation—e.g., the final guy getting off a vehicle, jumping from an aircraft, rear guard on a patrol, etc.

Taliban: Militant, anti-Western Muslims with extreme religious views; in serious conflict with Shiites

TDy: Temporary Duty

Three-Shop: Operations and Training Section of the staff

TO: Table of Organization

TOA: Table of Allowances

TO&E: Table of Organization and Equipment

Two-Shop: Intelligence Section of the staff

U.K.: United Kingdom (England, Wales, Scotland, and Northern Ireland)

UN: United Nations

Unass: To jump out of or off something

UNREO: United Nations Relief and Education Organization

USAF: U.S. Air Force

USASFC: U.S. Army Special Forces Command

USSR: Union of Soviet Socialist Republics—Russia and neighboring countries before the fall of communism there

VTOL: Vertical Takeoff and Landing

WARNO: Warning Order; an informal alert, written or oral, that informs personnel of an upcoming operation or activity

Watch Bill: A list of personnel and stations for the watch

Watch-and-watch: A watch bill that requires personnel to be off only one watch before going back on again; used as a punishment or when a shortage of personnel requires such scheduling; AKA heel-and-toe

Waypoint: A location programmed into navigational instrumentation that directs aircraft, vehicles, and/or vessels to a specific spot on the planet

Whaler Boat: Small craft loosely based on the types of boats used in whaling; they are generally carried aboard naval and merchant vessels and are diesel-powered

WIA: Wounded in Action

WMD: Weapons of Mass Destruction—nuclear, biological, etc.